Too Hot to Hold

Ricci Cummings

This book is dedicated to my loving, supportive family and friends. You have granted me the space and given me the courage to bring this story to life. You gave generously of your time, expertise and patience. I treasure you all.

CHAPTER ONE

Darien put her coffee on a nearby table, stood, and walked to the window, turning her back to the men who were engrossed in discussing the law firm's new case. Her new case. She caught snatches of Jim's explanation. When the fire was first reported. How it had burned. Why the insurance company suspected arson. She heard the words, but they careened off the edges of her consciousness and spun away in random directions. They were sounds drained of meaning.

She tried to steady herself, but outside the window, the rain-swept Providence riverfront and its upscale businesses were shimmering, blurring, whirling before her eyes. And there it was — the familiar ache in her chest and the clammy dampness of her hands. Color slowly faded to gray. Darien pressed her face to the cool, firm surface of the window. She did not want to hear about a fire.

She took a few deep breaths and closed her eyes, trying to will herself back from the precipice of her fire world to the everyday reality of the law firm. But it was worse that way. To her horror, the menacing orange and red flames exploded into view. An eerie, soft sound like the beginning of a windstorm arose. Darien knew from experience that if she let this go on, the wind would wrap around her and rise to a deafening howl, and she would slide through it from reality into the nightmare.

She had to stop this. Darien massaged her temples with a slow, steady rhythm, as if a motion anchored in the physical world could erase images that dwelt in a different dimension. She slowed her breathing and concentrated on each breath, three counts in and three counts out, hoping it would still the painful skidding of her heart. Slowly, the tension in her neck and shoulders relaxed as Darien fought down the panic. The lurid colors of the fire world receded and the familiar view from the window came back into focus.

Dear God. It had been years since this had happened in public. She could not let it happen here, not in front of her client, and most especially, not in front of her boss. She would be fine. All she had to do today was listen. She could do that. And she would find a way to avoid working on this case. She could do that, too. She just needed a minute to steady her world.

Taking a shaky breath, she turned and walked the few steps back to the men, who were still intent on their discussion. Edward Rankin, her silver-haired mentor and the senior law partner at the prestigious Rankin & Rhodes law firm, cast a concerned look her way. Was her disarray so obvious? She tried her best to compose herself into the capable, professional, hard-working senior associate that Edward relied on to keep his corporate clients happy. She gave him what she hoped looked like a reassuring nod.

"Please excuse me for a few minutes," she said. "I need to return a call from a client and it's time sensitive. I'll be right back."

Without waiting for a response, Darien stepped into the hall, shut the door behind her and leaned heavily against the wall. She closed her eyes tightly and marshalled every last bit of her resolve against the fear that threatened to overwhelm her. She concentrated on her breathing. Slow and steady. She could get through this.

Chance Deckert had not been waiting long at the law firm, but he'd already looked through his texts and examined the hunting scenes of dogs and foxes on the wall, and now he was inspecting the contents of the candy jar. He glanced at the handsome antique clock on the wall of the reception room, which was impressive all right, but time was time no matter how it was measured. He'd spent too much time sitting around and was impatient to get started on his new assignment. He stretched his long legs, ran his fingers through his hair, and then flipped through the pages of an article about some guy who caught a big fish in some river. The magazine was lame and so was the story. He knew a thing or two about fishing, and …. His thoughts were interrupted as the conference room door opened at long last and he tossed the magazine onto a table and stood.

She was tall and willowy. And she was gorgeous, with coppery hair pulled tightly back from her face and knock-out amber-colored eyes. She was wearing a slim, stark black suit that looked formal and professional — could she be a lawyer? Could she be *his* lawyer, his partner on this case? His smile grew broader as he started toward her. This could be interesting. Then he stopped short.

She wasn't looking at him. Her gaze was unfocused, she didn't seem to be looking at anything. She was holding herself stiffly, and after a few uncertain steps, she rested her back against the wall and closed her eyes. Her hands were balled into tight fists. Her face was contorted with something. Pain? Grief? Fear?

He looked around. There was no one in the reception room but him and a receptionist who was simultaneously talking on the phone and typing.

As he watched, wondering what if anything he should do, the young woman took a long, deep breath, relaxed her hands and opened her eyes. And then she saw him.

She blushed a deep crimson and looked away. Then she straightened her shoulders and walked quickly down the hall toward what appeared to be a suite of offices.

Several minutes later, he heard the sound of footsteps approaching the conference room, and looked up to see her walking back down that same hall, eyes straight ahead and a composed, in-charge expression on her face. If he hadn't learned over the years to trust his impressions and his ability to read people, he might have had his doubts. But he knew what he'd seen. That was one incredible transformation. She opened the door to the conference room and disappeared behind the ornately carved door.

Chance stood for a moment, staring at that door. He turned toward his seat, hesitated, and then turned back toward the door. He wished — what? He felt — what? He shook his head almost imperceptibly, and then went back to his seat.

Jim Plattman, their stout, perpetually rumpled client from the Property and Casualty division of Monitor Insurance, was deep in conversation with Edward. He nodded to acknowledge Darien's return, and then retrieved a toffee from his pocket and popped it into his mouth. He adjusted his wire-rimmed glasses and paused for a minute to review his notes.

"So just to review the high points in case you missed anything, Darien, this fire was in a tourist hotel on Block Island, off the coast of Rhode Island. We can discuss the details more fully later, but for now, what you need to know is that we don't believe the fire was accidental. The Fire Marshal thought that it might have been purposely set, and then rigged to look like an electrical fire. Because the fire was caught early and didn't consume the structure, we think he had plenty of evidence to support that conclusion. But he's still considering a determination that the fire was of undetermined origin because he's not sure his case for arson is strong enough.

Jim paused briefly to collect his thoughts. "Monitor recognized a pattern. We've had two other large hotel fires in Rhode Island, both of which were found to be of undetermined origin because of the massive damage. But the evidence at the scenes of both fires pointed strongly to an accidental fire of electrical origin. This struck us as quite a coincidence."

"Indeed," said Edward.

"Most important from my perspective, all of the fires have the potential to result in big losses to Monitor. Your firm has a lot of work to do on this one. In a nutshell, we need you to prove that this fire was arson in order to avoid a large insurance claim, tie it to the other two fires so we don't have to pay out on those either, and then try to figure out who is behind it all."

"Darien," he said, turning her way, "my supervisor is the reason you've been asked to join us today. He liked the work you did on the Mullins flood case. You were responsive, you got excellent results and you kept the costs down. And you're dynamite in a courtroom. He's convinced that you're the person for this job and so am I." He fished in his pocket for another toffee, unwrapped it and popped it into his mouth with one smooth, practiced motion.

"Now I know it's unusual to send the lawyer out to the site to investigate along with the rest of the team," he said looking in Edward's direction. "But Darien's presence on the site will focus the investigation on the facts we'll need to nail down in order to prove the arson. Also, her input and skills will be critical in interviewing witnesses." He glanced at Darien and then focused his intense gaze on Edward.

"This is very important to the company. I really can't emphasize that strongly enough. And time is of the essence. The site is secured but the Fire Marshal is waiting to turn it over to us. We needed Darien out there yesterday."

Edward nodded in response. "Your call, Jim. And the timing shouldn't pose any problem. If you need her out there right now, you've got her," he said. He glanced at Darien, who had remained silent.

"Good, good," Jim replied. "I appreciate top service, and I know I'll get it from your firm."

Edward's secretary entered and spoke softly in his ear.

"Call for you, Jim. Why don't you take it in the guest office so that you can have some privacy," Edward said.

Jim's brows furrowed at the interruption, but he stepped out into the hall.

This would be her only chance, now, while Jim was out of the office. Darien quickly ran through her options. She would have to be her most persuasive. She settled on a strategy and squared her shoulders.

"I really appreciate Jim's confidence in me, but he needs someone to get on this right away, and that's a problem," she said in the most confident manner she could muster. "My time's already committed to several projects, one of which, the Newville case, is really urgent because the trial date is near. I don't see how I'd be able to take this project on and give it the attention it clearly requires. But I can think of several excellent lawyers in the firm who'd be available to start work immediately, and I guarantee that Jim will be pleased with their work. Edward, what would you think about using…"

His face was a study in displeasure and disappointment. Darien's voice faltered as she felt her resolve unraveling, and she nervously twisted her mother's antique emerald ring. She was letting him down and she knew it. How she loathed lying, particularly to this man for whom she had such respect. She wished she could be honest with him about her refusal to take on this case, but knew with certainty that she could not. After so many years of silence, she would not have known how to begin.

"Darien," he said, lowering his brows, "we're talking about what could turn into a major account for the firm. And it's a client that looks to you to do their work. That will be a weighty mark in the plus column when you come up for partnership. I am confident that you will do your usual outstanding work. I'm sure that we can rearrange your work schedule to accommodate this good client.

"I'm sorry, Edward," she said, "but it's simply impossible. Trial preparation is too far along and there's no one who can come up to speed quickly enough. As much as I'd like to do this, we'll really have to find someone else to…"

"That's no excuse, and I think you know it." He took a few steps in her direction and stared down at her with a puzzled expression. "Jenny is working on that case and she could step in on short notice and handle the trial. And you heard Jim as well as I did. He thinks you're the one for the job. He won't take no for an answer and frankly, neither will I."

She took a step back. "I don't think you understand…" she said.

"No, you're the one who doesn't understand, Darien. This isn't what I'd expect from any associate. And it most certainly is not what I'd expect from you. The client is paying the money, and if the client wants you to do his work, your job is to figure out how to make that happen and then to prove to him that he made a wise choice. You've always told me that you wanted to be a partner here. Well in this law firm, partners make business, not excuses."

Darien turned away from the anger that had transformed her mentor's face. He was right, of course. And she needed this job in ways he could never begin to imagine. It was safe and steady ground. The rules were clear. She knew exactly what was expected of her and she knew precisely where she belonged.

Turning to Edward, she said with quiet resignation, "Of course I can redistribute my work. I'll make myself available at Jim's convenience."

"Indeed," Edward said. "Now if you can make up a list of your most pressing cases…"

"Sorry for the interruption," Jim said, striding back into the room. He stopped short and looked keenly from Darien to Edward, and then back again. "Everything okay here?"

Edward replied, "Everything is quite okay. Just working out some details."

Jim looked unpersuaded, but after hesitating briefly, he continued. "Well, then, where was I… Oh, yeah. Darien, I was going to bring you up to speed on the team. As you know, Edward, because this case is so high-dollar and important to the company, we've brought on board that independent arson investigator that you recommended. Never used him before, but we're always on the lookout for new talent. Name's Chance Deckert from out in Montana," he said, turning to Darien. "His family are old friends of Edward's wife, Maggie, and Edward assures me that he's worked with Deckert on other arson cases with good results. He comes with top recommendations, and a price tag to match, I might add. After I finished my call, I asked your receptionist to give us a minute and then to show him in."

Finally. Chance stood, retrieved his briefcase and followed the receptionist into the conference room. He glanced briefly at the substantial old conference table and rich green upholstery of the surrounding chairs, the fine wood paneling, and the pictures of somber old men hung on the walls, and then went directly to Edward and extended his hand in greeting. "Great to see you again. It's been a while." Turning to Jim, he said, "And it's good to meet you in person, Jim. Always enjoy putting a face to a voice on the phone. Sorry about the casual clothes. The airline misplaced my luggage and said they'd deliver it to the hotel this evening. But I sent my supplies ahead, so I'm good to go."

"This is Darien Dalton," Edward said, gesturing in her direction. "She's the lawyer assigned to the case. Darien, Chance Deckert."

Chance silently gave thanks to whatever fates had brought this good fortune his way. It was her. He turned and looked at Darien, who seemed lost in thought. As their eyes met, her polite smile froze briefly in place and then disappeared. Her eyes opened wide in recognition and her mouth rearranged itself into a tight, straight line.

Chance drew in a sharp breath. Those amber eyes were dazzling and appeared huge in a delicate face grown pale and drawn. His heart gave an odd jolt and seemed to bump around a bit in his chest before settling back in place. What the hell? He reached deep down to find his customary cocky self-assurance around women, and found that it had gone missing in action.

"Good to meet you, Darien," he said. "I understand we'll be working closely together." He gave her a crooked smile that seemed to overshoot professional without quite reaching personal. "I'm looking forward to it."

Darien's brow furrowed. She took a small step back. There was nothing wrong with the words and nothing out of order that she could put her finger on. But despite the innocent appearance of his remark, there was an undertone that didn't seem quite right.

"How do you do." she said.

"I do just fine, thanks," he replied.

Darien hesitated briefly and then, giving him the benefit of the doubt, extended her hand.

His smile deepened as he took it in his work-worn grasp and held it the slightest bit too long.

Darien withdrew her hand and returned to her chair. She studied him as he took a seat. He was a tall man, well over six feet and powerfully built, dominating the spacious office that seemed too small to contain him. He was dressed in a white cotton shirt rolled up at the sleeves to reveal muscular forearms, jeans and dusty cowboy boots. His windswept shock of sandy hair was a little too long. His smile was a little too bold. The contrast with the formal suits and restrained demeanor of the others in the office was stark. He was, she thought, all wrong for this place and time, and yet there was something so confident and sure about the man that he seemed to redefine the standard of what was appropriate.

She dropped her eyes and looked away. It would be one week at most. Seven days. She could handle the fire and she could handle this disconcerting fire expert as well, whether he stayed in his lane or not. She hadn't gotten this far in the combative world of litigation by being weak. She could be as tough and single-minded as she needed to be. She would be fine.

Seven in the evening. Shifting in her seat so she wouldn't draw unwelcome attention, Darien looked out the window, sighed and massaged her temples. The sun had set and the sky had turned to indigo. She would have bet good money that this day could not get any worse, but then, why should her luck change at this late hour? It had taken every last bit of self-control that she possessed to split her mind from her emotions, allowing her mind to think about the fires, while isolating her memories and emotions from the chasm that beckoned at the edge of those thoughts. She was exhausted, and she had the start of what would undoubtedly be a truly horrendous headache. On top of that, thanks to this new project, her workload was in disarray. She'd annoyed Edward, the partner she most admired and her mentor at the firm. And now Chance was hungry. Great.

"There are plenty of places around here," Edward assured him. "Darien will be pleased to take you and Jim for some dinner. Just let her know what you'd like to eat and I'm sure she'll be happy to oblige."

"Count me out," Jim said, hiding a yawn behind a beefy hand. "Sleep is higher on my list right now than food. But how about you, Chance? What's your pleasure?"

Darien was surprised. Judging from Jim's remarkable girth and from the number of cookies and toffees she had seen him put away during the day, she would not have expected anything to come up higher on his list of necessities than food. She looked hopefully at Chance. Surely, he would choose to punt, too. He had been doing most of the talking for the past hours, explaining his strategy for the investigation and answering innumerable questions from Jim. He should be flagging. Yet to Darien's dismay, the only visible sign of the long day he'd put in was the stubble that appeared on his jaw. He looked for all the world as if he'd just awoken from a refreshing nap and was raring to go.

"I'm sure Darien and I can work that out," he said.

She smiled politely to cover her disappointment. He had better like fast food. She felt rubbed raw, all bared nerves. She had been too exposed today. She needed to be by herself.

"One last thing," Edward said. He reached for a large manila folder on his desk. "Unfortunately, there aren't too many hotels open on Block Island at this time of year and they're booked solid for the weekend portion of your stay. But I have a home in Old Harbor that you can use while you're out there. It'll give you a convenient base of operations for the investigation. It's comfortable, spacious, so you'll both have plenty of privacy. There's a family, the Olsens, who look after the place for us. They live right near the ferry drop. Sally will have it all set up for you and will give you the key. She'll also help out with anything, including shopping and cleaning. Just let her know what you need. And as you've seen in the documents, her husband,

George Olsen, is the senior member of the volunteer fire department. Since the Fire Marshal is on the mainland, George will be your main contact on this case."

He started to pass the folder to Chance, but changed his mind and took it back. Edward rifled through the pages until he found what he was looking for.

"This is the address and GPS coordinates for our place. I've also included some directions and a map of the Island, just in case. You can't miss it, it's right on the beach." He took a few minutes to review the map with them, while Jim looked over their shoulders.

Darien was oblivious to the explanation. She was busy absorbing this unwelcome information about their accommodations. Her mental image of the two of them safely settled in one of the hotels in Old Harbor, preferably in the two rooms most distant from each other, had provided some measure of comfort and safety. She would have her privacy. She could keep her distance and her secrets. She had not counted on this beach house business. Darien went back to her seat and took refuge in her documents.

"We keep a car out there that you can use while you're on the Island. You'll find the key on a hook in the back hall. Make yourselves at home. I'll check in with you tomorrow night, and Maggie and I will be out in a few days." Edward headed toward the door with Jim in tow.

"Don't forget to call me every night and report on what you've learned," Jim called back over his shoulder. "It's critical that you keep me in the loop. I want to know everything, and I mean everything, in real time."

And then Edward and Jim were gone and she was alone with Chance.

"So, what did you have in mind?" he asked.

"What I'd really like," she said, "is to order a salad and then take an hour or two in my office to tie up the loose ends. If I'm going to spend the next week out of the office, I have a lot of work to finish up and reassign before I can leave. I'll join you for dinner if you really want me to. But I'll only have to come back here when we're done, and it's been a long day already. If I finish my work now, I can get some sleep before we meet here early tomorrow to drive to the ferry."

"Fair enough," he said. "Mind if I keep you company in your office for a while? I have some documents I want to review before tomorrow. You can add a roast beef and cheese sub with the works to that salad order."

Darien hesitated. This did not sound like a good idea. Something about him made her feel unsteady. Why couldn't he work in his hotel room? Providence was a small city; surely he could find someplace else to work.

"I think you'd be more comfortable working in your hotel room or in a guest office," she said. She looked meaningfully at the door.

"No thanks. I feel plenty comfortable right here. And I'm sure I can work more effectively if I have my lawyer handy-by in case I need a consultation." His voice was all innocence, but his eyes sparkled with mischief.

"All right then," she said. She rose from the chair and, without looking back to see if he were following, strode quickly through the richly appointed halls of Rankin & Rhodes to her office.

Darien sat at her spacious, orderly desk and put on her horn-rimmed glasses. She ordered dinner, turned to her computer and reached for one of several neatly organized stacks of papers.

"You can work there," she said, gesturing in the general direction of a sturdy round table surrounded by four simple, upholstered chairs. "Let me know if you need anything. And feel free to let me know when you're done with your work. I'll be happy to show you out." Very happy, she added silently.

She put him out of her mind and went to work. She typed several memos to her colleagues, bringing them up to speed on re-assigned matters, and reviewed the contents of her inbox. She doggedly worked her way through the piles of papers and case binders on her desk. She absolutely refused to be distracted by Chance.

And he was a bigtime distraction if ever there was one. Chance seemed oblivious to the rules of common courtesy and tact. He moved unabashedly about her office, leafing through her law books, studying her university and law degrees that were housed in simple silver frames and hung neatly along the wall across from her desk, and inspecting the muted still-life paintings that she had selected from the firm's library. His unrestrained curiosity seemed to be as limitless as her backlog of work. And where was all that work he had to do, anyway?

As she finished a particularly lengthy memo and the last of her salad, he pulled a chair up to the desk and seated himself across from her. He propped his elbows on the table and rested his chin in his hands. She could feel his eyes on her as she filed the memo in a bulky file and put it aside. Finally, with a resigned sigh, she raised her eyes and looked at him. Sometimes the best way to deal with a pest was to let him get it out of his system.

"Well?" she asked.

"Why does your office look so impersonal? I don't get any sense of who you are by looking around."

"I don't know what you mean," she responded. "You aren't really proposing to discuss interior design at this late hour, are you Chance?"

He laughed. "It's just so blank and empty, somehow. Everything looks like standard issue from the law firm. Nothing personal. No books other than your law books. And no photographs. Not even a picture of you, not to mention a picture of your boyfriend."

If he was looking for a picture of her boyfriend, he would be looking for a very long time, she thought. There could be no place for a boyfriend in the life she had pieced together for herself. She had surrendered whatever right a person could have to that kind of happiness long ago.

"Not that it's any of your business," she said, "but I don't have a boyfriend."

He took a minute to consider this information. "Is that right? Well then, how about pictures of friends, of good times, parties, adventures? Where are the pictures of the lawyer at play?"

She was silent.

"How about your family? Any pictures of them?"

His question caught her off guard and the flash of pain left her breathless. This inquisition had gone far enough.

"I really don't have time for this." She picked up a pen and, clutching it far more tightly than necessary, turned to some papers on her desk. She knocked over an etched glass container that held her paper clips.

"Sorry," he said. "Looks like I've crossed some kind of line. I'm just trying to get to know you. We're going to be spending a lot of time together." He smiled, righted the container and started to put back the paper clips.

"I don't want to be rude, Chance, but this isn't about getting to know each other. I have a job to do. I intend to do that job well. That's all you need to know about me."

He reached across the desk and took the pen from her hand. Carefully, he placed it on the desk next to the orderly rows of papers.

"Come on Rennie," he asked. "I find it hard to believe that you're this serious lady lawyer twenty-four hours a day, seven days a week."

The use of the nickname brought her up cold. It did not belong here, in this office. It belonged in another time, another place. She was very still for a moment.

"The name," she said finally, pronouncing each syllable with care, "is Darien. Don't ever presume to call me that again. And while we're setting the ground rules here, please know that I don't care what you choose to believe about anything other than this fire. Period."

She stared at him in stony silence.

"Something just doesn't add up, Darien. You act as if you have a wall of glass around you, tall as this office and thicker than those books on your shelves. And I haven't seen you smile since I've been here."

"You're way out of line, Chance. And as a rule, I smile when I have a good reason to. Right now, I most assuredly do not."

"Well, Darien," Chance said, fixing her with a thoughtful gaze, "you are partial to drawing lines and making rules, aren't you?"

"I don't recall inviting you to advise me on my mental health, Chance," she said in a carefully controlled voice. "I thought that your area of expertise was arson. You should learn to limit yourself to what you know, or better yet, limit yourself to what you're being paid to do."

"Maybe that's where we're different," Chance said. "I don't limit myself. I never have. I live for the present and what's right there in front of me. I make it a rule to take my pleasure where and when I find it. And I do find it, Darien."

His confident smile was infuriating.

"Fair enough," she retorted. "In case you have any thoughts to the contrary, consider this notice that you should look elsewhere for your pleasure this time. We play by very different rules. I don't hear anything in your self-serving little template for the well-lived life that makes even the least bit of sense in my world."

Chance studied her flushed face for what felt like an eternity.

"Fire and ice?" he asked finally.

"If that's how it makes sense to you, feel free to think of us that way," she answered.

"Fire melts ice," he reminded her.

"And when the ice melts, it puts out the fire. Now please go."

He rose, gathered his jacket, and turned back to her. The confident smile had disappeared. And then he was gone.

CHAPTER TWO

Chance didn't know which fire he found more intriguing, the fire on Block Island that he'd been hired to investigate, or the one that he'd seen flare briefly in Darien's eyes when he'd called her Rennie. The memory of that moment was nudging at the edges of Chance's consciousness when he awoke.

He'd never seen anything quite like those eyes. They were almond shaped, a true yellow-gold that reminded him of amber. And they had been, with this one exception, curiously opaque — asking nothing, conveying nothing. Perhaps, he thought, he'd seen in that one unguarded moment a glimpse of the person who lurked beneath that carefully managed façade. Now there was a good thought to start the day with.

Chance glanced at his watch on the bedside stand. Six a.m. He ran his fingers through his tousled sandy hair. No time to work out. He'd grab a shower, check out of the hotel and then head over to the office to meet Darien. Whistling to himself, he turned on the water, hot and hard, just the way he liked it.

Darien let the steam work its magic. The hot water was soothing, washing away the last vestiges of sleep and restoring her to the world of the day. She knew who she was in that world. She was Darien Dalton, senior associate, professional, competent, poised, reliable. Her nightmare world and the haunted woman who inhabited it — those were creatures of the dark hours, and she had grown adept at keeping them there. She greeted each dawn with relief.

She toweled herself off briskly and, entering her sparely furnished bedroom, turned on some music while she dressed. The strains of Duke Ellington greeted her, and with great determination, she hummed along. She would focus on the music. This would be fine. She stepped into her jeans and added a slim white cotton sweater, securing the tiny buttons while she slipped her feet into canvas sneakers. Then, brushing out her damp, tangled hair, she mentally ran through a list of what she should pack.

With some effort, the duffel was retrieved from the top shelf of the closet. Quickly and efficiently, Darien worked her way through her drawers and selected jeans, T-shirts, warm socks and sweaters, and slipped them neatly into place. She added a few items appropriate for interviews. Then, opening another drawer, she paused and her pace slowed as she lingered over the piles of silky, sheer lingerie. Hesitantly, she slid her fingers over a delicate, pale-yellow garment, conscious of the sensual feel of the fabric against her skin, and found to her surprise that her cheeks were growing warm. Refusing to let herself think about why, Darien scooped up what appeared to be an adequate supply and, without looking too closely at her selections, added them to the duffel. The remainder of her supplies were quickly located and packed. She pulled on her coat, and grabbing a muffin in one hand and her duffel in the other, headed to the nearby bus stop and boarded the bus.

By the time she reached her stop, Darien had finished both the muffin and nearly a quarter of a stack of documents pertaining to investigations of the other fires. She took off toward the office at a brisk walk, struggling with her bulky duffel and brushing muffin crumbs as she went.

He was waiting outside the office, lounging against the wall and so intent on what he was reading that he didn't see her until she was nearly upon him. But she saw him. You really couldn't miss him, she thought. In the slanted sunlight of early morning, in this ordinary place among these familiar people, his presence was jarring. The freshly combed sandy hair, the soft brown leather jacket, the jeans that stretched tightly over his powerful thighs — none of these served to disguise or even mute the raw sensuality that was the core of this man. He charged the space around him with a primitive energy, and as she entered that space, her steps grew smaller and her pace slowed. Darien paused briefly. Then, lifting her head high, she strode purposefully up to Chance, looked him squarely in the eyes, and gave him a formal nod.

"Let me help you with that," he said, reaching for her duffel.

"I can manage it," she said.

"I am trying to make a peace offering," he said. "I feel like we got off to a bad start yesterday. Let me do my penance."

She hesitated, and then let go of the duffel.

Chance turned and led her to a dark racing green Jaguar sports car parked at the curb. It was low to the ground and looked like it could do zero to sixty in a few seconds. Darien ran a finger over the sleek body and then seated herself in the cream leather interior. "Where'd you rent this?"

"Edward offered me the use of one of his cars while I'm out here on business. He and his wife are good friends of the family. My Mom and Maggie were college roommates back in the day, and have been like sisters to each other. Just last month, Maggie spent a few days at our ranch."

She stored that bit of information away to consider later.

"No space for my tools, but I sent them ahead." He keyed up the car's GPS and said, "Looks like we shoot straight down 95 South to North Kingstown, and then pick up US 1 to Narragansett. From there, it's not far to the Point Judith Ferry." The engine roared to life and the car swung out into traffic.

"Do you and Edward do much work together?" Chance asked, when they had left Providence behind and were speeding down the highway toward Point Judith.

"Why do you ask?"

"Just making polite conversation. Have I run afoul of another rule?" Chance asked.

Darien considered a retort, but decided the wiser move was not to take the bait. Her silence was answer enough.

"When he called me to talk about this job, he said that the client had specifically asked for you on the team and that he thought you were a good choice," Chance said.

"Edward's been a mentor to me at this firm," she answered. "He's a tough taskmaster and won't accept anything less than your very best effort. But he's been good to me. He's given me a chance to show what I can do, and that's more than many associates get. He's taken the time to teach me, to introduce me to his clients and colleagues. I owe him a lot."

"Have you met his wife, Maggie?" Chance asked.

"Yes," Darien replied. "Edward's brought her to firm events, of course, and they've been kind enough to invite me to their home."

"She's a second mother to me and, I'd wager, to most everyone else she knows. She's forever lecturing me on my wayward ways, but she's good people," Chance said.

"The best," Darien agreed.

They rode in silence for several miles. Chance seemed lost in thought.

"Have you reviewed the material on the two previous fires?" Chance asked, breaking the silence.

"Yes" she replied, "the ones in Newport and Watch Hill. I noticed that the properties appear to have different owners, but there are plenty of ways to obscure the identity of the true owners if they're inclined to do that. Do you agree with Jim's conclusion that they're related?"

"I do," Chance replied. "There are too many coincidences. Some of them we touched on back at your office. First, these fires all involve property that recently changed hands. That's suspicious in itself. Almost seems as if the properties were purchased with arson in mind. Then again, all involve old, outdated buildings. The hotel on Block Island dated from nearly seventy-five years ago and had lots of commercial drawbacks. It did a good business in its day, but with different facilities on that property, it would have doubled the revenue. In fact, the same could be said for the other commercial structures that burned. All were on very valuable pieces of property. All were insured for the maximum coverage, and were possibly over-insured, making it certain that the new buildings could happen if the old ones burned." He was silent for a few minutes, thinking it over.

"I'm more interested in the similarities among the fires themselves, but there's not much to go on. I didn't inspect the other sites, but I've reviewed the reports from the firemen and from the investigators. They have some interesting features in common. In both fires, as in the Block Island fire, the fire alarms failed to go off and the sprinkler systems didn't engage. There were explanations, but I'm not buying them. Both of the other fires were found to be of undetermined origin, although both appeared to be electrical fires. But I'm not so sure about that, Darien. If you read the investigations, it's clear that the structures were almost completely consumed, making it very difficult to determine the origin of the fires. I am hoping that you will be able to take a fresh look at the interviews with employees, with neighbors, with anyone who might have seen something suspicious." He grew silent as he negotiated a particularly tangled stretch of traffic. "And I've already started to put together a list of potential interviews for this fire. We can compare thoughts on the most effective way to proceed."

"Here's the crux of it," he continued. "Each fire has its story to tell, if you're willing to listen. You just need to know the right questions to ask, the right places to look. And that's our job. We're going to eat, drink and sleep this fire. We're going to live this fire. And when it's all over, I promise you that we'll have our answers."

She'd grown very quiet.

"Not the most entertaining conversation you've had lately?" he asked.

She didn't reply.

"Guess I come on pretty strong when I start talking about fire, but that's how it is for me. My folks say I've let it become an obsession and they aren't any too happy about that. Could be they're not far off the mark. But there's something about the heat, the intensity, the power of the thing. It has a hold on me that I can't explain. Long ago, I decided that it made no sense to fight those feelings, and I've been studying fires ever since."

"No problem, I was just taking it all in," she said over the lump in her throat. She could hear the hollow tone of her voice, and even to her own ears, it rang false. Furtively, under the guise of adjusting the fabric that held back her hair, she wiped the trickle of perspiration from her face. She felt light-headed and sick to her stomach.

She'd be hearing a lot more about fire in the days to come, Darien thought with dread. She would be immersed in a fire investigation that would occupy her days, and was bound for the foreseeable future to this man whose world rotated on an axis of flames. And it seemed that when the subject was fire, his words alone were enough to summon the abyss that lurked in the recesses of her mind. Entering the actual site of the fire — well, she would neither waste her time nor dissipate her courage by wondering what horrors awaited her there.

"Mind if I put on some music?" she asked brightly.

Perhaps it had been a shade too brightly. Chance looked at her with a puzzled expression.

"Sure," he replied.

She reached for her phone and selected a playlist. Sarah Vaughn started to sing "What a Difference a Day Makes." Darien stared out the window in silence. As she had done so many times before when circumstances required, she purposefully calmed herself and willed herself to slip into the music. Focus on the notes, which were now skimming lightly over the surface of her consciousness. Take it from the surface and let it seep deeply into her mind, her soul. Let the music take control. Only the music. No thought. No pain. No fear. Just sound, melody, tempo. Mile after mile after mile…

"The ferry's this way, Chance," she said, guiding him toward the long line of cars waiting to drive onto the ferry. You wait in line with the car, and I'll go ahead and get the tickets."

"You know your way around here," he observed, choosing to let her long silence pass unremarked.

"I've spent a lot of time on the Island, especially in the off-season, when the crowds haven't moved in yet," she explained. "I feel at home there. Sometimes I think I should try new places, plan a vacation elsewhere, but I always find myself back on the Island. If you've not been there before, you're in for a real treat." She unfolded herself from the low-slung car, and made her way to the ticket booth.

Yes, I am, Darien, you'll get no argument from me on that point, Chance thought. He watched with pleasure as she moved toward the ticket booth. The coppery curls appeared to be throwing off sparks in the early spring sun. She was clearly a woman to be reckoned with. Despite her slender frame, she had a poised, assured presence. He sensed that she was competent and accustomed to taking control, and made no apologies for either. But then again, she carried herself with a fluid grace that struck him as profoundly sensual. The combination of the power and sensuality intrigued him, excited him. Oh, yes, he was in for a real treat, and he planned to enjoy every minute of this stay on Block Island.

Chance reached over to open the door for her and Darien slipped into the seat. She handed him the tickets, and then rolled down her window to enjoy the sounds and smell of the ocean. He followed her lead.

"Nothing like this in Montana," he observed. "You love the ocean, don't you?"

Darien smiled. "Am I that obvious?"

"Let's just say that that's the first real smile I've seen on your face since we met last night, and although I'd like to flatter myself and think that the prospect of spending time with me put it there, I expect you'd disabuse me of that notion real quick."

"I do enjoy the ocean," she said, choosing to ignore the flirtation. "It has so many moods — serene, turbulent, ominous. Seems that no matter what I want, I can find it there."

"Sounds like you have more than a passing acquaintance with the ocean. Did you grow up on the coast? Is your family still there?"

"Yes, I did," she said. "But enough of that. You need to be paying attention to getting this car settled on the ferry. You don't want to put any dents or scratches in Edward's very expensive, very well-maintained car, especially if you want to remain his number one choice in the expert arena."

Chance turned his attention to the task. Once the car was safely parked in the bowels of the ferry, he and Darien grabbed their jackets and followed the crowd to the upper decks.

"I'd prefer to sit outside on the top level," Darien said as they climbed. "Gets pretty breezy up there. You can sit in one of the glassed-in levels if you want to avoid the wind."

"Why Darien, are you trying to get rid of me?" he asked with a disarming smile.

She gave him a level look. "Why ever would I do that?"

"Why ever, indeed?" he said, following her up the stairs. He sat down next to her on the bench, and followed her gaze over the harbor and out to the ocean. The sea was deep green shaded with gray, and farther out, whitecaps were forming.

The thunderous sound of the ferry's horn scattered the gulls that had been hovering just off the decks of the ferry, and sent them screeching and soaring for safety. The massive engines rumbled as the ferry slowly pulled out into the ocean and pointed in the direction of Block Island. Darien looked back at the retreating shore. Then, resolutely, she turned and focused her attention in the direction of Block Island. There was no turning back now.

They sat in silence, taking in the beauty of the ocean under the mild rays of an early-spring sun. The ferry motored through Point

Judith Pond, and then through the Point Judith Harbor of Refuge, and left behind the last sanctuary before the open waters of Block Island Sound and the Atlantic. For an unbroken eighteen miles there would be no shelter for unwary mariners engulfed by the dense fogs or caught in the violent squalls that traversed the area. Darien wrapped her jacket more closely around her.

Eventually, Chance stood up, stretched, and then looked down at her. "We've been sitting all the way from Providence, and my legs are telling me that that's about enough sitting for one day. I know you lawyers are used to sitting in front of dusty books for hours on end and that you're more inclined to exercise your mind than your legs. But how about humoring your investigator. I'd like to see the rest of the boat and could use a guide. I'll make it worth your while. I'll buy lunch!"

"That's very generous of you, Chance, particularly since you know as well as I do that lunch for both of us is paid for by the client."

"Good point. How about the pleasure of my company then. Payment enough for services rendered?"

She looked up and searched his eyes suspiciously. Was there a message for her in his choice of words? The hazel eyes that met hers sparkled with amusement.

"That proposal contains a questionable assumption — namely, that your company would be a pleasure," she responded. "However, I'm willing to overlook that point for now and agree to show you around, contingent only on your good behavior. Deal?"

"You drive a hard bargain, counselor, but it's the only bargain in town, so call it sold."

She stood and started off in a circuit of the deck, with Chance close at her side.

"These ferries are a lifeline for the Island," she explained as they walked. "They run all winter, despite the incredibly rough seas they have to cross. The Island is surrounded by waters whose currents and tides can be challenging to navigate. These ferry captains are highly skilled and experienced, and take great pride in their work."

"I find that reassuring," Chance said dryly.

"You should," she said. "It's a vibrant maritime region, but historically, this area saw its share of shipwrecks."

They stopped at the railing to watch the seagulls soar toward the deck in hopes of a meal, and then swoop skyward once again, only to resume the incessant circling and screeching. The wind was cold on the deck, blowing in fitful gusts and whipping about the clouds that increasingly were obscuring the sun. She shivered in her thin jacket. Chance, who had been standing uncomfortably close to her, moved even closer to protect her from the wind. She shifted uneasily away from him.

"Let's move on to the lower level. You'll find your lunch there, and we can warm up a bit," she said.

"Lunch it is," he said, and followed her as she strode briskly toward the door to the lower deck.

They proceeded down a narrow flight of stairs to the deck below. It was warmer here, as the walls were largely glass that admitted the weak rays of sun, but blocked the blustery wind. They both unbuttoned their jackets and walked the expanse of the deck, looking out at the churning waves on the ocean.

"In the summer, this ferry will be jammed to capacity," she said, trying to make polite conversation. "Occasionally, the ferry fills and cars simply have to wait for the next one. At the height of the season, they take reservations. Not so many people at this time of year, though. We're probably carrying some fishermen. It's a little early, but the striped bass and bluefish may be starting to run now."

He looked around with interest. When they'd completed the circuit, he turned to her expectantly. "Where's that lunch?" he asked.

Relieved to have something concrete to focus on, she directed him to the food line and followed close behind. She selected her food and then caught up with him at the cashier.

"That's not much of a lunch," he said, studying her bagel.

"Sure you have enough to hold you?" she asked, looking with disapproval and a fair amount of envy at the tray he had piled high with everything that caught his eye. "You do insist on doing everything full out, don't you." It was a statement, not a question.

"There's no other way to do it."

"I see," she said. "Are you acquainted with the concept of restraint, or with the idea of moderation?"

"Can't say as I am," he replied. "Are you acquainted with the concept of throwing caution to the wind?"

"Not even remotely," she answered.

"Well, we'll have to work on that, won't we," he said in a mock serious tone of voice.

"The only work we'll be doing will be related to the case, Chance. End of discussion."

"Yes, Ma'am," he replied with his lazy smile.

She selected a booth that gave them a clear view of the ocean. They ate in silence, both engrossed in the view.

"I'm going to head back up to the top deck," she said, when she'd finished the last of her bagel. "I'll take some hot tea up with me to help me stay warm. You're welcome to stay down here if you're more comfortable and I'll come down for you when we reach the Island."

"Wouldn't think of deserting my partner," he said. "We're a team now." He smiled down at her and then walked off in the direction of the stairs.

Darien sighed wearily, and then followed him.

They reached the top deck and found their space on the bench. She sipped the warm tea and stared out at the ocean in silence. The sun had broken though a rent in the cloud cover and shone warm on her face. That, together with the hypnotic motion of the boat and the comforting smell of the salt air, lulled her into drowsiness. She'd been up so late last night. What with jousting with Chance and worrying about her time on the Island, she'd been too wired to get to sleep when she got home. Small wonder she felt so tired. She'd just rest a few minutes. Gradually, her eyes closed and she slipped into sleep.

The blast of the ferry horn jolted her into wakefulness. She opened her eyes and found that the sun had slipped behind the clouds, leaving the day raw and chill. Turning, she saw that Chance was looking down at her. She could feel his touch on her forehead, on her cheeks, as his fingers brushed her wind-tangled hair back from her face. She was nestled against him, protected from the cold, her head resting comfortably on his broad shoulder. Much too comfortably. Darien sat up abruptly, looking around her to get her bearings.

"I see we're nearing the Island," she said quickly to cover her confusion. She must have slept for quite some time. "We should get into the car so we don't hold up traffic leaving the ferry." She stood and turned toward the stairs.

As he rose to join her, the ferry gave a small lurch and Darien stumbled toward him. He put his arm around her to steady her, and then pulled her close. Darien removed his arm and turned to him, her face serious.

"Look, Chance, I know you're busy taking your pleasure where you can find it and all, and this is your idea of fun, but it's not mine. Before we get on the Island, we need to come to an understanding. We have a serious job to do here. This is a business relationship and your behavior is completely unprofessional and inappropriate. I don't like it. I don't want you to do it anymore. Can I make it any clearer than that?"

He was grinning that lopsided grin.

"I'm willing to buy that you don't want me to do it, Darien, and I respect that. I reckon it doesn't fit with your rules, right? But I don't believe for a minute that you don't like it."

"Thank you for sharing your opinion with me," she said coldly. "And while we're on the subject, I have an opinion that may interest you. I 'reckon,' as you so colorfully phrase it, that out on the ranch in Montana, you've been hanging around the cattle and the horses too much. Well, Chance, I'm not one of your heifers or fillies in heat, thrilled to pieces when that old bull or stallion comes sniffing around. I'm your colleague and we have an important job to do. Now get your thoughts out of the barnyard and settle down so we can get some work done."

She turned and walked off in the direction of the car. His laughter followed her. He was still smiling when he caught up with her.

As soon as he'd unlocked the car, Darien opened her own door and stiffly took her seat. She was neither smiling nor laughing. She buckled her seat belt and stared straight ahead, expressionless, her hands held firmly in her lap. She would not think about the fire scene that awaited her on the other side of the ferry exit. She would not think about this impossible man with whom she would face that scene. She could not afford to do either. With steely determination, she started humming silently to herself. Humming "Summertime" from Porgy and Bess. It was an all-time favorite. She was concentrating on the notes, the melody, the lyrics. She could handle this. She would be fine.

CHAPTER THREE

The Jag seemed to shudder briefly as it inched forward in the long line of cars. They reached the exit and drove slowly off the ferry. Darien scanned the sky, which had darkened considerably and taken on a threatening cast. She pulled her thin jacket more closely about her. The late April sun was obscured by black storm clouds that hung low to the ground. They were in for it now, she thought. At this time of year, the weather on the Island was changeable and a storm could blow up out of a clear sky, lash Block Island with winds and rain, and then subside as quickly as it had appeared.

"Which way to the Olsen's?" Chance asked.

She studied the directions and pointed him to the right. "They're just a few blocks down this road. I'll look for the house number."

They pulled into the driveway of the weather-beaten, brown-shingled house just as the first drops of rain bounced off the windshield. A young woman appeared at the open door with a baby in her arms and a child at her side. A small puppy dashed into view and barked a frenzied greeting.

"Come in quick, before it really starts to come down," the woman called to them.

The rain began to spatter hard and fast. They jumped out and made a dash for the house. The woman shut the door behind them just as a roar of thunder rolled over the Island.

"Sally Olsen," the young woman said while pressing towels into their damp hands. "And you are Darien and Chance."

"Nice to meet you," Darien said as she toweled off her face. They took off their wet jackets and hung them on the hooks in the hall.

Sally's warm smile was welcoming and Darien couldn't help but smile in response. Sally looked to be about twenty-six or seven, only a few years younger than she was. Her round face, liberally sprinkled with freckles, was open and friendly. Her blond hair was cut in a breezy, no-nonsense style, and her jeans and plaid flannel shirt sported smears of what looked to be flour. Amusement lit up her frank blue eyes as she regarded her damp visitors.

"This is Lily," she said, looking down at the child in her arms who appeared to be about two months old. "And this is Bobby. Bobby, say hello to Miss Dalton and Mr. Deckert."

"Hi, Bobby," Chance said, extending a hand to shake. Bobby hesitated, and then gave him his hand. He looked about five, with tousled sandy hair and his mother's large blue eyes. Unlike hers, his eyes were serious, almost grave.

"You can call me Chance if it's okay with your mom," Chance suggested, looking at Sally for guidance. Sally nodded in agreement.

"I'm Darien," she said, also shaking hands with the solemn little boy.

"And this is Flash," Sally said, gesturing with her head at a multicolored, long-haired puppy who peered at Darien with a quizzical expression. "If you watch her for a few minutes, you'll understand the name. She comes and goes with a speed that boggles the mind."

"Please come in and warm up," she said, leading them into the cozy kitchen. The entire entourage followed. Darien looked around, taking in the scene. The kitchen, painted a sunny yellow, was bright despite the storm, filled with well-worn but comfortable furniture and stray toys. A bulletin board was covered with reminders, invitations,

Bobby's artwork. The good smell of the soup that Sally was cooking permeated the room.

"Maggie told me to expect you today, so I've cleaned up her place, stocked the shelves with groceries and done a bit of cooking for you. And before I forget, I'm supposed to give you the key for the padlock at the hotel. The guys put heavy chains on the door to secure the scene. You won't get far in your investigation without this." She walked to a near-by desk, retrieved the key and handed it to Chance, who nodded his thanks.

"If you like, the kids and I can drive down to Maggie's with you and show you around."

"No need to do that," Chance said. "I can see that you've got your hands full. Just give us the key, tell us what we need to know and we'll be on our way."

"I won't hear of it," Sally protested. "It's pouring out and you'll have a rough time finding your way with the limited visibility. Stay and have some lunch with us. By the time we're done, the rain'll have let up and you can go on your way. In the meantime, I can tell you about the Island and give you some pointers, and you can tell me about yourselves and your investigation. I'd love the company, and I'm sure Bobby and Flash would agree."

"We couldn't get much done at the site in this weather, anyway, and Jim told me that the site had already been secured against bad weather," Chance said. "So thanks, if Darien is on board, we'll take you up on it."

"All right, if it isn't any trouble," Darien said. "I don't want to be a bother. Can I help with lunch?"

"I can manage lunch, thanks, but I'd really appreciate it if you'd hold Lily for me. She's been fussy, and if I put her down, she's sure to howl."

Darien hesitated and then held her arms out awkwardly. Lilly squirmed for a moment and then snuggled against Darien. She brought Lily close to her, feeling the warmth of the tiny body in her arms and inhaling the sweet, fresh scent of the child. She felt the baby's feather-soft wisps of hair brush against her neck and cuddled her closer.

"You look so natural with her, like you've been holding babies all your life," Sally said, getting to work on the sandwiches.

She hadn't, of course, Darien thought. She'd had very little contact with babies in her life. Looking around the cozy little house, it struck her that she'd had little experience with families, either. It was true that at times she'd passed through other people's families, but she'd always felt like an observer, never a participant. Those times when she took stock and thought of her life, which were rare indeed, she thought of her work, her cases, sometimes her music. Families, babies — these were all noticeably absent from her thoughts and plans. She simply assumed that she would be alone, and life had done little to challenge that assumption. Darien looked down at the baby, who was resting comfortably in her arms and was drifting off to sleep. It felt so good to hold her, felt as if some of life's rough edges had been smoothed away.

"Bobby, we have some time before lunch. Maybe you could take Chance to your room and show him some of your collections," Sally said

"Hey, I'd really like that," Chance said with what seemed to Darien like genuine enthusiasm. "What kind of collections do you have? I used to collect baseball cards when I was a kid."

Bobby looked up at his mother and Darien watched as Sally met his gaze and smiled her encouragement. Bobby, his shoulders slumped and his eyes fixed on the ground, led Chance off toward the back of the house.

Darien cocked her head to one side, watching as they made their way to Bobby's room. He really was a piece of work. She would have sworn that kids didn't fit in with his pleasure-seeking ways. He seemed so shallow, so self-centered and so darn proud of it!

She looked up to find Sally's perceptive eyes searching her face. There would be no use trying to hide anything from this woman. She sighed softly and turned her attention back to Lily.

"You'll love the house," Sally said tactfully, carrying the sandwiches to the table. "It's gray shingles, with a huge wrap-around porch facing the ocean. It's one of the loveliest homes on the Island. Maggie did a beautiful job decorating it. She has a sure touch and it really shows."

She took the sleeping Lily from Darien's arms and placed her in the bassinet in the corner of the kitchen.

"Did you grow up in Providence?" Sally asked as they worked.

"No, I grew up in Connecticut, on the shore," Darien replied. "I've lived in Providence for some years now, although it's never felt like home." She was surprised to hear herself make this admission to a total stranger. She usually was such a private person.

"Friends can help make a place feel like home. Do you find the people there friendly?"

"I haven't really given that much thought," Darien responded.

"Well, I guess I can understand that. You must be real busy with a job like yours," Sally said. "Still," she said with a conspiratorial smile, "I bet you find time for a boyfriend. You must meet a lot of interesting men."

"No, not really. Work takes up pretty much all of my time. But I don't mind, I like my work. It's all I really need."

"I see," Sally said.

"So," Darien said a bit more loudly than she'd intended. "I think we're about ready for lunch, right?"

Sally nodded her agreement. "Let's do it."

"Chance, Bobby, time for lunch," she called.

Chance and Bobby emerged from the back of the house, with Chance deep in conversation about Bobby's shell collection. Bobby seemed downcast, and Darien noticed that he wouldn't meet Chance's eyes. He went directly to his mother and pulled his chair closer to hers before he seated himself.

Darien paused for a minute, on the verge of asking if anything were wrong, but then reconsidered. It really wasn't any of her business.

"How long have you lived here on the Island?" she asked her hostess.

"All of my life," Sally replied, as she passed the sandwiches and spooned out the soup. She cast a concerned looked at her son. "Wouldn't even consider living anywhere else. My husband George was born on the Island, as well. Bobby's never known another home, have you sweetie?"

Darien watched as Bobby slumped even further in his chair.

"Bobby," she said with an encouraging smile, "Why don't you tell Chance and Darien about school?"

"I don't want to," he said quietly, staring at the table. The furrows deepened between Sally's eyes. Bobby poked at his food without much interest.

"Bobby has quite a shell collection," Chance said. "He has a new one that's pretty special. Said he picked it up a few days ago on a field trip with his class."

"I didn't know that, honey," Sally said to her son. "I don't remember hearing you tell me about what you did during the field trip or about the new shell. Your class was going to the shore, right? Must have been somewhere along the shore if you found a shell."

Bobby paled and put down the spoon he was holding. He placed his hands carefully in his lap and didn't respond.

Chance and Darien exchanged puzzled looks. What was wrong with Bobby? Chance turned to Sally.

"You probably hadn't seen the shell because it wasn't with the rest of the collection," Chance explained. "I only found it when I took one of the shells over to the window to get a closer look at it in the light. The new one was tucked away in the corner, behind the curtain."

"I see," Sally said.

But judging from Sally's baffled look, Darien got the feeling that Bobby usually couldn't wait to share a special find with his mom.

Sally twisted a strand of her hair around her finger, released it, and then twisted it again. "Well," she said, as she reached for another sandwich. "I'm sure glad you have a new addition. And I bet you'll be able to add some good finds this summer, too."

Bobby didn't answer. He patted Flash, who had settled down beside him, and the puppy nuzzled him in return.

Darien found the long silence that followed increasingly uncomfortable. She tried to think of a neutral topic of conversation and could not.

Finally, Sally, placing a hand gently on Bobby's shoulder, turned to Darien. "I know that you're here to investigate the fire at the old hotel," she said. "The Islanders were sad to see it burn. We all have so many memories of that place. A lot of history there."

"I imagine it's fairly quiet on the Island this time of year. The fire must have been big news," Chance said.

"It was," Sally replied, glancing at Bobby before turning her attention back to her guests.

"We'll be going over to the hotel tomorrow morning to survey the fire scene. We'd really like to speak with anyone who might know anything about the fire and would sure appreciate whatever help you could give us in figuring out who those people might be. We know the hotel was closed for renovations, so we'll start with the workers who were doing those renovations. And Edward told me your husband heads up the volunteer fire department, so we'll want to meet with him as soon as possible. Maybe he'd spend some time with us at the hotel."

Bobby leaped to his feet, knocking his glass of milk to the floor and causing Flash to scramble under the table. "My Daddy doesn't want to go there," he said. "He doesn't. And you can't make him go." He stood defiantly, staring up at Chance.

Chance turned in his seat to face the little boy. "Easy, Bobby, no one's gonna ask your dad do anything he doesn't want to do."

Sally rubbed a hand across her forehead and closed her eyes for a moment.

"Bobby, if you don't feel like eating, why don't you go to your room and play for a bit. I'd like to speak with Chance and Darien for a few minutes, and when they've left, we'll finish baking those cookies."

Bobby kicked the floor with the toe of his sneakers.

"Go ahead now," Sally encouraged him. "We'll just be a few minutes." She reached for a dish towel and started mopping up the spilled milk.

Bobby looked at them and then walked off toward his room, glancing back at them over his shoulder as he left.

"What's up with Bobby?" Chance asked, lowering his voice and leaning toward Sally, "and what was that about his dad?"

"He just hasn't been himself for the last few days. He's in kindergarten and should be in school now, but yesterday and today he just plain refused to get on the bus and begged to stay home. He usually loves school. I let him stay home, but I just don't understand it." She paused and then sighed.

"My husband thinks it may have to do with Lily. You know, new baby and all, but I don't think so. Something just isn't right."

She gave a self-deprecating little smile. "Sorry, didn't mean to bore you with family worries."

"No need to apologize," Chance said. "We're just worried is all. We'll head out and let you get back to Bobby." He paused for a minute, looked down at the table, and then turned back to Sally.

"But before we leave, is there anything else you want to tell us about the fire?"

Darien watched as Sally, with a strained smile, changed gears and tried to put aside her concerns about her son. Apparently, sensitivity was not high up on the list of Chance's good qualities. She had a feeling that it might be a very short list.

"Well...I don't want to spread gossip," Sally said.

"I understand," Chance replied, "but if you know anything, we'd sure appreciate it if you'd share it with us."

Sally hesitated. "Well, there is something that's odd about the fire."

Chance sat up a bit straighter. "Like what, for instance?" he asked.

"I have a friend who works at the hotel. She cleans rooms and does whatever else needs to be done, and she had been real busy lately helping with clean-up for the renovations. She told me some things..."

"What kinds of things?" Chance asked.

"Well, odd things. Like that just before the fire, they had started to replace the office equipment that they used to do things like create different kinds of reports, manage the inventory for the hotel kitchen and book reservations. The old stuff had been removed, and the new stuff was in the hotel and ready to be set up."

"That doesn't seem odd to me," Darien said. "Makes sense that they'd want to upgrade the office equipment just before the busy season."

"Yes, but while she was cleaning, she spent some time dusting the new equipment. She said it appeared that they were planning to replace the equipment with this old, outdated stuff, just this side of junk. Now, what kind of sense does that make?"

"I see," Darien said. "Does seem kind of strange." She stole a glance at Chance to see what he made of this. He was leaning toward Sally, who had his full and undivided attention.

"Could she have been mistaken?" he asked. "Most of us aren't familiar with that type of equipment."

"I guess it's possible," said Sally. "But I doubt it. She seemed pretty sure of what she'd seen. Also, it's kinda peculiar…" she started, but stopped when she saw Bobby coming into the room. He walked up to his mother and put a hand on her arm.

"I think we'll continue this another time," Sally said quietly. She looked with concern at her son. "Bobby and I have some cookies waiting to be decorated. Maybe we'll bring some by for you when they're done. What would you think about that, Bobby?"

He nodded without much enthusiasm.

"Are you comfortable with the directions, Chance?" she asked as they walked toward the coat hooks.

"Looks straightforward enough," he said. "But I'd like to pick up this discussion another time. Another time real soon."

She nodded her assent. "Sure. Chance, I think you'd like the blue room to the left of the stairs. It's the largest bedroom and real comfortable. And Darien, if I were you, I'd choose the peach room. It's to the right of the stairs. It faces the ocean and has a gorgeous view. I think you'd really enjoy that room."

"That'll be fine," Chance said. He turned to Darien and added softly, "For now."

Darien refused to meet his eyes. She felt the color rise in her face and squelched a scathing retort. The man knew no shame.

"Sally, thank you for lunch and for all your work opening the house for us," she said in a carefully controlled voice. "Bobby, it was good to meet you and I look forward to some of those cookies." Both she and Chance shook hands with the subdued little boy.

"Don't you two be strangers now," Sally said.

They opened the door to find that the rain had settled down to a drizzle. Chance sprinted the short distance to the car and slid into his seat. Darien followed a short distance behind. She opened her door and seated herself stiffly, staring straight ahead.

"Where do you get off, Chance?" she asked with barely controlled fury.

"What's your problem, Rennie?"

"The name is Darien and my problem is you," she shot back.

"Ummm," he said, tapping the address into his phone's GPS.

"Didn't you hear what I said to you back at the ferry, or do you just choose to disregard it and make your own rules?"

"All right," he said with exaggerated patience, putting his phone aside. "I see you're all riled up and it's rules time again. What have I done this time?"

"I didn't appreciate that remark about the bedroom arrangement being fine for now."

He turned and met her eyes. "I was simply stating a fact, Darien. This is how you want it now and I get that. And if it's how you want it later, that's how it'll stay. I get that, too. But to my knowledge, there's no rule against two people having a little fun while they're working, and if at some point you're interested in a little of that fun…"

She glared at him. "This is how I want things now and I'm absolutely certain it's how I will want things later, so give it a rest."

"Look," he said. "Let's call a truce here. I expect that one thing we both see the same way is that we got some pretty interesting information from Sally today. Can I invite you to refocus that razor sharp mind and perpetual sense of outrage on the case at hand?"

"It hasn't escaped my notice that you only want to change the subject when the argument isn't going your way," she said. You act like an adolescent, and then when I call you on it, you're all innocence. Suddenly, it's all about business."

He regarded her steadily.

"All right then," she said finally. "The information. But I meant what I said, Chance. Watch yourself."

"Yes ma'am" he said with just the barest hint of sarcasm.

"For starters," he said, "take what she said about replacing the office equipment. That's classic in an arson. You remove the valuables to store for future use, and replace them with junk that you don't mind losing in the fire. It's especially intriguing because we're on an island. Either they've taken it off the island somehow or, if my hunch is right, they didn't have time or didn't risk that and have it stored somewhere here where we may be able to get our hands on it."

"Then let's plan to study the fire scene to see if anything else of value has been removed," Darien said. "And zero in on that point when we get to the interviews."

Chance nodded in agreement. Darien's glance lingered on him despite her best intentions. She looked down at his hands on the wheel. They were large, rough but well-formed. They rested lightly but firmly on the wheel. She looked away.

"And it sounded like there's more," he continued. "She stopped only because Bobby joined us. She has other information and we need to get it quickly."

"This is it," he said, turning abruptly off the road, and they pulled into a long driveway.

Darien leaned forward and peered through the drizzling rain to catch a glimpse of the house. Sally had told her to expect something special, but still she was unprepared for the sight that greeted her.

They were isolated here, removed from the tourists that crowded Old Harbor even when it wasn't the high season. The graceful lines of the old house were covered with weathered gray shingles. There were neat rows of windows, each flanked by freshly painted white shutters. The house was set well back from the two-lane road and fronted a broad, gently rolling growth of scrub that was typical of the Island. The back of the house looked out over a vast expanse of ocean, which now was a deep gray-green and flecked with white from the winds that swept in with the rain.

"I'll take the bags in," Chance said. "You go ahead and open the door."

Was that a peace offering?

"Thanks," she said.

She hurried the short distance to the door and put the key into the old lock. The hardware was obviously antique, probably brass. She swung the door open and stepped inside.

It was simply magnificent. With the exception of the kitchen, which she could see off to her right, the entire downstairs was one room separated into areas. The back wall was glass and looked out onto the ocean. Darien could see the wind-whipped waves surging up on the shore below before falling back to gather strength for the next swell. A door led out to a deep, wrap-around porch, on which Maggie had set out a comfortable arrangement of tables, chairs and lounges.

The living room was decorated in natural fabrics in various shades of beige. It was filled with comfortable furniture accented with colorful embroidered pillows and blankets in muted colors woven from what appeared to be the softest wool. Paintings of Block Island decorated the walls, including several of the bird life. The room held a variety of family photographs and mementos. Cozy and welcoming, it was true to Sally's description of Maggie's sure decorating hand. And best of all, there was a baby grand piano situated in an alcove, surrounded on three sides by glass and commanding a dramatic view of the ocean. What music she could make in this room!

Chance brought in the last of the luggage and she preceded him upstairs to find her room. Darien stood in the doorway, trying to take it all in. The room was light and feminine, with a delicate canopy bed and matching curtains at the window. The soft peach tones of the walls harmonized perfectly with the apricot and cream colors of the fabric on the bed and at the windows. She even had a desk. She stepped to the French doors and pulled back the curtain. A balcony ran the full width of her room, looking out over the ocean. After her sterile, tiny apartment, it would be such a pleasure to call this room her own.

Chance strode into the room and set her bags down pointedly in the middle of the floor. "I gather this is where you'll want these," he said.

She nodded decisively, looking him straight in the eyes, and then placed her briefcase on the bed.

"I'm going to use this time to review my notes and work on the strategy for the investigation. You might want to look at the witness interviews from the other fires. And I have a book on arson investigation that you should study. It'll help if you have some of the basics before tomorrow," he said.

"All right," she agreed. She would have said just about any-thing to move this along. She felt vulnerable with him in her bedroom. She twisted her mother's emerald ring nervously.

Chance started to leave the room, but then slowly turned in the doorway and looked back at her. She was startled to see his puzzled expression. He opened his mouth as if to speak, but then seemed to change his mind. He turned and walked out of the room.

CHAPTER FOUR

The delicious smells wafting up from the kitchen distracted Darien from her reading and she stood stiffly, stretching to relieve the cramped muscles. She was hungry. She glanced at her watch. It was almost seven. No wonder. And it had grown chillier. She pulled down a warm wool sweater from her shelf and slipped it over her head. She was not anxious to go downstairs and join Chance, but her hunger was stronger than her reluctance, and with misgivings, she left the relative security of her room for what was sure to be another sparring match. Damn that man.

She found him in the kitchen, stirring a bubbling pot on the stove and looking far too domestic and tame to be a problem for any woman. Appearances could be deceiving, but this was really the limit.

He turned when she entered the kitchen and smiled his most disarming smile. She noticed that he, too, had put on warmer clothes, and the rich forest-green of his sweater deepened and darkened the green of his eyes. He was a remarkably handsome man, if one cared to notice. And she most definitely did not care to notice.

"Sally is a seriously good cook," he said. "We owe her. I'm just heating up her seafood chowder. She left the makings of a salad and some great bread. We should be ready to eat in just a few minutes. How about some wine while we're waiting?"

Warily, she accepted a glass. She looked around the room. The table was set with simple mats with a woodland motif, and Sally had left an arrangement of fresh, early wildflowers in a rustic pottery vase. It looked casual, inviting. She was accustomed to eating on the run at her desk, or in front of the television with the national news for company.

"You look at ease in the kitchen," she said.

"I should," he said. "I come from a large family. We are five kids, all boys and close in age. Mom needed help, and besides, she thought we should be able to take care of ourselves when we left home. She used to say our wives would thank her someday. I don't cook fancy, but I cook good. I'll show off for you one evening while we're here."

He was working on the salad now. She knew she should offer to help, but she was fascinated watching him. If she had been asked to describe the least likely scenario for this evening, this would be right up at the top of her list. She looked up and met his eyes briefly, felt a sensation like riding an elevator that was dropping into oblivion, then looked away. She noticed that her glass was empty. That was obviously enough wine for one evening. She needed a clear head. It was definitely time to talk business.

Darien said, "I've been thinking about Bobby."

"It's an odd situation," he said. "There's something bothering that kid, and I doubt it has much to do with his sister. He was so guarded with me, and he was wound up tighter than a spring."

"I agree. I'm wondering if his behavior might be somehow connected to the fire."

Chance turned his attention to the mushrooms. "How do you figure that?" he asked.

"Think about it," she replied. "The field trip was on Monday, the same day as the fire. According to Sally, Bobby's peculiar behavior and clinginess started early on Tuesday, and he refused to leave her side either Tuesday or today."

"That's not a whole lot to go on," Chance said.

"Then there's the matter of that shell. He found it on the field trip. The field trip he won't discuss with his mother. The field trip that coincided with the start of his fears. According to you, it was a pretty special shell, Chance. Why didn't he put it with his collection? Or show it to his mom? Or, if he didn't want it, why didn't he just leave it on the beach, or throw it out? But he did none of those things. He just put it out of view, hid it behind a curtain, like he couldn't deal with it, somehow."

"That's true," he said. "And he was none too happy when I found it. When I asked him about it, he stammered for a bit and then finally told me when he'd found it, but then took it from me and put it back behind the curtain."

"The strangest thing of all, though, was Bobby's response when you mentioned his dad. He jumped right up out of his seat, almost like he was getting ready to defend him. Bobby forbade you from taking him anywhere near the scene of the fire. It couldn't be clearer that he doesn't want his dad within a hundred miles of that hotel. Why?"

"Not a bad question. Ought to be easy enough to figure out where the class went on that field trip. I suppose there's only one kindergarten on Block Island. Why don't you call the school tomorrow and check with the teacher. If they were in the vicinity of the hotel, it would be worth following up with Bobby. Maybe you can arrange to meet with him."

He tossed the salad and looked her way. "If you'll help me cart the food over to the table, dinner is served," he said.

She brought the salad to the table and then returned for the bowls of chowder. Chance insisted on carrying the bread, butter, salad dressing and wine all in one trip, precariously perched in his arms, but managed to deliver them safely to the table. Darien seated herself and watched as he poured her another glass of wine. She really should refuse, but it had been a long, stressful day, and the wine was excellent.

The chowder was real comfort food and the fresh baked bread was delicious. Her world seemed to be slowing down a notch or two, and although she suspected it was ill-advised around Chance, Darien could feel herself start to relax.

"So, tell me about Chance Deckert," she said.

"What would you like to know?"

"Where do you live in Montana, and what's it like?"

"Ever been there?"

"Never."

"We have a ranch in the southwestern part of the state, not far from Yellowstone. Lots of open space, no neighbors within thirty miles or so. It's rugged country, harsh and unforgiving, and it's kinda isolated, especially in winter. Plenty of cold weather and lots of snow. And the work on the ranch is tough." He seemed for a few minutes to be lost in thought.

"Despite the distances, everyone knows everyone. And everyone knows everyone's business. Families tend to stay put and kids carry on the family business. It's what's expected and it can get pretty stifling after a while." He took a long drink of his wine. "Yet there's so much about it that I love."

"Like what?" she asked.

He thought for a few minutes. "Well, we have the usual misunderstandings, but I think the world of my family. They're the best. And I like the big sky, the open spaces. No restraints. No limits. No entanglements. We rely on ourselves and we get the job done."

They ate in silence for a few moments.

"You said before that you were five brothers." She watched as he reached for the bottle of wine and poured her another glass. "Do your brothers still live in Montana?"

"Yeah, they all do. The older three are married and have built homes on our ranch. Seems like there's always a kid or two underfoot, and that makes Mom happy."

"Are they all still working the ranch, or have they taken on separate careers like yours?"

"They're all involved with different parts of the family business. I'm the family misfit, I guess. I like being part of our family, don't get me wrong. And I know my life away from the ranch is a puzzle to them. They don't get how I could want to do the work I do and go the places I go. They seem to hope it's a phase I'm going through and I'll come home to Montana, settle down with a good wife, raise a family and work the ranch with them."

She studied him for a moment, absorbing this information. "And is it? Will you?"

Darien was taken aback by his pained expression and momentary silence. She watched as he pushed the salad around on his plate.

"I don't hold out much hope for my family's vision." He paused and drained the wine from his glass.

"I tried," he said, staring intently at the glass. "I went through all the right motions. I found the right woman, I said all the right things and made all the right plans, but in the end, none of it was right." He put down the glass and met her eyes.

"All that my trying accomplished was to hurt a trusting girl and disappoint my family. I'm just not that man, and it's better for everyone if I don't pretend to be." He smiled, but the smile wobbled around the edges. "And I don't, Darien. I don't pretend." He turned his attention back to his dinner and lapsed into silence.

Darien knew from painful experience the need to take refuge in silence, and knew, too, that refuge was an illusion. There was no refuge from the truth. She finished her dinner in silence while mulling over this unexpected and poignant revelation.

"Now, on this particular cold, dark night, my mind is an open book and my motives are wholly innocent," he said, interrupting her thoughts. "I'm planning to clean up the kitchen and then take a long, brisk walk on the beach. You're welcome to join me, if you'd like."

"Thanks, but I think I'll take the opportunity to play the piano for a while," she said. "The one in the living room is a beautiful instrument, and it's been a long time since I've had the chance to play."

She left the kitchen, seated herself at the piano and ran her fingers lightly up and down the keyboard, listening with delight to the warm, resonant tone of the old instrument. Then she closed her eyes and started to play the blues. She began with some of her favorites, coaxing from the well-worn keys the aching notes of loneliness and melodies of loss. "Stormy Weather." "I Got a Right to Sing the Blues." "But Not for Me." Then she moved on to other beloved pieces, lingering over favorite refrains. She'd lost track of the time and had no idea how long she'd been playing, when she became aware of Chance close behind her. She stopped playing mid-song and put her hands in her lap.

"Don't stop on my account," he said. "I could listen to you play all night. You are very, very good, even if that is some of the saddest, most melancholy music I've ever heard."

"Thanks," she said, closing up the keyboard.

"You play as if you've been there."

"I play as if I've had many years of piano lessons," she said.

He shrugged his shoulders. "Well, if you're done playing, can I get you to change your mind and come out walking with me? It's a beautiful night. The wind's still up from the storm and the waves are rolling in. C'mon, it'll do you good to let the fresh air blow the cobwebs out of that high-priced brain of yours. I'll get your coat."

Well, maybe it was a good idea. The music had worked its magic for a while, but tomorrow, inevitably, would come, and she was still feeling uneasy at the prospect of all that tomorrow held. And a brisk walk in the cold and the wind would tire her out, help her sleep better. God knows that a good night's sleep would be a welcome change.

He held open her jacket, but she took it from him and shrugged into it. Then she followed him out the door and down onto the beach.

They set off at a brisk pace. He'd been right about the wind, she thought, turning up the collar of her coat against the raw night. It whipped the waves into a churning frenzy and set the broken clouds to scudding wildly across the sky. There was no light from the vast, opaque ocean to compete with the stars, so they glittered fiercely and seemed surprisingly near. The moon was a jagged sliver in the turbulent sky, now visible in its entirety, and now obscured by the clouds, casting ever-changing patterns of light and shadow on the beach. She hurried to keep up with his long strides.

They walked in silence for what seemed like a long way, with the sound of the roiling surf accompanying their footsteps. When he finally came to a stop, it took a few moments for her to sort out her surroundings. She was aware that the intensity of the wind had diminished. She saw that they were in a small cove, surrounded by cliffs and protected from the elements.

Darien turned toward Chance. He was leaning back against a bluff of craggy rocks and motioned for her to join him. She settled against the bluff some distance from him and turned her eyes to the ocean, trying to see by the wavering light of the moon. She could just make out the whitecaps on the waves. One after another, they threw themselves at the shore, as if struggling to escape their fate in the dark depths of the ocean, only to surrender to a pull stronger than their will and fade back softly into the night. The crash of the waves on the shore, followed by the soft murmuring sounds as they swept back out to sea, was hypnotic. She closed her eyes, lulled by the soothing sound, comforted by its predictability.

She felt his presence, sensed him standing in front of her, long before she opened her eyes. And when she did, he was there, standing very close to her and looking down at her with eyes soft with desire. Dark against the moonlit scene behind him, he looked solid and strong, steady in the midst of the shifting sands and ocean. He moved closer, and then slowly bent toward her.

The touch of his lips on hers was unimaginably gentle. It was less a kiss, and more a caress with his lips. It demanded nothing, took nothing. She had never dreamed a man could be so tender.

He broke the kiss and stood back in silence, searching her eyes. The wind suddenly gusted and whipped her hair across her face. Carefully, he brushed the tangled curls from her face, and then letting his hands slide down to her shoulders, he pulled her into his arms. He brought his lips to hers again, but this time they were hungrier, harder. He pushed her lips apart and deepened the kiss, pressing his body to hers until she felt herself growing as liquid and wild as the waves, as searing hot as the stars. She sighed, but the sound was taken by the wind and was lost.

If she let this go on for even one moment more, she would surrender whatever will she had to turn away from this man. That would be a mistake.

Darien pulled back from his touch and stumbled away from him toward the rocks of the bluff. She rested her burning cheeks against the hard, cold surface of the stone until she had regained her composure. Then, pulling her jacket tightly around her, she turned to face him. In the cold moonlight, she could see the question in his eyes. She had the answer to his question, all right, but he wasn't going to hear it. What good would it do?

Suddenly, she was terribly tired. "I'm going back to the house. No need to walk with me. I can find my way alone." Hadn't she always?

She turned on her heels and strode back toward the house. She could feel his eyes on her as she moved away from him. Was he laughing at her? Cursing her? She probably deserved both. He had been honest about who he was and how he saw his world. She'd been put on notice, and should not be surprised that he was a man who took so easily and cared so little. But common sense had been a casualty of the wind and the stars and the waves. She would not let that happen again.

So she wasn't interested. No problem. There were plenty of women out there who were up for good times with no strings attached. Passion without promises. No expectations. No commitments. He knew who he was, and he knew whatever kind of love he was capable of ran shallow and didn't take root. Like the tumbleweed on the ranch, he blew where the wind took him and then moved on.

Chance closed his eyes and tried to steady his breathing. His heart was pounding and he felt off balance, shaky. He wanted to call after Darien. He wanted her to come back.

What the hell! What was the matter with him? He ran his fingers through his hair and then stuffed them into the pockets of his jeans. He turned into the wind and started back to the house.

Darien went directly up to her room and shut the door firmly behind her. Quickly, she undressed and slipped into her nightgown, going through the motions mechanically, with no conscious thought. Then she slid beneath the soft, scented covers and lay awake, trying not to listen for his return.

Shortly, she heard the heavy door below close after him. Her heart gave an odd jolt as she heard him on the stairs, his step firm, determined. He reached the top of the stairs and then his footsteps faded as he turned in the direction of his room. His door creaked as it opened, and then she heard him shut the door behind him.

Darien lay still for a few moments, aware of the rapid pounding of her heart. Then, feeling foolish, she rose quietly from her bed, walked slowly to the door, and turned the key in the lock. As she stared at the old-fashioned, ornate key, she tried to be absolutely honest with herself. What was she doing? Was she locking the door to keep Chance out or to keep herself in? Uncertain, she turned and climbed back into bed.

CHAPTER FIVE

He was acting as if nothing had happened, but she shouldn't have expected anything different. Despite her restless night and the hours spent trying to understand that kiss on the beach, it was likely that for him, nothing out of the ordinary had happened. Nothing he hadn't expected, in any event, except perhaps her walking away.

"Coffee?" she asked him, lifting the pot and pouring herself a cup.

"Already had some," he replied, thumbing through some notes with a distracted expression. "Grabbed some of those muffins Sally baked, too. They're terrific. Maybe you could have yours on the road to save some time. I'm in a hurry to get out to the hotel and get started. I've already packed all our equipment and protective gear. I need time to study the scene, make sketches, take pictures, gather samples. Later today I have a phone meeting with the incident commander to get a briefing, and I don't want to be late."

"Fine with me," she said. "Do you want to fix something for lunch, or would you rather find someplace to eat?"

"I don't want to take the time to pack lunch now. We probably should have taken care of that last night."

She gave him a searching look. He was busy assembling his equipment. No hidden meaning there.

"We'll be sure to take care of it this evening," she said.

"Sure, okay. Ready to go?"

Darien drew in a deep, shaky breath. She wiped an invisible crumb off the counter and turned toward the door. As ready as she'd ever be. Which was not very ready. Not very ready at all.

She could smell the acrid odor of smoke long before they pulled up to the old hotel. Despite yesterday's rain, it hung heavy on the spring breeze. She tried to isolate the fact of the odor from all that it suggested. But despite her firm resolve, wisps of memories, pale and half-formed, drifted into consciousness and then receded.

She would simply have to try harder. Darien twisted her mother's emerald ring with nervous fingers and chewed on her lower lip. The queasiness in her stomach seemed to intensify with each passing minute. She swallowed hard.

Darien glanced over at Chance, who was intent on locating the hotel. Despite the chill of the early April morning, he was dressed in a faded black T-shirt and old black jeans. His freshly washed hair was still damp, and she could make out the tracks left by his comb. His eyes, almost gray in the early morning light, were clear and focused. He looked solid, confident. Firmly anchored in the present. Almost imperceptibly, she inched closer to him in the car.

"A remote location with an obstructed view," Chance said. "That made their work a whole lot easier. I think you've been over the reports from the fire commander. They received a call about the fire at 1:30 p.m. The cleaning crew had been in there working all morning to get the place in shape for the tourist season. According to the report, they left at about noon, so there was no one on the premises when the fire broke out."

"That was fortunate," Darien replied. Her voice sounded steady. That, at least, was a relief.

"More than fortunate, I'd bet," he said. "They probably planned it that way. These folks are interested in profit and there's no sense in complicating things if it's not necessary. That's not to say that they'd hesitate to hurt someone. They'd probably do whatever it takes to get what they want. Odds are good they decided to start the fire after the cleaning crew left to ensure that it would get a good start before anyone called it in. Also, unless they used some kind of remote trigger, they would have needed everyone out of the building in order to start the fire without being spotted. We'll want to figure out who was the last person to leave the hotel. That might be important."

She blinked her eyes hard and tried to focus on the conversation.

Chance consulted his directions and then turned down a road. "First firefighters arrived on the scene at 2:05."

"I noticed that," Darien said. "It doesn't make sense. This is a small island and the fire house can't be that far away. Why would it take so long for them to arrive at the fire?"

"Good question," Chance said. "I'd flagged that as something we should follow up on. Who saw the fire first? Who turned in the alarm? Why the delay? Block Island has a volunteer firefighter unit. I did some checking before we came out here and they have a good reputation. We'll have to catch up with them. They can flesh out the report and maybe come up with some helpful details."

"What else did you think was significant in the report?"

"They found a portable heating unit that the cleaning crew was using to stay warm. It was plugged in and turned on, and there were rags close by, which would have suggested that the fire was accidentally set. But the cleaning crew reported that they had turned off the unit. It's already been sent out for testing to determine whether someone poured an accelerant into the heater and on the rags and ignited it. We'll also want to know if it was operating normally at the time of the fire. Had it been sent out recently for repair? Had it been moved recently? Was it subject to recalls? Had it been modified? Can you look into that?"

Darien nodded yes. She fumbled for her phone and selected her music app. Without looking at the title or artist, she made a selection. The moody strains of an Etta James song filled the car.

"He reported that the fire was burning a deep cherry red and that it was throwing off large quantities of black smoke, and he suspected the presence of fuel oil. I checked out the heating system and it uses propane, so if true, that's a suspicious finding."

They rounded a curve and the hotel came into view. The charred section of the old building traced a jagged line that was starkly visible against the backdrop of the serene blue of the ocean and the lighter blue of a cloudless sky. It was covered by a dark blue tarp, which flapped disconsolately in the breeze. Bits and pieces of what had once been the gracious furnishings of the hotel were strewn about at random, some burned almost beyond recognition, others showing barely any sign of damage. An air of desolation pervaded the scene. Darien turned away, but she couldn't turn away from the memories.

Chance sat in the car for a few minutes, taking it in.

"We'll need the protective gear," he said. "I'll carry the cameras, notebooks and the shovels and heavy stuff. You take the toolbox and the sample containers. Be sure to bring plenty of evidence labels." He lifted his cameras from the back seat and grabbed the shovels and other tools from the trunk. Then he strode off toward the building.

Darien hesitated, watching as he unlocked the padlock and walked briskly in the direction of the burned portion of the hotel. She took the bulky specimen containers by the handles, scooped up everything else remaining in the trunk that looked like it was part of their investigation and turned warily in the direction of the hotel. Trying not to look too closely at the scorched building, and deliberately making her mind a blank so as not to think of what lay ahead, she strode rapidly after Chance.

"Put everything down here," he said. "First we'll do a visual inspection of the outside of the structure, and then we'll take a careful look at the material that was thrown from the building during the fire." He picked up one of his cameras and a notebook.

"This is a handsome old building," he said. "You can still pick out the clean, strong lines of the design. Made for gracious living back when summer people counted on formal dining for all meals, large bedrooms with plenty of storage for big wardrobes, and other home comforts. A bit of a dinosaur, but I bet it was really something in its day."

The stench of fire and charring was oppressive. Darien moved closer to Chance. Steeling herself, she risked a look at the building. In response, the earth heaved and rolled under her feet. She looked down again quickly. Her hands were clammy with perspiration. She wiped them furtively on her trousers. She had to stay in this world, in this reality.

"We'll need to rule out accidental causes of the fire, so we should be particularly vigilant for anything that will show that this wasn't an electrical fire," she said through the haze of fear that was enveloping her.

Chance seemed engrossed in his study of the outside of the structure. He was by turns snapping pictures and writing in his notebook. She watched as he moved around a corner to another view of the hotel and lingered while he studied it carefully.

Just as carefully, Darien kept her eyes locked on Chance. She did not want to look at the charred timbers, the blistered paint, the weirdly twisted metal ornamentation. She feared what she would see, but worse yet, she feared what might follow if she truly let herself look. God help her if she had to confront her own private, internal fire-scape here, fully awake in the stark light of day. Those images belonged in the world of slumber, where the raw horror was muted by the soft, dark edges of the night. If she let them seep through the boundaries of wakefulness…

He stopped writing and stood for a long time gazing up at the building. "Look at that window," he said. "Still has a few shards of glass, but most have been knocked out. You can see that the fire vented there. The wall is badly discolored and there is more evidence of burn in that area. And look at this."

He bent down and picked up a piece of broken glass and turned it over in his hand.

"What?" Darien asked.

"There's no soot staining on this glass, no crazing. What do you make of that?"

She concentrated on his words and tried to formulate a response. "The glass was knocked out before the fire started rather than blown out by the fire, probably to let some oxygen in to feed the fire and make certain it wouldn't burn out prematurely."

"Exactly," Chance replied. "But that is either a big-time amateur move or the work of someone in a huge hurry who is sacrificing caution for speed." He took some photos and drew a careful diagram of the area where the glass was found.

Darien had absolutely no intention of looking further at the offending window, the glass, or anything else to do with this fire, for that matter. Her grasp on the present, on reality, was becoming more tenuous by the minute.

He continued to move slowly and carefully around the outside of the structure, stopping from time to time to make a note or take a picture. For the most part, he was silent, his eyes and attention fully focused on his work. When he spoke, it was to mutter a comment to himself. He seemed to expect no reply. That suited her fine.

For Darien, time stretched and twisted like melted wax. She could not have said what hour it was or how long they had been there. The ground seemed to her more fluid than firm, and the light wobbled precariously. She was calling on every ounce of grit that she possessed to hold herself together. She stared fixedly at Chance. She did not know where else it was safe to look.

"Look at that," he said half to himself and half to her. "The fire marshal found this really telling and so do I."

Chance was studying the building intently. "We're all the way at the opposite end of the hotel from what looked to be the point of origin of the fire. And there's fire damage at this end, as well."

"That doesn't make sense," she said deliberately, carefully lining up the syllables one after another.

"It looks like we have two independent points of origin for this fire, not one. One at each end of the hotel. And I can't think of a logical explanation for why an electrical fire would start simultaneously at opposite ends of the hotel."

He stood quietly for a minute, clearly not expecting a response, and then jotted down some notes. "See anything else that doesn't fit?" he asked.

Bracing herself, she looked quickly up at the building and then fastened her eyes on the ground. Her heart was racing painfully and she felt hopelessly dizzy. Her hair was damp with perspiration. Cautiously, she leaned against the wall for support before she answered.

"The window is broken on this side of the building, as well. We'll want to check with the firefighters to see which windows were already broken when they arrived, just to be sure, but I'm thinking we know the answer to that question."

Something in her tone of voice must have caught his attention, because he turned a sharp look on her. "You're white as a sheet," he said, his eyes narrowing with concern.

"Nothing to worry about," she said in a flat, hollow tone of voice. "A bit too much wine last night, I think. I'll feel better if I don't pay it any attention and just keep going."

"You didn't have that much to drink," he said. "Did you sleep okay last night?"

"Don't flatter yourself," she replied with forced animation. "I slept very well last night." With an effort, she detached herself from the wall.

"What a waste," he said, turning back to his notes. "Some things are worth staying awake for."

She turned away.

"I've seen enough of the outside of the structure. I want to spend some time studying the furnishings and other materials that were tossed from the windows. Let's start over by the first broken window."

That was not going to happen.

"I have a few things I need to check on back at the office, Chance," she said in the steadiest voice she could summon. "I'll call in from my cell phone and join you in a bit."

"All right," he said, rifling through the pages of his notebook. "But try not to be too long. There's a lot to do here."

Darien walked unsteadily back to the car, trying to put as much distance as possible between her and the fire scene. Under no circumstances, she thought, would she look at anything more that day that was even remotely related to the fire. She had sense enough to know that she had reached the limit of what she could tolerate. No, the truth was she had passed that limit sometime earlier, and had been going on sheer nerve and determination. Both were exhausted now, and so was she.

She slid into the passenger seat, leaned back against the cool leather and tried to regain her composure. Slowly, blessedly, the waves of nausea and dizziness abated. She sat like that for several minutes, until she was quite certain that the laws of physics were in control of her world once again. Only then did she open her eyes.

Why had she thought that she could manage this situation? How had she been foolish enough to accept this assignment? Far better to have weathered Edward's wrath and disappointment back at the office than to have come here to Block Island. It was not that the fears or sensations were new. They were old companions of her youth that had accompanied her to adulthood, deepening with the passage of years until now, after so many years, they were as familiar as the reflection that greeted her each morning in her mirror. But she grappled with them alone, in the dark hours of the night, unobserved and unencumbered. She could not afford to lose control here, in the light of day.

Nervously, she fingered her mother's emerald ring. As she had innumerable times in the past, she asked herself if there were anyone she could turn to for help. She knew better, of course, but still could not surrender the comforting fantasy that someday someone would get close enough to her to know, and feel deeply enough for her to care. Darien thought of the careless, pleasure-seeking man she had left behind at the fire scene and her mouth twisted into a bitter smile. Chance Deckert was not a promising candidate for that position. Of that she had no doubt. He had been clear about what he was looking for, and it had precious little to do with caring. He had no interest in her as a person and would have no patience with her secrets. Here, as always, she was on her own with her ghosts, and on her own was the way she would have to deal with them.

And now, she thought, finally, here at this bleak site and in the company of this troublesome man, deal with them she must. She had no choice. Her job was on the line and her credibility was at stake. In the last analysis, they were all that she had and, realistically, they were all she could expect to have. The hard truth was, she simply could not afford to fail.

Darien sat very still, marshalling her resolve and strength. Then she retrieved her bag from the back seat, pulled out her cell phone, and called the office.

She didn't know how much time had passed when Chance slid quietly into the seat next to her. He was silent, listening attentively until she had completed her call.

"Nice job, counselor," he said.

Darien turned to him, expecting to see a mockery in his eyes. Instead, she found him looking at her with an expression of frank admiration.

"I like the way you handle yourself. I see why Jim was so intent on getting you to do this work."

"Did you find anything else of interest?" she asked quickly, meeting his eyes briefly and then looking away.

"I'll tell you about it over lunch," he said, starting the engine. "Let's drive back toward town and see what we can find open this early in the season."

She watched with an increasing sense of relief as the scenery flashed by, grateful for each mile that separated her from the desolate hotel. She had faced the worst in that fire-ravaged hotel and gotten through it, with Chance none the wiser. She could not surrender again to the old fears that had held sway for so long. She would complete this investigation and she would do it well. And then she could go home to the safety of her everyday life. Home.

They approached a small, gray-shingled restaurant with a weathered sign that hung crookedly over the door.

"Let's try that restaurant," she suggested. "The locals congregate there and the food is pretty good."

Chance maneuvered the car into one of the few available spaces and they entered. The conversation was loud and animated, punctuated by an occasional burst of laughter. Darien smelled something delicious — chowder? — and realized with surprise that she was hungry. The nausea had passed and her appetite had returned with a vengeance. They found a booth and reached simultaneously for the menus. Shortly, a plump, affable waitress appeared and took their orders.

"Sorry I didn't get back in time to help," Darien said when they were alone. "Lots of loose ends to tie up at the office. Did you find anything useful?"

"I agree with the fire marshal that the fire was likely incendiary, set on purpose," Chance said without hesitation. "I found evidence of accelerants. If I had to guess, I'd say it was a combination of fuel oil and gasoline. It's not unusual for arsonists to mix the two, because fuel oil is hard to ignite."

"And does that track with anything found at the sites of the other suspicious fires?" she asked.

"Not much to go on with those fires, but I plan to look over the notes again tonight. And maybe you could follow-up with some of the witnesses and ask a few more questions. Anyway, I feel like we're making good progress. Jim'll be happy. He's pushing hard to get this investigation completed. He wants to know everything and he wants to know it pronto. We'll give him a call this evening and fill him in."

Their meal arrived, and just as the waitress was setting it in front of them, a tall, thin young man with a mop of curly blond hair approached.

"Hey, George, how's the family?" the waitress said.

"Good, thanks," he said. "And you must be Darien and Chance. No psychic powers," he said with a chuckle at their startled expressions. "Not too many strangers on the Island at this time of year, and I recognized you from Sally's description. I'm her husband, George Olsen." He extended his hand.

"Good to meet you," Darien said, taking his hand in hers.

"Hi," Chance said, extending his hand as well. "We've already had the pleasure of meeting up with the rest of your family and, I am happy to report, with your wife's cooking!"

George smiled and nodded. "She's something, isn't she? Anyway, just wanted to welcome you, and to let you know that if there's anything I can do to help with the house, just give a yell."

"Thanks," Chance said. "Everything seems okay with the house, but I understand that you're with the volunteer fire department. I'd sure appreciate the opportunity to talk with you about the fire. Can you join us?" He gestured toward the empty space in the booth.

"Got to get back to work," said George, "but I'd be happy to talk with you later today or tomorrow. And Sally is planning to have some folks over this weekend for a cookout to start the season. It's an annual event, something of an Island tradition, and we'd be real pleased if you two would join us. Come by about three on Sunday, and bring your appetites."

"If we can take the time off, that sounds good," Darien said. "I'd like to see Bobby and Lily again."

George's smile faded and his mouth formed a thin, straight line. "Sure," he said. "They'll be there. Got to run now, but glad I had the chance to meet you."

After a pause, Darien said, "Doesn't look like things are any better with Bobby. I'd like to follow up on my hunch and speak with the teacher. I'd also like to spend some time with Bobby and Sally and see what I can find out."

"Good idea," Chance said. "Maybe tomorrow. And I want to talk with you tonight about interviews with witnesses and research that might be helpful. But today we need to start looking at the interior of the hotel." He glanced at his watch. "We'll head back right after lunch and see how far we can get."

No sense of foreboding. Nothing. She would be fine.

The bleak outline of the hotel emerged in the distance, harshly illuminated by the glare of the midday sun. Darien followed Chance from the parking lot to the building and approached the entrance. Not even the most tentative rustling of fear accompanied her.

"The Fire Marshal cleared the building and concluded it was safe to enter. Not enough structural damage to make it unsafe," he reassured her. "But stay close to me and try not to touch anything. And put on that safety gear." He gestured to the equipment on the ground. After she had done so to his satisfaction, he pushed open the old door and she followed him through.

"We'll investigate the fire from the outer edges of each floor to the area of most burn, and from the bottom floor to the top," Chance explained. He started to shoot pictures as they slowly covered the space from the entrance hall to the hotel desk. He kept up a running commentary while pointing out interesting features.

"Look here," he exclaimed, dropping to his knees. Darien knelt beside him. "Look at this burn pattern. It runs deep and is confined to a small area. And it spreads in a very narrow line. I'll come back later and get some samples of the wood."

"I read about that last night," Darien said. That's a sign that fuel oil was used as an accelerant. The fuel oil has so much staying power that the fire burns a hole straight down from where it was placed. You can have good wood right next to the burn area, like this," she said, pointing to a nearby spot with smoke damage, but no burn.

"Exactly," he replied while snapping a series of shots.

He put the camera down for a moment and thoughtfully studied the hotel lobby. "Something's not right," he said in a puzzled tone. "Something's off, but I can't put my finger on it." He looked around again and shook his head. "Don't know what it is. Maybe it'll come to me later, when I study the photos." He retrieved the camera and took a few more shots.

They moved carefully from room to room, taking notes and pictures to record their findings. The work went more slowly than anticipated, and by the time they had completed the downstairs, it was late afternoon.

"I'm about done here," Chance said. "Let's go upstairs and take a quick look. We can come back tomorrow and finish."

"Fine," she said, approaching the stairs ahead of Chance. She paused briefly before she started to climb, getting her bearings and making certain that the bottom stairs and railings were secure. Then, her gaze swept slowly up the still graceful sweep of the staircase, rounding the elegant curves and coming to rest at the darkness at the top.

The surge of panic that crashed over Darien was as inevitable as it was unexpected, and left her reeling with shock. She struggled frantically for breath in air now grown thick with acrid, choking smoke that seared her nostrils and burned her lungs. The world around her faded to a murky, muted gray. In lurid contrast, the stairs erupted in dazzling shades of orange and red, shot through with flames that leaped and twisted into grotesque forms. She could hear Chance describing the burn pattern on the stairs, but his voice was distant, remote, and barely discernible over the roar of the flames.

The voice of reason that served as her guide whispered, as it always did, that this was the dream and was not real. She could free herself from this world by awakening. But this time it was different. She was not asleep, not dreaming. She was wide-awake and slipping deeper into the fire-world.

Swiftly, Darien turned from the menacing stairs, strode through the room and out the door. She could feel Chance's bewildered gaze following her and hear him calling her name. Such a futile gesture! No power on heaven or earth could have held her there. He might as well have been calling to the moon.

The sky was the first true thing she saw, and it filled her line of vision, awash in the palette of rose, blue, and purple of late afternoon. She pulled the safety equipment from her face and threw it to the ground. Darien could feel the grainy sand beneath her and could hear the rhythmic pounding of the surf. She struggled to focus on the weight, the density, the solidity of this world. This was real. This could be trusted.

She leaned her back against the blistered wall of the old hotel and tried to steady her breathing. As the menace of the fire world receded, a new and disturbing threat took its place. She saw with painful clarity that she was losing control. She was coming unraveled, and she was doing it very publicly. She was going to lose everything.

"Hey." Chance's voice was filled with concern. Gently, he brushed a cool hand over her cheek. "Darien, what happened?"

She didn't trust herself to speak. She was still in transition between two worlds, and she didn't know from which her words would come.

"I'm fine," she said finally. "The smell of smoke got to me for a minute there. I needed some fresh air, but I'm fine now."

Chance studied her in silence, and she met his gaze before dropping her eyes.

"You are not 'fine'," he said finally. "And you haven't been 'fine' all day. You were pale as a ghost this morning, and now this. Come on, Darien. What's going on? No rules. No games. Just tell me the truth."

She wavered for a moment. Inexplicably, she was tempted to tell him, tempted to free the ugly secret from the shadowy recesses of memory and bring it out into the bright light of day. But what good could that possibly do? There was no way to change what had happened all those years ago. The truth didn't change with the telling.

Darien pulled away from the wall and stood as steady as she could manage. "It's over, Chance, that's all you really need to know. And it won't happen again. I can assure you that nothing will interfere with our ability to work this case."

"Do you honestly think that's all I care about — this case?" he asked.

She looked at him steadily for a long time, and didn't answer. Yes, if the truth were to be told, she honestly did. But today had not been a day for truth telling, and there was no particular reason to start now.

"I'll wait for you in the car, Chance. Don't hurry on my account."

Darien turned and headed off in the direction of the car. She could feel his eyes following her every move. She did not look back.

CHAPTER SIX

Darien awoke to the dark and silence of the night. She turned to face the glowing green face on the clock on her nightstand. Three a.m. She could try to get back to sleep. But she was probably awake for the day, and if she stayed here in bed, her thoughts undoubtedly would take her where she did not wish to go. Bad enough to live through that humiliating scene at the hotel. She had no wish to relive the moment in her mind. The only saving grace had been Chance's omission, in their debrief with Jim, of any description of her unprofessional behavior. That was an unexpected kindness. At least she could hope it would stay between the two of them and go no further. Small comfort, but a comfort nonetheless.

She glanced at the clock again. Better to go downstairs and get her mind engaged in some kind of activity. Maybe while she awaited the dawn, she could pick out a book from the library she noticed in the living room. No more remembering. No more worrying.

Darien sat up in bed and turned on her bedside lamp. Her clothes were scattered on the floor where she had left them last night. She was always so meticulous, so careful of her belongings. It seemed that here, nothing would be as it always was.

Ignoring the clutter, she pulled her robe from the bedside chair and fastened it firmly around her. The thin, silky yellow fabric did not provide much protection from the evening chill that permeated her room, but in her haste to pack, she had neglected to bring anything warmer. This would have to do.

Darien opened the door and stepped out into the hall. A soft nightlight illuminated the head of the stairs. As she approached it, Chance's door swung open and he walked out into the dim light, headed in the direction of his bathroom.

Darien stepped back in confusion. He was wearing a pair of briefs and nothing more. He was so close that she could see the awareness dawn in his eyes as his gaze met hers. And she could see, too, that awareness turn inexorably into something more. The invitation there was unmistakable.

Drawing a shaky breath, Darien turned on her heels and walked quickly back to her room, shutting the door firmly behind her and turning the key for good measure. She lay sleepless on her bed, lost in thought and lost, too, in feelings both strong and unfamiliar. And try as she might, she could not fit them into one of her tidy little compartments, and could not discover a useful rule to govern her feelings and her behavior. She was still awake when the sun rose over the horizon.

Later, she heard Chance whistling in the shower, heard him opening and closing drawers in his room, and waited until she heard him bounding down the stairs, taking them two at a time, before she stepped into her own shower. She pulled on her jeans and a soft yellow cotton sweater, and then headed downstairs to breakfast.

Chance was fixing bacon and eggs in the sunny kitchen. She noticed with displeasure that he looked well rested and eager to start the day. No sleepless nights for him. That man had no conscience.

"Good morning," he said, as he fixed a plate for her. "You missed a beautiful sunrise over the ocean today."

Darien seated herself at the table and looked with distaste at the plate he set before her. She pushed it away and said, "Chance, I want to talk about last night. We need to get some things straight."

His smile faded and he silently poured himself some juice and settled in the chair across from her. "Rules again? Is that where we're headed with this? Okay, Darien, exactly what about last night would you like to talk about?" he replied, grinding pepper liberally on his eggs.

"You're going to make this difficult, aren't you?"

"Not at all," he said, finally looking up to meet her eyes. "I'm more than willing to talk about last night." His eyes swept over her lazily, and she felt the heat rise to her cheeks.

"What should we talk about?" he continued in his slow, deliberate way. "Where should we start? Do you want to talk about the way that you looked at me, Darien? No? Well…"

"That's quite enough, Chance," she said sharply. "You see what you want to see, and that's your problem, not mine. I want to talk about consideration, about courtesy. Like it or not, we're both living in this house, in close proximity that can't be avoided. Privacy is hard to come by, but you are making it worse by refusing to abide by even the most basic conventions."

"And those would be?" he prompted.

"Those would be making certain that you're decently clothed when you're in public spaces. Pajamas, Chance. Try them."

"I don't sleep in pajamas," he said. "I sleep in my skivvies."

"You weren't sleeping," she pointed out.

"Look," he said, an edge creeping into his voice. "That's how I sleep and that's how I go to the john. None of your rules are going to change that. And while we're on the subject, that flimsy yellow thing you were wearing didn't leave much to the imagination, either. You don't hear me complaining."

She dropped her eyes. He was right, of course. Where humiliation was concerned, his instincts were unerring. Damn him!

"You have a nasty way of pushing the limits, Chance."

"With you, that's a short walk," he retorted.

"Why is it always all about you, about what you want, whatever the consequences for anyone else?" she said angrily.

"And why is it always a matter of right and wrong for you?" he shot back. "You're so busy figuring out what category to put things in, and what rules people should play by, that it's all lost on you. No fun. No pleasure. No life!"

"If you find me so ridiculous, why can't you just leave me alone?" she said.

They were both silent for a moment while her words lingered between them.

"I don't know the answer to that question, Darien," he said. "And I don't understand it any better than you do."

The anger drained from her, leaving confusion in its place. Darien sat immobile and silent, gazing at her untouched meal. Finally, unable to endure the silence any longer, she looked up at Chance.

"I asked you to respect my wishes. You'll either choose to do it or you won't. I don't think there's more to say, Chance. I suggest we get to work and try to get this assignment over with as quickly as possible."

"Fine by me," Chance said.

"I'm going to give Bobby's teacher a call this morning, and then I'd like to spend some time with Bobby," she said, assuming a careful, neutral tone. "I was thinking that I might take him on an activity, maybe a sail, to put him at ease. He'd be more likely to open up then."

"Fine," he responded. "No need for you to go back to the hotel. I can finish up alone. I think your work there is done." His voice, too, was studiously neutral.

Darien studied his face. Was he remembering yesterday? Was he trying to protect her? His expression communicated nothing.

"I'll be meeting with the electrician and with George late in the morning. We're going to spend some time working through this electrical fire theory. And I need to look more closely at the fire detection and fire suppression systems, which both failed. I should do that before you interview anyone about them. But I'd like to meet up with Bobby, too. Give me a call on my cell and let me know what's happening, and I'll try to join you," Chance said.

"Okay," she agreed in a civil tone. "That'll work."

"Good to know there's still something we can agree on," he said.

"I don't want to quarrel with you, Chance," Darien said. It was intended to be a simple statement of fact and nothing more. But the tremor in her voice, where had that come from? And the tears lurking so close to the surface, what was that about?

Hurriedly, she got to her feet and started toward the door to get her jacket. She removed it from the hook and turned to find Chance blocking her path, so close that she could hear the sound of his breathing, so near that she could see his chest rise and fall with each breath. She stopped abruptly to avoid touching him.

Chance reached out and caressed her cheek, turning her face gently up to his. Darien stood absolutely still, staring into hazel eyes grown surprisingly tender and savoring the warmth of his touch. Closing her eyes, she turned her face into his hand and brushed her lips across the callused skin. Then she pulled away and went quickly through the door to Maggie's car.

Sitting in the garage, Darien paused to remember. The sensation of his hand on her cheek. The way he had looked at her. The feel of his hand against her lips. She backed the car out of the garage and swung onto the road.

Her intuition had been correct, Darien thought, reviewing her notes. Bobby's teacher had confirmed that the field trip had been a nature study and that they had spent time in the vicinity of the hotel. They had planned to stay a few hours, but because of the fire, had been there only from approximately noon to one-thirty p.m., when she moved the children quickly but calmly into the waiting bus and off the property. In fact, she had remarked to the principal how very fortunate it was that they were there so she could call in the fire alarm before the fire had progressed too far.

Darien thought, too, that Bobby might have been on his own for some time. The children had not necessarily stayed together in a group, because they were searching for interesting specimens of shells and stones. The teacher assured her that they had all been within her sight at all times. Darien thought of a group of frisky kindergarten students turned loose on the beach and silently doubted that assertion.

The teacher also recalled that Bobby had been subdued on the trip home. She had not attached any particular significance to this behavior; it had been a long afternoon in the fresh air, and many of the children were drowsy. One or two had dozed on the way home. She had been aware that Bobby was reluctant to return to school and was planning to visit him at home over the weekend to see if she could be of assistance. She had no thoughts on what might be behind this fear, but did say that these things sometimes happened when a new baby arrived in the house. The teacher concluded by stating that Bobby was a "dear little fellow" from a lovely family, and that he was missed by his classmates.

Darien sat in the car mulling over this information. Then she dialed Sally's number.

"Olsen's'"

"Hi Sally, it's Darien."

"Hey, how's it going?"

"Fine. Look, I'm unexpectedly free this afternoon, and wondered if I could take you and Bobby for a sail around the harbor so you could show me some of the sights. Maggie and Edward offered the use of their sailboat."

Sally chuckled. "Have you seen that boat yet, Darien?"

"No, why?"

"Well, they have two. The little one is at least 32 feet. One person could handle it in a pinch, but it's best with a two-person crew. I'm pretty fair on a boat, and if you can sail, we ought to be able to handle it."

"Been sailing all my life," Darien replied. "We'll be fine. Chance may want to come as well."

"It'd be great to have him along and all, but doesn't he have some work to do on the fire?"

"To be honest, this is part social and part work. I called the school today and spoke with Bobby's teacher. Turns out the field trip was in the vicinity of the hotel. I think it's possible that he may have seen something related to the fire. I'd like the chance to spend some time with him, get to know him better, and maybe find out what he knows."

Sally hesitated momentarily. "That's a pretty scary thought. And why wouldn't he tell us if he'd seen something like that?"

"I don't know," Darien said. "But it sure would help to explain why he's so upset."

"I guess so," Sally said. "Maybe."

"Okay," she said finally. "Why don't you stop by early and I'll pack a picnic to take down to the harbor. I'll plan to drive so I'll have Lily's car seat available."

"That's really thoughtful," Darien said, "but not necessary. Don't want you to feel that you need to break out the supplies every time we get together."

"Nonsense," Sally said. "It takes me a few minutes to pull it together and I'm happy to do it. See you soon."

Darien finished the conversation and then dialed Chance's cell number. She told him what she had learned from the teacher and filled him in on the plans for the sail.

"I think you're on to something important," he said. "That would explain a lot about what we saw at the hotel. These guys may have been professionals, but they probably panicked when the class showed up, and started doing whatever they could to speed up the fire. If that's the story, the sloppy moves like knocking out the glass and starting fires at both ends of the hotel make sense. And Bobby could have seen something that would be useful to us."

"I think that's right," she said.

"I'll meet you at the dock at noon," he said. "I have some late afternoon meetings, but I'd really like that time with Bobby."

"No problem. Just be sure to bring some soft-soled shoes so you don't scratch the deck," she said.

"Thanks for the advice. Anything else I need to know about sailing?"

"I don't think so," she said. "We'll be sure to have a life jacket for you, so don't be concerned if you can't swim. Montana's pretty far from the ocean, eh?"

"That it is," he said. "By the way, Jim called me again this morning. He wanted to speak with both of us and wondered why you weren't at the fire scene. I told him you were meeting with the kindergarten teacher and then were going to try to meet up with Bobby. I said you'd done all you needed to do at the hotel and that you'd be investigating off-site for the next few days."

"Thanks," she said, chewing her lower lip. What was he doing? Was he protecting her from the fire scene? Was he giving her cover with Jim? She frowned. Not likely. Compassion and caring were not Chance's way. He was simply telling Jim the facts as he saw them.

"He wanted to confirm that I'd sent several samples back to our lab for analysis. He also had a few more questions about Bobby. He is particularly interested in that piece of it, and wants us to report back to him as soon as we know more."

"Maybe we'll have something more to tell him tonight. Let's see how it goes. Meet you at the harbor," she said.

A decidedly downcast Bobby greeted her at the door. Flash's frisky antics only served to highlight his serious mood.

"Why don't you move your gear to my car," Sally called from the house. "I just need another minute. My neighbor stopped in and offered to stay with Lily while we sail, and I thought I'd take her up on the offer."

In short order, the two women and silent little boy were in the car, headed toward the harbor. Inexplicably, Darien found herself pleased at the prospect of spending the afternoon with Chance and anticipating his arrival. As she smoothed her hair and tucked a few loose strands into her braid, she caught Sally's eye in the mirror and turned quickly away from the young woman's amused smile. But the smile was contagious, and ruefully, Darien smiled, too.

The marina on the Great Salt Pond appeared on their right. There were a surprising number of boats for so early in the season, Darien noted. The boats rode easily in the soft swells of ocean, rocking gently from side to side. She recognized the reassuring sound of the halyards clinking against the masts, which glittered silver against the deep blue of the sky. There was a good breeze. And it looked as if the tide was coming in, but she would have to check the tide charts to be certain. She would also want to check the depth charts before they left the slip, but she expected that Sally was familiar with any dangerous areas.

Just as they arrived at the picnic table, Chance pulled smoothly into the parking lot. For the first time that day, a small smile crossed Bobby's worried face. "Chance is here!" he said.

"Why don't you go to greet him," Sally suggested. "I know he'll be happy to see you."

"Bobby seems to have taken to Chance," Sally said quietly to Darien. She was quiet for a minute. "How about you, Darien? Have you taken to Chance? Seems to me that he'd be pretty hard to resist."

At Darien's uncomfortable look, she raised a hand to her mouth and shook her head. "I really am sorry. I'm used to Island life. Everyone knows everyone's business. I shouldn't have pried into your private affairs. Please forget that I said anything."

"No need to apologize," Darien said. "I suppose you could call him an attractive man. But we are here to work on this case. This is purely a professional relationship. Nothing there to resist."

The women looked at Chance as he approached. He had changed out of his work clothes and was wearing a fresh pair of jeans and a heavy navy hooded sweatshirt that stretched over his broad shoulders. The breeze ruffled his soft sandy hair. He moved with an easy animal grace and flashed that crooked smile as he drew nearer.

"Understood," Sally replied, turning her attention to the brightly patterned tablecloth. But her smile was not lost on Darien.

"I finished early with the electrician, so I thought I'd hustle down here so Bobby could take some time to show me around the boat before we sail," he said to Darien and Sally. "Good to see you again, Sally."

She smiled at him.

"Can I speak to you for a minute?" Chance asked Darien. Excusing herself, she followed him some distance from Sally and Bobby.

"Just wanted to let you know that everything George and the electrician said confirms the arson. I'll go into more detail when we're alone, but I'm thinking now that it's critical that we find out what Bobby knows. I believe he has the missing pieces that will help us fill in the puzzle."

She nodded and turned to go back to Sally and Bobby.

"One more thing," he said, catching her by the shoulder and turning her gently back in his direction. "I went into town after the interviews and made a purchase. A bathrobe."

"Thank you, Chance," she said in her most professional manner.

His hurt expression cut through her resolve as if it were made of gossamer. Against her better judgment and against all common sense, she found herself moving closer and laying her hand on his arm. Just briefly. Just for a moment. Then she turned and walked away.

"Let's enjoy our picnic and get onboard," Darien said, her voice unnaturally husky. She started setting out paper plates and napkins with a great show of activity.

The picnic passed amicably enough, with conversation focused on the party the Olsen's were giving on Sunday.

"We'll be disappointed if you both don't show," Sally said. "You're the only off-Islanders who'll be there, and the only source of stories that haven't been told and retold through time immemorial. Most of those stories weren't that good the first time. We need some new blood!"

"Thanks, we'll try to make it," Darien said. "Depends on how the work is going, but we'd love to be there."

"Hey Bobby, maybe we could head over to the boat and do some exploring. I'm betting you've been on board before and can show me around," Chance said, looking to Sally for approval. She nodded her agreement with the plan.

"We'll clean up and meet you there," she said.

"She's beautiful," Darien said as she and Sally came on board. She glanced at Chance, who was studying the rigging. "Clean lines, but beamy, so they'll be plenty of room below." She trailed her hand admiringly over the gleaming brightwork.

"And every high-tech piece of equipment known to man," Sally said. "They spared no expense. You're as safe as it gets on this boat. I checked the tide charts after you called. High tide is in an hour. I know the harbor well and there are few shallow areas or obstacles that you need to be mindful of." She ran through the brief list, pointing them out.

Darien noticed that Chance was listening carefully. "You can go below and have Bobby complete your tour while we get underway," she said.

"Yes, ma'am," he responded smartly. He didn't move.

She gave him a pointed look. "Below," she repeated.

"Would it help my credibility any if I were to tell you that I was captain of my sailing team at college, and have sailed trans-Atlantic twice?" he asked.

Darien stared at him in surprise. "You're from Montana."

"Well, I am, Darien, but although it clearly strains the limits of your credulity, from time to time they let me out. On one of those occasions, I went to college in New England, where there's ocean to spare. And by the way, folks do sail on lakes, even in Montana."

This was a scenario that had not crossed her mind. She had him pegged as a man of the wild outdoors and backcountry, through and through. "And where did you go to school?"

"Yale," he said. "Despite the fact that I was from Montana, they decided to take a gamble on me. But they did draw the line at my bringing those steers and stallions you mentioned. I had to leave them at home with the family."

Sally looked confused.

"It's a private joke," he told her. "Not really worth going into, is it, Darien?"

She was off-balance and he knew it, she thought. He had so many moods, so many facets. Each time she thought she had him figured out and could manage to stay clear of the force field that surrounded him, he turned a different, unexpected surface her way and she was drawn irrevocably closer.

"Not worth going into," she said quickly. "I'll get the gear ready in the cockpit, Sally, and you can take the cover off the main sail."

"Bobby, why don't you help me with this line," Chance said, and the two of them set to work.

A few minutes later they were underway, skimming through a universe of sea and sky that held no place suitable for the charred ruins of a hotel or the splintered fragments of a woman's memories. The brisk wind caused them to heel hard and, from time to time, sent a chilly spray of water their way. Chance was at the helm and seemed easy with the control of the boat. Darien smiled a rare smile and felt herself relaxing.

The four sailed in compatible silence for some time, enjoying the warmth of the sun and the smooth, silent speed of the boat.

"Darien, will you take the wheel?" Chance asked sometime later.

Darien agreed, and watched as Chance settled down comfortably next to Bobby.

"So," he began casually, "I'd like to hear more about the field trip your class took last Monday."

Bobby stiffened and the grin disappeared from his face. He said nothing.

"I understand that your class was doing a science project. That must have been neat. What kinds of things were you looking for?" Bobby sat still and silent.

As if he didn't notice, Chance continued the one-sided conversation. "I remember one of my favorite science projects. We were looking for tadpoles. After we managed to corral a few and take them back to the classroom, we got to watch them turn into frogs. It was pretty interesting."

"My favorite was when my class went to the marsh and we counted up how many different kinds of birds we saw," Sally said. "It was the first time I really looked carefully at the birds and realized how different they were from each other. I've been hooked on birdwatching ever since."

Chance and Sally exchanged glances. Chance nodded, prompting her to continue.

"Honey," Sally said encouragingly, "where did you find that pretty new shell? Was it down near the hotel? I'd sure like to know, because I'd like to look for another like it. It's so special."

"Don't go there, Mommy," Bobby cried, suddenly animated and quivering with emotion. "You can't ever go there!"

Sally reached out an anxious hand to pull Bobby to her, but Chance stopped her with a gesture of his hand.

"I think there is something about that trip that scared you, Bobby, and I want to help you," he said quietly. "It makes us all sad to see you so worried, but we can't do anything if you don't tell us what's wrong. Did you see something on that trip that you want to tell me about?"

Bobby was on his feet in an instant, and he burst into sobs. "I didn't see anything. I didn't! Nothing happened! I didn't see anything!" He could barely speak through the sobs that shook his small frame.

Chance moved quickly, lifting the terrified little boy into his arms and holding him close. He let Bobby cling to him while the child wept, his arms tight around Chance's neck, his head burrowed into the man's shoulder. Chance gently stroked Bobby's hair and whispered words of comfort. Sally, shocked by the intensity of her son's response, put her arms around Chance and her son, holding both of them close in an effort to provide some comfort.

Bobby was the key to this case, Darien thought. They would need to discuss that theory with Jim tonight, but there was no question remaining in her mind. He had seen something on that field trip, something so bad or so scary that he was afraid to speak its name. And given the proximity to the fire, both in terms of space and timing, it wasn't hard to guess what he might have seen. But she needed facts, not guesses. She needed to tie those facts up in a neat little parcel, label them 'arson' for the jury, and then bring in the verdict.

Darien tried to focus her thoughts, but for the moment, the facts had lost their customary allure. She could not take her eyes off of Chance, who was gently cradling and comforting the terrified little boy, while talking softly with Sally. Darien thought of the panic-stricken, wild-eyed child that inhabited her night-world, the screams that tore her from sleep, and the searing flashes of memory that kept her from returning. The only comfort that child had known was in the order and predictability of a carefully circumscribed life. Her heart ached as she sailed the boat cautiously through the waters off Block Island and watched the three people entwined in each other's arms. And she didn't really understand why.

CHAPTER SEVEN

There was an odd smell in the air, like nothing the child had smelled before. It stung her nose and brought tears to her eyes. She rubbed at her irritated eyes and put down her book. Curious, she opened the door to the family room and stepped out into the downstairs hall.

The smell was stronger here, and there was something else, too. The air was smoky, making it difficult to draw a clear breath. A haze hung over the narrow hall, and everything looked different somehow, unfamiliar. Alarmed now, the child started down the hall toward the stairway.

"Mom," she called loudly. There was no response. "Mom."

The smoke was growing thicker as she approached the staircase. She walked by the living room and peered intently in, but the outline of the sturdy old furniture was barely perceptible through the shroud of smoke.

Fear made her walk more quickly. Something was very wrong here.

She reached the bottom of the stairway and looked up uncertainly. Through her six-year-old eyes, it looked the same as always, yet different. A faint haze was suspended high up, near the ornate molding next to the ceiling. Her parents were taking their Sunday afternoon nap and she and her little sister, Abby, had strict orders not to disturb them. Still…

"Mom, it's Rennie," she yelled up into the darkness at the head of the stairs. "There's smoke everywhere down here. Please come quick. Dad. Dad!"

There was no answer. This was very strange. Surely Mom and Dad would hear her calling, and would want to come down and see what was causing the smoke.

She hesitated, considering. She would go upstairs. She would knock on her parents' door and ask them to come downstairs. That would be okay, wouldn't it? They wouldn't be angry, would they? Reluctantly, she started slowly up the tall staircase.

A fierce concussion rocked the staircase as the fire burst through the ceiling from the kitchen and exploded into the upstairs hallway. The flames leaped and twisted before her horrified eyes, blood red at the edges, and white-hot at the center. The child froze where she stood, staring at the menacing spectacle. Slowly but inexorably, the flames snaked their way down the old staircase.

'Mommy! Daddy! Abby!" She screamed in terror. "There's a fire! Fire, fire!"

The smoke was becoming thicker and she was finding it difficult to breathe. The air was scorching hot. Flying bits of fabric and wood burned her as they grazed her frozen form. And a strange, eerie noise, a whoosh not quite the sigh of the wind, and not quite a moan, enveloped her.

"Rennie?"

Peering through the flames and smoke, Darien could just make out the form of her little sister. She was standing directly behind the flames at the top of the stairs, her hair still tousled from sleep, dressed in her fuzzy pink pajamas and clutching her favorite doll.

"Rennie, hot," she called plaintively.

"Get away from the fire, Abby," Darien shouted frantically. "Go get Mom and Dad. Hurry, Abby, go!" she cried.

"Rennie? Rennie, hot!" Abby said again. "Hot!"

The flames continued their ominous march down the stairs toward Darien. She saw to her horror that they were moving backward, too, toward Abby.

"Rennie, Rennie, Rennie!" Abby's terrified cries rang in her ears over the roar of the fire.

She had to do something. She had to help Abby. She had to help Mom and Dad. She willed herself to move again. Balling her little fists in sheer determination, Darien forced herself forward against the heat and smoke, and tried to climb up the stairs to reach her sister, but the hot flames drove her back. She tried again, but gagged on the smoke and could not continue. She was growing lightheaded and confused. It was increasingly difficult to see Abby through the raging fire, but her sister's cries still carried on the fire-wind.

Behind her, Darien heard the splintering of wood as the firemen tried to break through the door. She turned in their direction, and then back toward the stairs. The fire was perilously close to her now, reaching out to her like the tentacles of the monster she had read about in one of her storybooks. She was gasping for breath and was dizzy, and felt like she might throw-up. But she had to get up the stairs to Abby.

She could hear the firemen calling to her from the door, yelling at her to come away from the stairs, to run outside. Didn't they understand? Abby, Mom and Dad were upstairs in the fire. They needed her help. She had to help, she had to save them. She turned her back to the fire to tell them no, she had to get her sister, she couldn't come just yet.

The child felt a searing pain tear at her back as the fire surged toward her, and her shirt burst into flames. The smell of burning flesh permeated the air. The first fireman reached her and wrapped her tightly in a blanket to smother the flames as he pulled her from the inferno. She struggled wildly against him. "Abby!" She screamed. "Abby, Abby, Abby, Abby..."

"Wake up. Wake up. Darien."

The voice was deep, worried, hovering just beyond recognition somewhere between sleep and wakefulness. As it called to her, the thick smoke thinned to a swirling mist and lightened from darkest black to silver. And she knew with certainty, although she could not have said why, that the way out of the fear was through that voice.

"Darien. Wake up. Open your eyes."

She moved soundlessly through the silvery mist toward the insistent voice. It was nearer now, guiding her out of the haze and away from danger. And then the mist parted. She stepped through hesitantly.

Darien opened her eyes and looked about in confusion. The room was dark, but the moon gleamed through a gap in the shade, illuminating the scene in a cold, pale light. There was no familiar staircase, no smoke, no fire. She struggled to sit up.

That house no longer existed. It had been the dream again. The old dream, and yet different this time. It had never gone so far before. She had walked that narrow hallway countless times, smelled the smoke, approached the stairway. She had called in vain to her parents, her fear mounting as the silence deepened. The fire had erupted in all of its fierce fury more times than she could remember. And yet it had gone no further. Through her screams and terror, she would know that it was the dream. Some part of her, even in the deepest sleep when she had fully given over to the past, would know. And she would force herself to awaken. But not this time.

Someone turned on the bedside lamp, and illumined in the harsh light she saw Chance. The last remnants of the dream faded. Not the fire. Not even her apartment in Providence. She was on Block Island, in Maggie and Edward's home, in the peach-colored room. She closed her eyes against the light and lay back on the pillow.

"Sorry, I thought the light would help," he said as he snapped it off. He sat down on the bed and put a hand on her trembling shoulder. She could feel his warmth through the thin fabric of her nightgown and realized that she was icy cold.

He sat quietly, giving her time to regain control. "That was some nightmare, Darien," he said at last. "Would it help to tell me about it?"

Darien tried to bring her breathing under control. "No," she said dully, "no, it won't help."

"Sometimes it's good to talk. It seems less frightening when you put it in words and the nightmare loses some of its power."

"No, not this time," she said vaguely.

"Open your eyes and look at me, Darien," he said more loudly. "You're not really awake yet. Come on, look at me."

She forced her eyes open again. He sat on the edge of her bed, very close to her, and she could hear the soft, even sound of his breathing. He was as she had seen him the evening before, nearly naked, roused from bed. In the cool light of the moon, his body looked chiseled from stone, hard, solid. So unlike the images of her nights, half-real, half imagined, insubstantial. She could feel the terror of the dream start to recede.

She reached out a tentative hand to his chest and touched him. The hand, at least, grew warmer. She thought that she could feel the racing of his heart. Not stone. Not a dream. Flesh and muscle.

The touch lingered and became a caress. She looked up to see hazel eyes that glittered with passion, and lips that had parted at her touch. His breathing had grown shallow and ragged.

To lie in his arms all night, firmly secured to this world by his touch, and anchored to this reality by his presence. To sleep with the living, to be one with them, for just this one night. To be free from the fear, free from the memories. The comfort and safety would be worth anything she had to offer.

"Stay with me tonight, Chance," she whispered to the form etched darkly against the moonlight. "I…" She hesitated, reached for the top button of her nightgown, and then averted her eyes. "Please."

He studied her face in silence for a very long time.

"No, Darien," he said at last, taking her hand firmly in his. "Not now. Not like this." He brushed his lips over her fingers, and returned her arm to her side.

She turned away in embarrassment, too mortified and heartsick to speak the words that might reclaim her dignity. She waited, very still, for him to leave.

Instead, he climbed into the bed next to her and gently took her into his arms. She hesitated for a moment, confused by his unexpected response, but deeply grateful for his presence. Then she turned to him and snuggled close, drawn to his warmth, his strength.

"Try to get some sleep," he said. We have a busy day tomorrow."

"I don't want to fall sleep," she said against his shoulder. She didn't need to explain why.

"I'm here with you. It'll be all right. You rest now."

She was asleep almost before the words were out of his mouth. He looked down at the beautiful young woman cradled in his arms in the moonlight. The coppery curls glowed softly on the pillow. Careful not to wake her, he pulled one arm free and caressed the soft skin of her cheek, and then traced the line of her lips. His hand moved down to the scalloped neck of the silky blue nightgown, and slid over the soft curve of her shoulder. She sighed in her sleep and moved closer.

Reluctantly, he pulled his hand away and held her close again. You, Chance Deckert, are one crazy fool, he told himself. You are going to hate yourself in the morning. You sure picked a helluva time to develop a conscience.

He bent down and brushed his lips over her hair, inhaling the fresh fragrance of jasmine. He had never needed a cold shower this much in his life, and hopefully, never would again. And then he, too, slept.

CHAPTER EIGHT

She had been so hopeful that she could control this problem during their brief stay on Block Island. Sometimes months at a time would pass without the fire dream. And sometimes she could awaken at the first hint of smoke, before the child started her fateful trip to the staircase. And sometimes — but then, what did it matter. Last night had not been 'sometimes', and Chance had been there.

Chance. She brushed her fingertips over the sheet next to her. He'd been gone when she'd awoken, but the scent of him lingered on the pillow, musky and male and vaguely unsettling in the peach-colored, decidedly feminine room.

How was she to understand what had happened between them last night? Or more to the point, what hadn't happened. Her behavior had been embarrassing and utterly out of character. But although she would have given the world to consign last night to oblivion, at least she could understand the fear and need that had driven her into his arms.

But Chance, well, that was a different matter entirely. Chance had not seemed to her a particularly complicated man. To the contrary, he was easy to read and had given her a road map that first day in the office. He was self-absorbed, pleasure seeking, careless of feelings and heedless of the consequences for anyone but himself. He put his cards on the table, and if a woman wanted to pick them up and play, so be it. But now this bewildering unwillingness to take from her, when it was offered, all that he had been seeking.

She was confused and weary, but one thing was clear. She could not stay here in bed all day. There was work to be done, and at some point, she would have to face him. Reluctantly, she left the warmth of her bed.

He was already downstairs, seated at the table sipping coffee and reading the paper. He looked up when she entered the room, and his eyes swept slowly over her, taking in the damp hair caught back in a braid, the navy turtleneck sweater and the faded jeans. "Good morning," he said, and then he fixed her with a long, level gaze. The ball was in her court.

She poured herself a cup of coffee while she considered where to start. She crossed the room to the table, seated herself opposite him, and then looked up to meet those searching eyes.

"Chance," she began carefully, "I want to thank you for last night."

He said nothing, but continued looking at her with an inscrutable expression.

"I want to thank you for what you did," she said. "And," she added after an awkward pause, "I want to thank you for what you didn't do."

"Darien," he began, and reached for her hand.

She pulled her hand back abruptly, side-swiping the napkin holder, which skidded across the table and landed on the floor.

Chance lapsed into silence. When he spoke again, his voice had grown cold. "You're welcome for last night on both counts," he said.

He looked down at his paper, and she thought with relief that the conversation was over. She turned away to butter her toast, and was surprised when he spoke again.

"But," he said in a deceptively soft voice, "don't make the mistake of expecting me to turn away again. The next time you invite me into your bed, and there will be a next time, Darien, count on getting what you ask for."

Her body tensed as she struggled to bite back an angry retort. She continued buttering her bread as if the exchange had not taken place.

When she had composed herself, she said, "I'm going to stay here for a while. I want to nail down the ownership question. Before I left the office, I left instructions to hire private investigators at the sites of the other fires, and asked that they check land records and certain other documents to fill in any gaps on what I'm finding online. I want to call back and see how that's coming. Then I plan to head over to the town hall here to do some research. Depending on what I learn, I'll probably have some follow-up to do."

"Sounds good," Chance responded. "I wanted to take a last look at the hotel to see if I can nail down exactly how the fire was set. I want to take another look at that lobby, too, and see if I can figure out what feels off. Then I'm going to meet with George and some of the other volunteer firemen to go over their report, and see if I can jog their memories."

"We should get back to Sally and Bobby, too," Darien suggested. "At lunch the other day, it sounded like she had some additional information and she might be able to suggest other people we should interview about the fire. And Bobby — well, I don't want to upset him again, but I'm so certain that he holds the missing piece to this puzzle."

"Why don't you call and set something up with them for late afternoon, say three or so. I can meet you there and we can talk with them together."

"Okay," she said, "I'll call you to confirm the time."

"We need to get back to Jim at Monitor tonight around seven. He was pretty emphatic about wanting to hear everything we learn today. I think we can finish up by then."

"Fine," she said.

He rose from the table and walked over to get his jacket. Darien reached for the paper and pretended to read intently while she waited to hear the reassuring thud of the door closing behind him. Instead, she heard the sound of his footsteps heading away from the door and coming closer, until they stopped directly behind her chair. She sat up stiffly, but did not turn around.

Darien felt the heat of his hand as rested it on her shoulder. He lingered there for a brief moment, and then she felt his fingertips slide slowly and sensuously up her neck, unleashing a searing cascade of sparks. She closed her eyes, helpless to control the spasms of pleasure that shot through her. And then he pulled his hand away.

"It will be that good, Darien. I promise you." And he was gone.

Darien waited until she heard the roar of the Jaguar's engine receding in the distance before she attempted to stand. Her legs were shaky beneath her as she walked over to the study, carrying the papers that had arrived by Fed Ex from her law firm only that morning. She opened the package and quickly skimmed the contents. She needed to put that man out of her mind and concentrate. These were the deeds, mortgages, insurance documents and various papers related to the other properties and could be significant. Taking a deep gulp of coffee, Darien tried to turn her attention to her work.

Two hours later, Darien was still sitting in that same chair, reviewing yet again the pages of notes she had taken in the course of the investigation. It was like a shell game. Layer after layer of owners, boards of directors and executives. If her information was to be believed, the buildings that had burned had no ownership or management connections in common whatsoever. Where was the common thread? She removed her glasses, and rubbed her tired eyes. Time for a break.

She got to her feet, poured herself another cup of coffee, and took it out onto the patio. The ocean was tranquil today, an endless succession of lazy, deep green waves slowly unwinding under the cloudless blue sky. A few sailboats were visible on the horizon. Darien turned her face up toward the sun. What was she missing?

Half lost in thought, she watched the sandpipers scuttling about at the ocean's edge. They were so tiny and had such short little legs, one would have expected them to move slowly. And yet, they scurried swiftly about, covering surprisingly large distances quickly and effortlessly. Appearances couldn't be trusted. She had to dig deeper. With a last look at the ocean, Darien headed back into the house, and from there, to the town hall.

And there, sitting at a high desk amid the dusty volumes of town records and reviewing the land records for the hotel, she found her first clue. She squinted at the page. Surely, she had seen this name before. She marked the page and read further. Glancing at her watch, Darien gathered together all the books she had carefully marked with bright yellow post-its and headed off toward the copier, humming under her breath. Copies securely in hand, she headed quickly home to confirm her recollection. Yes, there was the name again. And again. And yet again.

At two o'clock she sat up a little straighter and smiled grimly. It was a good start. She had half an hour before she needed to leave for Sally's, and she was going to spend it walking along the ocean. She had earned the respite.

The low-slung Jaguar was already parked in the driveway of Sally's house when she arrived. As soon as she stepped from the car, she could hear the raucous sounds of Chance, Bobby and Flash roughhousing in the backyard. She followed the noise around the side of the house, and spotted Sally seated comfortably in the shade with Lily resting in her arms, watching the action with an amused smile.

"Come join me." Sally patted an empty chair nearby. "There's coffee or juice in the house if you'd like any."

Darien crossed to the chair, careful to avoid the tangle of man, boy, dog and ball that were whizzing across the grass at a dizzying speed.

"Am I late?" Darien asked, glancing at her watch. It was still not quite three.

"No, Chance said he finished up early and thought he'd come by and play for a while. He's just a big, overgrown kid himself," she said, laughing as he ran by with Bobby and Flash in hot pursuit.

"Ummm," Darien said skeptically.

"Point taken," Sally replied. "I hope you two are planning to come to our cookout. Great food, and you get to bring some of it! Good company, too."

"We'll have to see how we're coming on the work," Darien replied. "We're out here to do a job, and we're under instruction that time is of the essence. Sooo…"

"So nothing," Sally retorted. "What are you bringing?"

Darien laughed. "If we do come, what could you use? I'm an adequate cook, but Chance has allowed as how he's pretty good, and I propose that we give him a chance to prove his boast."

"Sounds like a plan. Speaking of work," Sally said after a pause, "how's it coming? Have you learned anything?"

"Between the documents and the interviews I've conducted, I'm starting to make some connections. But there are some big gaps. I was hoping that we could continue the conversation from lunch the other day. About the fire."

Sally thought a minute. "I think I told you everything I know," she said.

"There was something more that you were going to say when Bobby — when Bobby got upset."

Sally's smile faded at the mention of her son's current problem.

"Please, Sally, try to remember. It may be something helpful. What else were you going to tell me?"

Sally thought intently for a minute. "I'm sorry, Darien. I do feel like there was something else, but I can't for the life of me remember what it was." She looked at Darien's disappointed expression. "I'll try to remember. Promise. And meanwhile," she said, looking at the baby who was stirring in her arms, "how about holding Lily while I get the troops some refreshment?"

Sally brought out cookies and juice, which they ate sitting at the old-fashioned picnic table. Lily cooed and smiled in Darien's arms while the conversation flowed easily around them. Darien glanced over at Chance, who was deep in conversation with Bobby, his face still flushed from the exercise, his soft, sandy hair rumpled and glinting in the sun. He had pulled off his sweatshirt, and the powerful muscles in his shoulders rippled beneath the thin white tee shirt as he reached out for his juice.

"Want to hold Lily while Darien helps me clean up?" Sally asked Chance. "Or are you uneasy with babies?"

"Are you kidding? Uncle Chance?" he said, swinging his long legs over the bench and coming over to where Darien was sitting with Lily. Expertly, he took the baby from her and lifted Lily to his shoulder.

"Done like a pro," Sally observed admiringly.

"We have five little kids at the ranch, although it's a moving total, because it seems like someone's always having a baby. Babies are second nature to me now. When I'm not traveling, I'm the first-string babysitter and I love every minute of it. My nieces and nephews are terrific kids."

"Well, maybe one day you'll have kids of your own," Sally said, starting to pick up the plates and cutlery.

Darien was sorely tempted to remind them that first, he would have to settle down with one wife, and that seemed an unlikely prospect in the extreme. But she held her tongue and carried the glasses into the kitchen.

"He is great with kids," Sally declared, coming through the door with a load of dirty dishes.

"So who else is coming to this party?" Darien responded, running water in the sink for the dishes.

Sally picked up a dishtowel and gave Darien a sidelong glance. "Gracefully changing the subject…" she began, and then proceeded to describe her friends and neighbors.

As they finished up the dishes, Bobby, Chance and Lily, accompanied by Flash, came in the door. In answer to the women's unspoken question, Chance nodded a furtive no. Bobby's high spirits had disappeared, and he appeared anxious and uneasy. He moved next to Sally and took her hand.

"Guess it's time for us to be going," Chance said, handing Lily back to Sally. "Bobby, I'll see you at the party this weekend?"

"Yeah, sure," Bobby said listlessly.

Sally put Lily down in her infant seat. "Goodbye Chance, Darien," she said, hugging each in turn. "So happy we'll see you at the party. Chance, you've been volunteered to bring a dish. Bring whatever you like."

She turned and put an arm on Bobby's shoulder. "Let's get Flash a snack and some water."

"We'll see ourselves out," Darien said.

They walked out to their cars together.

"No luck?" Darien asked.

"He just clams up tight when I mention anything related to the fire," Chance said in frustration. "I don't know how to reach him."

"I think you're doing just fine," she reassured him. "He likes you and he's at ease with you. He's learning to trust you. He'll open up to you soon."

"I guess one out of two isn't bad," he said, shooting Darien a meaningful look.

She looked at him, unsure how to answer.

"See you at home for dinner," he said, breaking the awkward silence. "I'm cooking. I'll stop on the way to pick up some supplies, and then we can trade notes on what we found today. We can call Jim together."

She nodded and got into the car for the brief trip home. She had some time before Chance returned. She would shower and change into something fresh. Had she brought that soft amber sweater, the one that everyone said matched her eyes? And the white linen trousers that were so flattering? Unexpectedly, she felt her face grow heated and flushed. Darien rolled down the window and let the cool air blow on her burning cheeks. It didn't help at all.

CHAPTER NINE

Darien took another sip of wine and settled herself more comfortably on the kitchen stool. She'd been watching Chance as he moved about the kitchen preparing their dinner, and from time to time had made the requisite remarks intended to keep up her end of the conversation. But silently, beneath the amiable chatter, she had been hard at work trying to characterize this puzzling man. She hadn't got it quite right yet, but she was getting closer.

Maybe 'John Wayne goes to Yale'. She looked at Chance thoughtfully. Not bad. Not bad at all. In fact, it was pretty good. She nodded to herself with satisfaction.

"Can I assume that that's a 'yes'?" he asked.

"What's the question?"

He shook some spices onto the fish fillet that he was preparing to bake. "It doesn't work that way, Darien. First you tell me the answer, and then I'll supply the question."

She laughed out loud and he looked up in surprise. He seemed about to say something, but then turned his attention back to the fish.

"I think I'll pass on that offer," she said. "But I do have a question of my own. What can I do to help?"

"Before we go any further with dinner, let's give Jim a call and bring him up to speed on the investigation. Okay?"

She nodded.

Although Chance seemed prepared to engage in the requisite small talk with a client, Jim seemed anxious to get to the point. "What do you have that I haven't heard?" he asked.

"Well, we've been wondering why the alarm, detection and suppression systems didn't work. The smoke detectors were properly placed, but fire damage may have prevented an audible signal, and in any event, it's a remote location and no one was around to hear it," Chance said. "It wasn't connected to any monitoring service. The rep from the service says that contract was terminated recently, but management denies terminating." Scanning his notes, he continued, "The sprinkler didn't work because the water for the fire suppression system had been turned off."

"Who did that and when was it done?" Jim interrupted.

"To be determined," Chance replied. "The electrical system was old but checks out — no problem there. But here's what's really important. The portable heater was damaged in the fire, but we could tell the safety devices had been tampered with, and I'm still waiting for the lab report, but I'm sure the heater and the rags nearby had been doused with an accelerant."

"Anything else?" Jim asked. "What's happening with the kid?"

"We haven't been able to get anywhere with Bobby. He was on the school trip that day and for sure he saw something, but he's too afraid to talk."

"Okay, keep on it," Jim said. "And Darien?"

"Hi Jim," Darien said. "I have been looking through land records and other documents, and I realized that the same notary's name appears on all of the documents. That would be a really strange coincidence if the owners of the three properties were truly separate entities. I guess it's possible, but highly unlikely. I'm going to follow that thread and see where it leads. I'll interview the owners of the properties. It looks like they all worked with the same agent at Monitor, which is another interesting fact. I'm going to look into that further as well. I think I'm closing in on the kinds of connections that might tie all three fires together."

"That all sounds promising," Jim said.

"Anything else you'd like us to look into?" she asked. Hearing nothing, she continued, "Okay. And you'll be up on Saturday with Maggie and Ed. Great. We'll talk more then. Thanks, Jim." She hung up the phone.

"You've made a lot of progress," Chance said. "Sounds like you have some thoughts on where this is heading."

"I do," she said. "I just need a little more time to follow up on some leads. I hope that when everyone gets out here this weekend, I'll be in a position to offer a pretty strong hypothesis on who's behind these fires."

"Speaking of a little more time, that's about all I need to get this dinner on the table. I don't need any help with the food," he said. "The fish is ready to bake, and the potatoes are already roasting. I'll fix the salad and we'll be good to go. But I'd be much obliged if you'd play the piano for me while dinner's cooking."

She hesitated briefly, and then agreed. "What would you like to hear?"

"Anything you'd like to play," he said. "Until I heard you playing the other night, I hadn't really realized how much I missed music. At the ranch, we all play together. That's not to say that everyone in the family plays well. It'd be fair to say we run the gamut from pretty good to needs improvement. My brother Jed plays a really hot sax. On the other hand, when my dad picks up the bass — well, let's just say he's been known to make some unusual sounds." His smile was genuine, but tinged with nostalgia.

She had seated herself at the piano and was lightly fingering the keys. Chance was seated on the piano bench next to her. "What do you play?" she asked.

"Trumpet," he said. "When I was a little boy, Louis Armstrong was my hero. I would rush home from school to listen to his music for hours on end and wonder how he could coax those incredible sounds from his horn. I couldn't wait until I was old enough to take lessons. I think I still have my first trumpet stashed away somewhere at home."

She started to pick out a Dinah Washington tune.

"That must have been fun," she said. "Playing together as a family, I mean."

"It was," he agreed. "Sometimes I'd play along with my jazz records, or just play by myself if the mood came over me. But I really enjoyed the times when we would get together as a family to make music. Even though the music wasn't always good, we always had a lot of fun making it happen. Did your family play together?" he asked.

"Just me," she said as she played, her voice as melancholy as the music. "It was always just me."

He gave her a quizzical look, but she was too engrossed in her music to notice. Nor did she notice the man who emerged from the inky darkness surrounding the house, peered furtively in the window at both her and Chance, and then melted into the shadows of the gathering night.

He was as good as his word. The fish was moist and done to perfection. The potatoes were well seasoned, the salad dressing homemade, and the wine that accompanied the meal went down far too easily.

"That was really delicious. And since no good deed goes unpunished, you have now earned the honor of cooking our contribution to George and Sally's party." She smiled.

Chance laughed. "I'll probably be sorry I started this cooking thing," he said, "but you've got it."

"Great. And the other thing you've earned is a rest. Let me handle the clean-up." She reached for Maggie's apron and tied it securely around her waist.

"Sounds good," Chance agreed. "I've been wanting to look through Edward and Maggie's records. They have some great jazz. I'd be curious to see what else they have." He walked off in the direction of the living room.

Darien gathered up the dishes, rinsed them slowly and stacked them in the dishwasher. She was in no hurry to finish. There was something oddly comforting in being part of this domestic ritual. She liked sharing her meal with someone. She liked the companionship. She liked the conversation. And against all odds, not to mention all reason, she was starting to like the man.

Drying her hands on the apron, Darien scanned the area to make certain that she had gotten all the dishes. Chance's jacket was draped carelessly over a stool, where he had tossed it when he started to cook. She retrieved it and turned toward the pegs in the hall to hang it up for him. The cotton fabric was soft to the touch. Impulsively, she rubbed it across her cheek. That now familiar scent of musk, his scent, rose from the jacket. With a determined gesture, she folded it and quickly replaced it on the stool. Then she turned out the light and headed for the living room.

The moon shone through the wide expanse of the windows, illuminating the room with the softest suggestion of light. Chance was sitting in the dark, his silhouette barely visible against the shifting shadows of the night. She paused for a moment while her eyes grew accustomed to the dark, and then hesitated, uncertain, in the deepening silence of the room. She closed her eyes and listened to the familiar, evocative refrain of 'At Last', feeling the longing and need that resonated in every note. The throbbing rhythm of the music worked its way inside of her. And then, he was standing beside her.

She felt his hands, strong and insistent, grasp her shoulders and guide her deeper into the moonlit room. They stood facing each other, linked only by his touch. She searched his eyes, seeking — what — reassurance? Passion, raw and demanding, looked back at her. Quickly, she looked away.

Chance moved his hand across her shoulder until it came to rest on her chin. He forced her to turn her head and look at him, and did not release her until it was very clear that she had read the message in his eyes. He removed his hands, and this time, she did not look away.

Then slowly, deliberately, he gathered her into his arms and started to move in time to the music.

She lifted her arms around his neck and rested her cheek against the soft cotton sweater, savoring the sensation of this nearness. He held her tightly against his body, so tightly that she could feel the muscles ripple in his chest, the long, hard line of his thighs. Where his body touched hers, small fires flamed, burning her, melting her, until she could barely stand. Each rhythmic movement triggered a new firestorm. His hand held her firmly, locked tightly around her hips, forbidding her from pulling back. She could hear the sound of her breathing, ragged, uneven.

She moved sensuously against him. Secure in his arms, she felt so attuned to the man that the boundaries between them were melting. They were fusing together in the mysterious darkness. They were becoming one person, a molten being fashioned from the fabric of their passion.

She felt Chance lift her effortlessly into his powerful arms and then, through the haze of her desire, realized that they had left the living room and were climbing up the stairs. "What are you doing?" she asked in confusion.

"We'll be more comfortable in my room, baby" he said, his lips moving against her hair. His voice was low and rough.

It was only one sentence. Only a few simple words, really, and nothing more. And yet, once said, the events of the evening were irrevocably transformed. All the possibilities suggested by that night together — the companionship, the trust, the intimacy — evaporated. What remained was the harsh reality. The evening had been a carefully calculated prelude to lust.

"Put me down, Chance," she said sharply. He kept climbing. "I said, put me down," she repeated.

She could feel him stiffen with anger and frustration. He reached the landing and abruptly, he released her.

Darien struggled to get her footing. She was trembling and her legs seemed unwilling to support her. She grasped the railing, steadied herself and then turned to face him.

She could barely make out his face in the dark, but his eyes were glittering dangerously and were focused implacably on her. She shifted uneasily, aware of his bedroom a few short steps down the hall.

"I told you, Darien, that the next time you invited me into your bed, I wouldn't turn away and that you could count on getting what you asked for." His voice was as hard and unyielding as the iron banister against her back.

"But I didn't ask you," she protested.

"Oh, but you did, Darien," he said, moving directly in front of her and placing his hands firmly on the banister on either side of her. "Some invitations don't need to be put into words. You invited me when you put your arms around me and pressed yourself against me when we danced. You invited me when I could feel how hot you were burning, how much you wanted me. That invitation was about as clear as they come."

Darien lifted her chin and regarded him steadily. "There was no 'invitation', Chance. There was no 'pressing', there was no 'hot' and there was no 'burning'. There was just a dance. Nothing more."

The contempt in his eyes labeled the lie for what it was. "Do you really believe that, Darien?" he asked coldly. "Because if you do, there's not much else worth saying. You can lie to me all you want. But don't make the mistake of lying to yourself. The only person you'll fool, the only person you'll cheat, will be you."

He turned on his heels and walked rapidly down the stairs. She heard the door slam behind him, and listened as the sound of the Jaguar grew faint. He was headed into town. She knew exactly what he was looking for. And, with equal certainty, she knew that he would find it.

Darien walked numbly toward her bedroom, and without bothering to turn on the light, seated herself on her bed. She had to sort this out and make some sense of it.

She thought about all that Chance had said. She could not dispute a single word. His accusations had the unmistakable ring of truth. And then, she thought about all that he had not said. He had not said anything about constancy. He had not said anything about caring. And his silence on those subjects said more than all the hurtful words he had spoken.

An invitation. Knowing what she did about this thoughtless man, and knowing too that an 'invitation' would result in nothing but misunderstanding, heartache and despair, how could she have let things go so far?

Chance turned the car toward town, rolled down the windows and pushed the accelerator to the floor. He could not understand that woman at all. And he was fed up with trying.

The car picked up speed. The roar of the wind in his ears and the powerful sensation of unfettered speed as the Jag pierced the silent night was all he wanted now. That, and whatever pleasure he might find in town, far from a woman whose passion could flare at his touch, and then fade in the time it took to lift her into his arms.

CHAPTER TEN

The smell of smoke hung heavy in the air, and the curious child left the family room and started to walk down the hall. Darien whimpered in her sleep. It was the dream again, and she had to wake up.

The child was moving toward the staircase and was calling to her mother. Darien tried to force her way to consciousness, but it was like trying to rise to the surface of a vast ocean from the murky depths below. Finally, with great effort, she opened her eyes.

The last traces of the dream faded into the shadows of memory. Darien started to sit up, but had raised her head only a short way from the pillow when she found herself slipping back. Her limbs seemed to have no mass, no substance, and would not support her. She felt so very weak.

She tried to think, but she was lightheaded and dizzy. It was difficult to get her breath. She could not focus her eyes. And what was that irritating odor?

She was too sleepy. She would worry about it tomorrow. Now she would rest.

No. Darien forced her eyes open. She had to stay awake. Something was very wrong. She forced herself to focus, to think. What was happening?

Half-formed words slipped over and around one another, coming together in strange combinations that made no sense, and then rearranging themselves into a kaleidoscope of random patterns. She struggled to find some meaning, to order the chaos. The answer was there, lurking just beyond her grasp, taunting her as it flashed and faded in the recesses of her mind.

Gas. Not smoke, but gas. She was smelling gas. Her bedroom was filled with gas. And she had to get out.

Summoning every bit of strength and resolve, Darien tried to get up from her bed, but her mind no longer controlled her body. With a fierce effort, she was finally able to maneuver herself sideways and roll from her bed, landing hard on the cream-colored carpet. She lay still for a brief moment, exhausted by the effort and gasping for breath. Then, struggling to her knees, she started to crawl in the direction of the balcony. She felt so heavy, so drowsy. More than anything, she wanted to lay her head on that welcoming carpet and surrender to the darkness that was starting to envelop her. But she could not give in. She kept moving determinedly toward the window, toward the fresh air and safety.

She could see the French doors to the balcony in front of her. But try as she might, she was unable to reach the latch and could no longer summon the strength to rise from the floor. The fog in her mind was wrapping itself around her and obscuring the familiar room, but peering through it, she spotted a heavy, ornate metal doorstop close to the door. With the last of her will, she reached out and seized the statue, and swung it weakly at the door. She heard the sound of glass splintering, felt the shards of glass that sprayed about her, and then breathed deeply of the cool, fresh air that poured in through the breach.

In a few minutes, her head had cleared sufficiently for her to focus her thoughts. She got to her knees, pulled herself up by the doorknob, and with shaking hands turned the old key in the door. Mercifully, the shattered door swung open and she stepped out onto the balcony.

A rush of cool night air greeted her. Reaching out a hand to grab the back of a sturdy chair, she steadied herself and, when she was ready, pulled herself to the front of the chair and sat down. She leaned back in the chair and breathed deeply. She would be fine.

Gradually, Darien became aware of the stiff wind that was blowing in off the ocean, and of the waves cresting and then breaking on the beach below. She needed to move. She had to get out of the house and to the beach. She was not safe here. The house was filled with gas, and a house filled with gas could explode. She had no idea how long the gas had been leaking or how much gas had accumulated.

Then she hesitated. There was something she needed to do first. Yes — she would see if she could locate the source of the leak quickly and try to turn it off. She owed Edward and Maggie that much.

The stove. That was the most likely source of the gas. That was where she would start.

Darien took several deep breaths. Then, leaving the doors to the balcony flung wide open, she raced down the stairs into the kitchen. The odor of gas was intense.

First, she released the latch on the large window over the sink and threw it open as wide as it would go. She gulped several deep breaths of fresh air, and then walked quickly to the stove. She tugged it away from the wall and the problem was immediately apparent. The gas line was nearly disconnected. Fighting against the dizziness that threatened to overwhelm her again, she tightened it, and after one last look around the kitchen, staggered out of the house. When she reached the beach, she fell gratefully to the cool, damp sand.

Darien pulled the warm wool blanket closer about her and sipped the steaming cup of tea. She rolled the cup back and forth in her chilled hands, grateful for the warmth, and then settled more comfortably onto the beach blanket. She was feeling much better now, and the troubling haze that had made it so difficult to think was clearing.

"We got here as quick as we could when we got your call. Feeling better?" George's brows were drawn together in concern.

"I'm fine," she said to Sally's husband. "I'm absolutely none the worse for wear. But I didn't call. My phone is still in the house."

"You didn't call? But then who called?"

"I don't know," she said. I assumed all the gas in the house set off some kind of alarm somewhere."

"I'm pretty sure someone called it in. I'll check it out when I get home."

George ran his hand through his yellow curls, taking stock of the whereabouts of the other members of the volunteer fire department who had responded to this call. "They've opened all the windows and the house is airing out quickly. Sure you don't want to wait in the truck?"

"No, thanks, I prefer to be outside," she answered. "I have the blanket and the warm clothes your men brought me from the house. I can stay on the beach until the house is safe."

He shrugged. "Suit yourself. We'll stay until the gas company rep gives the all clear. First thing tomorrow, you'll want to nail some wood over the broken glass on that door."

She nodded. "Thanks so much for your help, George. I appreciate…"

"What the hell is going on here!" Chance demanded.

Darien and George looked up in surprise. They had not heard his arrival over the sound of the waves.

"Didn't expect you back," George said. "Darien told us you were gone for the night. Nothing to worry about, Chance. We had a little excitement here, but everything's okay now."

"What kind of excitement?" he asked, his voice tense and angry. "And why didn't you call me?" he demanded, turning his attention to Darien. She felt his eyes raking over her, taking in the wool blanket wrapped around her, the thick wool socks on her feet.

"There was no need to trouble you," she said firmly, holding his gaze with her own. "There was a gas leak. Someone called the fire department. Everything is okay now."

"A gas leak?" Chance asked incredulously, turning to George. "Someone called the fire department? You don't think that's suspicious?"

"A call came in about midnight," George said. "I don't know who called, but I'll check it out. Darien said that she woke up and found the house filled with gas. She broke the window to the French doors in her room to get some fresh air. Then she located the source of the leak and tightened a loose connection to the gas line."

"She stayed in that house and went looking for the gas leak? She should have called the fire department right away and gotten out. What the hell was she thinking?"

"Well, she was already outside when we arrived," George continued. "She was a little shaky, but she'd taken care of everything and had the situation well under control. My men opened the windows and aired out the house. You should be able to go back in any time now."

"There's no need to talk about me like I'm not here," Darien said. "I'm quite alive and quite capable of describing and accounting for my own actions. If you have any questions about how I handled things in your absence, Chance, kindly address them to me."

Chance turned to Darien and the tension in his shoulders went slack. "Are you all right?" he asked quietly.

"Yes, Chance, I'm just…"

"I know, you're just fine," he said impatiently. "You're always just fine. But how are you really feeling?"

"I'm really feeling just fine," she said, looking at him steadily. "Don't waste your time worrying about me, Chance. I'm sure that after your trip to town, you have other things that you'd prefer to think about tonight."

He was silent for long minute. George looked from one to the other in confusion.

Then Chance turned his attention back to George. "Tell me again about the gas leak." George repeated the description, and Darien confirmed it.

"How does a line that was perfectly functional at dinner time come loose a few hours later and leak gas? How does that happen?"

"What are you saying, Chance?" Darien asked sharply.

"We never lock the door. Not out here. What I'm saying is that that after I left tonight, someone came in and loosened that connection. And then that someone called it in. I'm saying that someone is sending a warning."

Darien looked at him skeptically. "Why would anyone do something like that?"

"I think that you're getting too close to the people who are responsible for the fire at the hotel and at the other sites. I think that someone is aware of that fact, someone who has a great deal to lose if you find all the pieces of this puzzle and fit them together. And I think that that someone wanted to slow you down from getting any closer."

"That is just ridiculous, Chance," she protested. "You've been watching too many bad movies. It's probably an old stove and the connection has loosened over time. No one is trying to warn us. It was simply an accident."

Unpersuaded, Chance turned to George. "I don't want to alarm you or Sally, but you may want to keep a close eye on Bobby. He seems to know something about the fire." He left the rest of the thought unspoken.

George rubbed his face wearily. "Maybe that's good advice. I don't know what to think any more about that fire. And Bobby..." He sighed heavily.

One of the firemen came up to George with a representative from the gas company. "All clear," he said. "They can go back in the house, and we can go home."

"All right," he replied. "Chance, I want to talk with you more about this. And I'll mention it to the police chief. You should probably make some time to meet with him in town." And then George headed back to his truck.

Darien got to her feet, clutching the heavy blanket around her.

"I'll bring in everything else, Darien. You head up to bed," Chance said.

"I just need to pick up a piece of plywood and a hammer," she said, her voice betraying the exhaustion that she was fighting.

"You need to pick up what?" he asked in disbelief.

"I knocked out the glass in the French door, and I want to nail some wood over it for the night."

"Sleep on the couch," he said. "We'll fix it tomorrow."

"I want to sleep in my own room," she insisted, shamed by the tremor that had crept into her voice.

His fixed her with a searching look. "I'll take care of it," he said. "You go on upstairs and get into bed."

She sat rigidly on the edge of her bed, wrapped in the warm sweater and holding her blanket tightly around her, unwilling to surrender either until he had made the repair and was out of her room.

Chance hammered in the nails and covered the jagged hole. "I'll clean up the glass first thing in the morning," he said. "Try and get some sleep." Then he just stood there, looking at her. His eyes were clouded with some emotion that she could not readily grasp. She didn't know what he was feeling. And she didn't care.

"Thank you," she said. "I appreciate your help with this. Now please leave, Chance."

"Darien," he began.

"Now," she insisted. "Leave now."

He stood there, not moving.

"Look," she said, clutching the blanket more tightly about her and glaring at him defiantly. "I know exactly what you're thinking, and it's not going to happen. Take my word for it and save us both a lot of trouble."

"Do you?" he asked.

"Yes, I most certainly do," she retorted.

"And what would that be?"

"Don't ask me to embarrass us both, Chance, by putting it into words. There is nothing to be gained by stating the obvious. And you are nothing if not obvious. We both know what you're thinking now."

"I wouldn't be so sure of that," he said.

"Well, I am sure. I am very, very sure. There is nothing hidden or complicated about your thoughts, Chance Deckert," she said.

There was a long pause while he considered his response. When at last he broke the silence, both his tone and his expression were dead serious.

"You're so intent on reading my mind, so certain you know my thoughts. But being certain doesn't make it so. The truth is that you're not doing a very good job of mind reading, and even if you were, you wouldn't learn the important things there. Stop wasting your time by trying to read my mind, Darien, and try reading my heart."

He turned, walked out of the room, and shut the door firmly behind him.

Exhausted, she unfolded the heavy blanket, shrugged out of the warm clothes, and put them carefully on the chair beside the bed. Then she pulled down the covers and fell into bed, weary beyond anything she could have imagined. As she drifted into sleep, she thought she could make out the faint, sensuous sound of music in the distance. It was the song she and Chance had danced to. She felt him reach for her, take her into his arms, hold her close to him. And then she slept.

Chance poured a double shot of the Jack Daniels over ice and stared moodily into the glass, considering. Then he poured a little more and returned the bottle to the table. He had a feeling that it would not be the last time he'd lift the bottle that night.

Out here on the porch, the wind off of the ocean was blowing hard and turning colder, but he did not mind the cold. He welcomed it. He was a man who needed to cool down. He raised the glass, tossed back the whiskey, and felt the slow burn of the liquor as it went down. He put the glass back on the table, reached for the bottle, and refilled his glass to the brim. Then he ran his fingers through his hair in pure frustration and walked over to the railing, staring unseeing at the dark, roiling waves.

The trip into town had accomplished nothing. He'd stopped at the first open place for a drink. As always, although it had been late, there had been women lingering at the bar, waiting, hoping. And, as always, there was someone pretty enough to catch his eye. It was a familiar story by now. Smiles that promised everything a man might want with no strings attached. Willing arms and eager lips. Good times.

But this time, when he looked down into those ice blue eyes, he saw only the glow of almond-shaped amber eyes looking back at him. When he tangled his hands in that glossy jet-black hair, he felt soft copper curls slip through his fingers. And when the music stopped and she pressed closer to him, he felt — nothing. Muttering something incomprehensible, he had turned and left.

He could have lost Darien that night. If she had not woken up when she did, if she had not had the good sense and courage to get out safely, if someone had not made that call, he could have lost her. For just one moment, he let himself face what that would have meant. His heart constricted painfully. It was as if he'd taken a hard blow to the chest and had the wind knocked clear out of him.

The cold gusts off the ocean were picking up and whipping over Maggie's comfortable porch. Chance looked down and saw that his glass was empty again. He leaned against the railing, brooding. What was he doing? What the hell was wrong with him? Whatever it was, the usual remedies hadn't worked their magic. The fast car hadn't helped. Neither had the fast woman. And the whiskey sure as hell hadn't helped.

Abruptly, Chance tossed the remaining ice cubes over the railing. Then he turned and went back into the house. He climbed the stairs deliberately, and paused at the top on the landing. He stared for a long time in the direction of her room. Slowly he turned away, and then he walked swiftly to his bed.

CHAPTER ELEVEN

She was already in the kitchen, showered and dressed, when he came down for breakfast. He looked at her in surprise.

"Thought you might want to sleep in and take it easy this morning," he said. "You didn't get much sleep last night. And you probably breathed in a fair amount of the gas."

"I'm just fine," she said, looking up from the notes she was reviewing. "I have a lot of work to pull together before Edward and Maggie come up tomorrow with Jim. They'll be expecting a detailed description of what we've found, and a summary of our conclusions and next steps. And then there's the client drill. If I know Edward, we'll be entertaining Jim and showering him with the red-carpet treatment. He has the potential to be a very big client."

"All the more reason to take it easy today," Chance said. "The next few days'll be pretty tough. Makes good sense to catch a break while you still can."

She looked back at her notes and then up at Chance. "I need to get into town early to track down a few details, and then head back here to make some phone calls to interview witnesses to the other fires. If I'm tired, I can rest after lunch."

"Okay, counselor, how about we negotiate some middle ground here. We work in the morning, and then head over to Mohegan Bluffs for some lunch and a nap. I hear it's something I shouldn't miss. There'll be plenty of time to work later in the afternoon if you haven't finished up."

"I don't nap in the middle of the day, Chance," she responded curtly.

"Then some rest and relaxation," he said patiently. "Surely, even successful, busy lady lawyers can stop to smell the daisies for a few minutes."

Her brows furrowed in exasperation. If she didn't agree, he was going to stand here and pester her all day, and she wouldn't be able to get anything done. "All right," she said with a notable lack of enthusiasm. "Whatever." She rubbed a hand across tired, aching eyes.

"Meet here at one?" he asked.

"Okay."

"And Darien, just in case there's anything to my notion that someone doesn't want you to get closer to the truth, be careful."

"There is absolutely nothing to your notion, and I'll be just…"

"Fine," he finished for her. "I know, you'll be just fine. But humor me. Watch your back."

She was still shaking her head as she walked out the door. She got into the car, put on a Charlie Parker track, and set off toward town.

The weak early morning sun was powerless to burn away the fog, which hung heavy and low. It blurred the edges of the trees and muted the colors of the landscape, making the familiar vaguely unfamiliar. There was no traffic at this early hour, and she had the narrow road to herself.

As was her custom, Darien started to plan. She ticked off a list of the tasks and then proceeded to organize them in the most efficient order. She had two people to interview in town. Next, she wanted to have a brief visit with Sally and Bobby, assuming Bobby was still out of school, because she'd thought of a few questions for each. And then she needed to check in with the associate at work that was monitoring the work of the investigators in the field.

That done, she began to mull over her evolving theory of the case, making a mental note of the gaps. And there were some big ones. She would return to those gaps later and think how best to fill them in.

She was deep in thought when she rounded a turn in the road to discover a large truck askew across both lanes of the road. It appeared to have spun out and come to rest in the worst of all possible places, where she could not get around it to continue into town. She slowed and came to a stop some distance from the truck, chewing her lower lip in exasperation. This was the kind of thing that inevitably happened when she was in a hurry and had a lot to do.

She looked at her watch and frowned. Would she have to turn around and circle the entire Island to get to town? Or was there some way through the center of the Island? Darien fumbled in her brief case for her phone, put on her glasses, and muttering to herself, tried to find an alternative route.

She looked up for a moment to get her bearings, and noticed that two burly men had stepped from the truck and were headed in her direction. Although there was nothing outwardly unusual about their deliberate, unhurried pace, a sense of urgency and dark purpose seemed to be radiating from beneath their surface calm. She felt an ominous prickling at the back of her neck. There was something about this that was oddly familiar. What was it?

Alert and inexplicably on edge, she put down the phone. The truck. It had something to do with the truck.

They were getting closer now, so close that she could make out their features. Even at this distance, their expressions seemed hard and furtive, their stance menacing. The vague feelings of anxiety were rapidly slipping over into alarm. Maybe she should turn around and leave.

Oh, really, she thought, bringing herself up short. Get a grip. Talk about melodramatic. She'd been around Chance entirely too long and now she was starting to think like him.

That was it. It was something Chance had said.

She tried hard to remember. The day of the fire…the reason for the delayed arrival of the firetrucks. She and Chance had discussed that delay on the way out to the Island from Providence. And then she remembered the answer. A truck had been blocking their path. A truck had broken down across both lanes of traffic, blocking the firetrucks and causing them to take a longer route to the fire.

The truck. The truck. Something about the truck. Had Chance learned something about the truck? The name of the business? No, the witnesses could not recall a name on the truck. But the color — that was it — they were certain of the color. It was white with blue lettering.

Darien looked at the truck and then felt a shock of recognition. It was a dirty white, with dark blue letters.

Going on instinct, Darien threw the car into reverse and backed up until she had reached a spot where she could turn around. She made a hasty U-turn and gunned the motor. The car took off, spraying sand in all directions and putting distance between her and the truck. She glanced in the rear-view mirror and saw the two men standing in the road, watching her hasty retreat, unmoving.

When Darien felt it was safe, she pulled over to the side of the road, killed the engine, and put her head down on the steering wheel. It hurt to breathe, and her heart was pounding wildly. There were beads of perspiration on her forehead. She waited, with her eyes closed, for calm to return. Then she sat up and took stock.

Around her, the sun continued its struggle to break through the fog. The birds were singing their morning songs, the ocean was rolling gently in toward shore, and the occupants of the nearby houses were starting their days with a hearty breakfast. The scene was familiar, reassuring, benign.

I am an idiot, she said to herself. A complete and total idiot. I just pulled off a dangerous, harrowing escape from an encounter with two tired, overweight truckers whose old rig had broken down, and who doubtless were hoping for a lift to town or some other help. Nice job,

Darien. The FBI will definitely be calling, if the CIA doesn't recruit you first. She gave a short, humorless laugh.

When her breathing had steadied, she started the motor and headed toward town. But she went the long way around.

It was after one o'clock and he was nowhere to be seen. Darien checked her watch for the third time in as many minutes. Wasn't that just like the man! First he pesters her until she agrees to join him, and then he leaves her high and dry.

She paced to one end of the kitchen, turned around, and retraced her steps. Then she repeated the circuit. Wearily, she rubbed her sore eyes.

Darien was on edge after her jarring, early morning encounter with the men in the truck. And she was upset with herself for acting like such a fool. But most of all, if she were truly honest with herself, she was exhausted from the effort of pretending that Chance's whereabouts last night were of no concern to her. It did concern her. It concerned her very much. And each time today that she'd had nothing to occupy her mind, the image had risen, unbidden and hurtful, of Chance taking another woman into his arms. Chance kissing another woman. Chance.

She heard the Jag pull into the driveway and then Chance hurried through the door. Her tired eyes swept over him and took in his relaxed, rested appearance. His white cotton sweater looked soft and fresh, and set off the tan from his days at the site. And although he was indoors, the sandy hair that fell so carelessly over his forehead still appeared to glow with the warmth and light of the sun. At a minimum, he should have had the good grace to show up with the hollowed-out cheeks, gray pallor and bleary eyes of a man who'd been out carousing half the night.

To add insult to injury, she didn't need to look in a mirror to know how she looked. She looked like she felt, absolutely wretched. She was pale, her eyes swollen and red from lack of sleep, her face puffy. She was, in short, a mess. Despite what they taught in law school, there really was no justice.

Darien snapped, "You're late."

"Just a few minutes," he said. "I stopped to get some food for a picnic."

"I was planning to bring leftovers," she said.

"I drove right past a store on my way home from the site, so it wasn't any trouble. And I'm not planning to spend my afternoon at the best spot on the Island eating leftovers. Now if you're through fussing, let's get a move on."

Chance turned and really looked at her for the first time. "And you should change out of that heavy wool sweater. The sun's broken through the fog and it's warm out. You'll swelter in that thing."

"The sweater will do nicely. And I don't require your advice on my wardrobe." she retorted.

"Suit yourself." He shrugged. "Let's go." He reached for the beach blanket that Maggie kept on a shelf near the coats, and headed out toward the car. Darien followed.

"Bad day?" he asked as he pulled out of the driveway and onto the street.

"Not at all. Why do you ask?"

"I've seen happier faces on a cow that's just been branded, and you near bit my head off in there," he answered. "At least tell me what crime I've committed so that I can defend myself."

"Guess I am a little on edge," she admitted.

"Anything in particular?"

"No. Well, yes. A strange thing happened on the way into town. It really didn't amount to anything other than a case of jittery nerves, but still, I can't shake it."

"Want to tell me about it?" he asked. Although he'd adopted a light tone, his voice had gone serious, and the smile was gone from his lips.

Darien described her encounter with the truckers. "I felt so foolish once I'd had time to consider the situation. They're probably sitting in some truck stop by now, laughing and shaking their heads at the crazy woman who ran off instead of offering to help. They're probably thinking that it must be one of those flighty summer people come up early to air out a cottage, or someone's slightly unhinged Auntie. I don't know what got into me."

"Describe that truck again, Darien." He clearly was not amused.

She did.

"Did you get a look at the license plate?"

"No."

"Can you describe the two men who got out of the truck?"

"I think I can. Yes."

"And could you…"

"Stop it, Chance," she broke in. "You're making too much of this. I told you it was just a case of over-active nerves. Let's just forget it."

"Come on, think about it, Darien. First, on the way to a fire, the firetrucks were blocked by a white truck with large blue lettering. Second, we decide that the fire is suspicious and start closing in on a likely scenario. Third, you are pulled over on a lonely stretch of highway by a white truck with large blue lettering."

"It's just a coincidence," she said.

"I'm a scientist, Darien. I don't believe in coincidence. And I'd bet that you didn't get where you are as a lawyer by placing too much faith in coincidence, either."

She lapsed into silence.

"Look Darien, I'm not trying to scare you. But I want you to take this situation seriously. We're going to let the police know about this. We'll put a trace on that truck and see what we can learn about it. And I want you to describe those men to the police."

"Okay," she agreed reluctantly. "But on Monday, Chance. Not today."

"First thing on Monday," he said.

"First thing. And for now, can we just drop it and enjoy the Bluffs for the afternoon?"

"Consider it dropped," he agreed, and gave her a reassuring smile. "Until Monday."

Darien turned her attention to the scenery. "There's the turnoff," she called after a few minutes.

Chance eased the Jag into the vacant parking area.

"In the summer, this lot is filled with cars and bikes and tourists," she said. "Looks like we have the place to ourselves."

"You carry the blanket and I'll take the food," he said.

She stepped out of the car into the bright sunlight. "You were right," she said. "I should have changed. It's really warm here, and this wool sweater is bulky and hot. Not to mention itchy."

Before she could stop him, he had peeled off his white cotton sweater. "Here, put this on. I'm already too warm so I don't need it, and you'll be more comfortable."

She looked uneasily at his powerful chest and arms, which glowed a soft copper in the warm sunlight. Obviously, he had been removing his shirt at the site and the sun had done its work. Then she looked around the deserted parking lot.

"You can change in the car," he said, laughing. "It's okay. I promise I won't peek."

She blushed and snatched the sweater from him impatiently. Then she got into the car, pointedly refusing to turn back to see if he was keeping his promise.

She emerged and adjusted the sweater. It was huge on her, but with the sleeves pushed up it would do, and she was much more comfortable.

"Thanks," she said, as graciously as she could manage.

"You're welcome," he said. "I'll never wash that sweater again. Now lead the way. You're the one who knows the Island."

Blanket in hand, she headed off in the direction of the staircase. "I always like to stop first at the overlook," she said. "It's a spectacular view, and you can orient yourself. The cliffs rise about 200 feet straight up from the ocean, so once you're down there, the view is very different."

Darien led the way from the lot to the small area at the top of the Bluff and gazed down with sheer delight. No matter how many times she stood at this point, she was thrilled by her first glimpse of the sweep of the shoreline and ocean below the towering cliffs. And despite all that had passed between them, despite last night, she was deeply pleased to share this feeling with him. She looked over at Chance.

He turned to her and smiled that crooked smile of his. "You were right, it is spectacular," he said. He reached over, put his arm around her waist and pulled her closer. They stood like that in companionable silence, taking in the quiet beauty of the setting. For a brief moment, she let her head rest against his chest, savoring the feel of his warm skin against her cheek. She felt the muscles bunch in his shoulder as he pulled her closer. If she turned her face only the smallest bit toward him, her lips would brush against him, would learn the taste of him. Darien shivered. Then she pulled away.

"Over there," she said, pointing the way, "is the Southeast Light. A few years back, the erosion was so bad that the lighthouse was in danger of toppling into the ocean. They actually repositioned it on firm ground by moving it three hundred feet on a hydraulic lift. It's a fascinating old lighthouse. You should plan to take a tour next time you come back."

"No reason I have to see it alone," he said. "I've been thinking that we could stay on the Island for a few days after we wrap up this case and you could show me the sights. I'm sure Edward would give you a few days off after all the hard work you've done here."

"Umm," she said.

"I take that as progress," he said.

"Progress?"

"Yes. At least it wasn't a flat out 'no.'"

She felt her cheeks grow warm. "Speaking of progress, we'd better get a move on. We have about two hours to mean low tide, and once the tide turns and starts coming in, it's just a matter of time until most of the beach is under water again."

They started off together with Chance in the lead. She was try-ing hard not to watch the way the muscles in his back rippled as he worked his way down the steep, winding staircase. Or the way his shoulders narrowed down to the lean waist that was just visible above the waistband of his jeans. Or the way the sunlight glinted off his taut skin. And she was failing on all counts.

Better that she keep her eyes on the stairs so she wouldn't lose her footing. And while she was on the subject of 'better,' it was better that she keep her mind off the thought of a few days alone on Block Island with that man. What a monumental mistake that would be. She looked up at Chance and took in the animal grace with which he navigated the plunging staircase. A monumental mistake, but a tempting one. Fortunately, she was far too prudent and sensible to make such a mistake.

They reached the bottom of the staircase and found a secluded spot in the fold of the cliffs. They spread the beach blanket and settled their belongings. "What's your pleasure, Darien?" he asked. "Do you want to eat or take a walk?"

"I'm hungry," she said. "What did you get for lunch?"

"Thought you preferred leftovers," he teased, reaching for the bag.

He pulled out a selection of fresh baked breads, cheeses, and fruit, together with a bottle of Medoc, and put them on the blanket. "Plates, cups and whatever are in the bag," he said. "This is a self-service picnic. Help yourself."

She ate in blissful silence, enjoying the delicious food, the gentle play of the ocean breeze in her hair, and the cries of the gulls as they soared above. It was such a relief to escape the problems of last night and the morning. She could feel herself relax as the tension melted away in the warmth of the sun.

She finished the last tasty morsel of cheese and sat quietly, tak-ing in the scene around her. Small wonder this place was special to her, Darien thought. In part, it was the rugged, natural beauty of the Bluffs. But more profoundly, it was the peaceful feeling they evoked in her. The cliffs towered protectively above her and seemed to wrap themselves around her, to enfold her, to shelter her. She felt safe.

"See the ship way out there?" he asked, pointing far out to sea. "The first time I saw the ocean, I was about five. I remember spotting a ship way off at the edge of the horizon, just like this one, and thinking that it was sailing off the edge of the world." Chance put his arm around her and pulled her against him, until her back was resting comfortably against his chest. Together, they gazed at the distant boat.

"Tell me about your trans-Atlantic trip," she said. "That must have been quite the adventure."

"We've talked enough about me," he protested, his lips in her hair. "Tell me about you, Darien."

"There's really not much to tell," she said, looking out to sea. "I was brought up in New England, on the Connecticut shore. I went to law school. I work at a law firm in Providence. I…"

"Tell me about your family," he interrupted.

She hesitated. "I was raised by my grandparents. They were very good to me."

"I hear a 'but' lurking in there somewhere," he said.

She scooped up a handful of sand and let it slip through her fingers. "I never wanted for anything and they loved me very much. But I wouldn't call my childhood normal, either."

"How do you mean?" he asked.

"My grandparents were older and led a settled, quiet life. They really weren't prepared to have a child at that stage of their lives. I was on my own a lot and learned to entertain myself with my music and my books. But it was a good, secure life and I was happy in my way."

"What happened to your folks?"

"My life really doesn't make a very interesting topic of conversation, Chance. The days are uncomplicated, predictable, and full of hard work. It suits me."

"And your nights?" he asked, brushing her hair back off her shoulder. "Tell me about your nights, Darien."

"Nothing much to tell. I relax. I read. I plan the next day."

Chance laughed. "You are a puzzle, woman," he said, turning her around until she was facing him. "When we're together, I never know who I'll be talking to. Will it be the prim, orderly lawyer who lives by her intellect and her rules? Or will I meet up with the woman who plays the blues straight from her heart, and whose passion flashes into fire like dry tinder touched by a match?"

"Well, fortunately for you Chance, you're not being paid to figure me out. You're being paid to figure out the fire." She turned away so that her back was to him, but let him pull her against him once more. They watched in silence for several minutes as the boat receded further from shore, on its way to some distant and unknown destination.

"Nothing happened last night," he said into the silence.

She hesitated, absorbing this unexpected bit of news. The witty, casual retort that she wanted to make died unspoken, unable to work its way past the lump that had formed in her throat.

His fingers traced a line from her wrist up toward her shoulder. Darien drew in her breath sharply and tried to ignore the warm, liquid feeling triggered by his touch.

"You don't have to account to me for your whereabouts or your actions," she said quietly.

He continued as if she hadn't spoken. "I realized that everything I wanted was at home," he said. "I just wanted you to know, Darien." His hand traveled to her cheek and caressed her softly.

Everything he wanted. What did that mean? Everything that he cared for? Everything that he held dear? Or everything that he wanted to lure into his bed for a night of raw, hot sex?

Darien sighed. On the surface, the man seemed like an open book. Yet she spent so much time trying to read between the lines of what he said and did. And the more she tried, the more the truth eluded her.

What was it that he'd said about her reading his mind? He'd said she would learn nothing important there, and had asked her instead to read his heart. Right. How could she be expected to do that, when no matter how hard she looked, or what angle she looked from, she could not seem to read what was written on her own heart.

The warmth of the sun was making her drowsy, and she was so cozy there in his arms. He enfolded her like the cliffs, sheltering her, protecting her. Her eyelids fluttered and then they closed. The last thing she was aware of was the gentle caress of his fingers across her cheek. It felt so good. And then she slept.

The sound of a small plane flying into the Block Island airstrip woke her. Darien opened her eyes slowly against the bright glare of the sun and tried to get her bearings. She'd been sleeping! That was really odd. The sleep that often eluded her at night was all but impossible during the day.

She looked down and saw Chance's arms holding her. Small golden hairs curled and glinted against the brown of his skin. And behind her, pressed against her back, she became aware of the rise and fall of his chest. She thought she could feel the slow, steady beating of his heart. And for just a moment, it felt as though it were beating in time with her own.

"Feel better?" he asked.

She sat up and turned to face him. "Guess I'm not immune to napping after all," she said. "What time is it, anyway?" She tried to look at her watch, but was foiled by the sleeves of the over-size white sweater, which had slipped down over her wrists while she slept, and were now dangling below her hands.

Chance laughed and obligingly rolled up the sleeves for her. "Next time, don't be so quick to dismiss my advice about dressing for the weather. We learn these things early in Montana."

She ignored his comment. "Three o'clock. We still have time on the beach before the tide rises too high." She got to her feet. "Let's clean up lunch and take a walk on the beach. I need to clear my head before I get back to work."

Darien started to assemble the remains of their feast, but was distracted by the loud, agitated cries of a large flock of gulls that were hovering over the ocean, just beyond the most distant breakers. She turned to watch as they gracefully circled a school of tiny fish below.

One-by-one they would break off from the flock and streak down on their prey, tracing a stark, white arc against the faded blue of sky and the deeper blue of the ocean, and then rise in triumph back to the flock with their prizes clutched firmly in their beaks. She stood watching, on the wind-swept expanse of beach, trying to etch the scene onto her memory. She would savor this moment some dark, rainy day spent behind mountains of work at her desk at Rankin & Rhodes.

She didn't know when Chance had come up behind her, but she felt the pressure of his hand on her shoulder, warm and insistent. She did not resist as he turned her toward him and gathered her into his arms. She could feel the heat of his bare flesh through her thin cotton sweater, and the guiding pressure of his hand as he lifted her face for his kiss. When his lips found hers, the kiss was as gentle and soft as the rustle of the wind through the long sea grass that grew on the Bluffs.

She felt his arms tighten around her as his kiss deepened and then became more urgent, and felt too the first tentative stirrings of her own desire. Abruptly, Chance pulled back and released her. She could hear the sound of his ragged breathing and saw his shoulders rise and fall as he struggled to regain control. Gently, she reached out and touched his cheek.

With a harsh cry, he pulled her tightly against him until she could feel his desire, rock-hard, demanding. His lips found hers again, but this time the kiss was wild, hot, hungry. Darien moaned softly as her body erupted in a hot rush of passion. She was aching with the need for him, trembling with the desire for his touch. Without taking his lips from hers, Chance lifted her into his arms, turned toward the blanket, and dropped to his knees. Then he broke the searing kiss and laid her down on the blanket.

Her eyes were still closed but the rest of her, every last aspect of her being, was fully open to the man and whatever this moment with him might hold. She was aware of nothing beyond Chance kneeling above her, waiting for the touch of his hand on her flesh, waiting for the feel of his body on hers. And when that moment stretched out over time, thin and taut as a rope fraying under unbearable strain, she opened her eyes and looked up at him.

He was staring fixedly at her shoulder, which was bare and exposed where his white sweater had slipped down. She took in the expression of shock on his face.

She had forgotten. For one brief, unguarded moment she had allowed herself to forget. And now…

Darien didn't need to follow his gaze to know what he was looking at. She knew only too well. Although she never looked herself, and although she carefully arranged matters so she would rarely have to see, it was endlessly and mercilessly visible in her mind's eye. The scar. The dull, angry red stain with jagged edges that slashed across her back and shoulder. All her fear, loss and guilt, the sorrow in her heart and the shame in her soul. Her most closely guarded secrets seared into her skin and given form and substance, and then made visible in that lurid scar for all the world to see. She sat up and pulled the sweater over her shoulder, clutching it tightly against her throat.

Darien stared, unseeing, at the sand. The wind had picked up and was blowing the sand into intricate, shifting patterns, but she was oblivious. She was seeing another day in another place. She was seeing a little girl walking heedlessly along a smoky hallway toward her destiny.

"That's quite a scar, Darien. The kind of scar caused by a fire, the kind of scar caused by a third-degree burn." he said.

She was silent.

"You were in a fire. You got that burn in a fire." He stopped, absorbing the implications of his words.

"My god, woman," he said in a puzzled voice, "what are you doing here? Why are you working on this case? Why are you putting yourself through all of this?"

Still, she said nothing.

"This makes no sense at all. The firm never should have sent you. You're the last person on earth who should be investigating a fire."

He stopped short, as the truth of the matter became clear to him.

"You never told Edward, did you? You didn't let on that there was a problem. He wouldn't have sent you if he'd known. He can be a hard man, but he's not cruel."

He grabbed a handful of the warm sand and let it sift slowly through his hand. "And me, Darien. When were you planning to tell me? Don't you think that's something I would have wanted to know? Do you think I'd have let you within a hundred miles of that charred hotel if I'd known?"

Darien didn't answer. She was sliding inexorably into the vortex of a past that was more real than her present, and could not find a foothold to anchor her to the world she had inhabited a few short moments earlier.

He studied her dazed expression. "Who's Abby?" he asked.

The unexpected question pierced the smoky haze that had enveloped her and jolted her back to reality, leaving her breathless from the rapid, disorienting transition. Her face crumpled, but she struggled to maintain her composure.

There was, in any event, no purpose to be served by speaking. What was she to tell him? That Abby had been her little sister? But Abby wasn't anyone anymore. Abby was dead these many years, killed in that pitiless fire together with everyone Darien had cared for. Killed, in every sense that really mattered, together with Darien herself.

"How do you know about Abby?" she asked in a voice that was little more than a hoarse whisper.

"You were calling her name when I woke you up from the nightmare," he answered. "The nightmare — it was about the fire, wasn't it? The same nightmare that woke you last night. The same nightmare that you have most nights, isn't that true, Darien?"

She turned and stared at him, anguish etched deeply into every contour of her face. When she spoke, her voice was barely audible.

"I can't talk about it, Chance," she said. "I never could."

"You can't afford not to talk about it," he said. "You're paying too high a price for your silence."

She looked at him wearily, unable to deny the truth of his words but unable, after so many years, to break the silence.

"Talk to me," he said. "Tell me. You can trust me."

His words cut through the thick steel bands of her isolation as if they had been strands of tinsel. Darien reached beyond the silence, beyond the guilt, beyond the fear, searching for the right words and the courage to speak them.

And there, witnessed only by the towering cliffs and the indifferent ocean, for the first time ever, she did.

The sun was sinking below the horizon, tingeing the sky and the ocean with deep rose shot through with traces of gold. Darien cast a sidelong glance at Chance's profile as he drove home along the winding beach road. Why this man, she asked herself. And why now?

She leaned her head back against the headrest and closed her eyes. Great, she was making like a lawyer and cross-examining herself. Next thing you know, she'd be asking herself to swear to tell the truth and nothing but the truth.

And yet, today, she had told the truth. For the first time in a very long time, someone knew the truth. Well, that wasn't strictly correct. It was not just 'someone.' It was Chance. Which brought her back to the question. Why had she opened her soul to this reckless, self-centered man, and all but issued him an invitation to come on in? Why?

She opened her eyes again and looked over at the person she had chosen to trust with her secret. He reached up and brushed a stray lock of hair out of the clear hazel eyes that were fixed firmly on the road. Those eyes that could grow hard and cold with anger one minute, flash with raw passion the next, and then look with infinite tenderness on a frightened little boy.

She knew why, all right. God help her, she knew why. But there'd already been quite enough truth for one day.

CHAPTER TWELVE

A few hours later, Darien stood in the steamy shower, savoring the languid sensation of streams of hot water coursing over her body. The scent of her jasmine soap permeated the air of the small room.

She rarely showered at night, but tonight was different. Slowly, lingering over each movement, she lathered the fragrant soap onto her body. Then she stepped back into the spray of hot water and let it play across her skin. She watched silently as it washed the sand and grit of the day down the drain, together with the last vestiges of her common sense.

She was going to do this.

Darien turned off the shower and stepped out onto the throw rug. She toweled her tangled hair dry and then caught it up in a thick white towel.

That done, she turned deliberately to the full-length mirror on the door and considered her reflection. Her eyes swept over her full, up-turned breasts, her slender waist, the curve of her hips. Was she beautiful? Was she desirable? Or was the hideous scar all he would be able to see? She chewed her lower lip nervously.

She reached for the terry robe and wrapped it firmly around herself. She left the steam and the scent of jasmine behind, and turned down the hall to the little peach room overlooking the beach.

She would not be spending the night in this room. Not this night.

Darien unwrapped the towel from her hair and worked out the worst of the tangles with her fingers. She retrieved her hairdryer from the closet, plugged it in and started to blow out the long, coppery curls. The rhythmic strokes of the brush marked time with the slow, steady beat of her heart.

She had daydreamed about this moment so many, many times over the years. But those dreams had been without substance, half-formed images, short on detail and shorter still on conviction. She never could get past the moment that he, whoever 'he' might prove to be, would see the scar and the truth it symbolized. Her daydreams had been spun of silent longing, mysterious sensations, and precious little else.

But one thing she had always known with the absolute certainty. When she gave herself to a man, when she made love to a man, it would be a moment anchored in shared trust and respect, and it would be an expression of abiding love. The 'I'm in this for the long run' kind of love. The 'you can count on me' kind of love.

Her hair was dry. Darien set the hairdryer aside and went to the drawer where she kept her negligees. She considered the contents thoughtfully, and then removed her favorite. It was fashioned of the softest, pale yellow satin and seemed to glimmer with the light of a myriad of fireflies. The sensual feel and cut of the fabric were set off with ivory lace trim at the bodice, but otherwise the delicate garment was starkly simple. She stroked the silky fabric with her fingertips. Darien stepped into the gown, aware of the cool caress of the satin as it slipped over her heated flesh.

She had been so sure it would be that way. Well, she'd been half right, anyway. It could be like that for her. In the short time that she'd known Chance, she was starting to care for him in that way. She would have wished for the time and opportunity to let those feelings grow and deepen. But she knew that would not happen.

Still, she had gone so far already, had committed herself so irrevocably to the man. She had given him her trust, her memories, her secret. He knew her as no other man or woman ever had. That was true intimacy. Having opened her heart and her soul to him, why would she hesitate to open her body?

Darien reached for her perfume. She touched the stopper lightly to her wrists and her throat, and then replaced it in the bottle. She paused for a moment and reconsidered. She slipped the straps of the negligee off her shoulders and let the garment slip low on her chest. She touched the perfume stopper to the swell of her breasts. Then she replaced the delicate straps.

And what of Chance? What would this night mean to him? She faced the question squarely. It was not a particularly difficult question to answer, as he had been honest from the first day they'd met. He took his pleasure freely, and then he moved on. He had told her that first night on the Island that she would find her way to his bed, and he had been right. He would feel passion. He would feel desire. Perhaps he would feel the heady rush of success. He surely would feel tenderness, and possibly affection. Nothing more than that. Could that be enough?

Darien put a touch of blush on her pale cheeks.

Well, she would have to care enough for both of them. She could do that. And she could pretend. She had grown very good at pretending. Just for tonight, just this one time, she could pretend he really cared. It would be enough for now. No need to think beyond that.

In fact, when she got right down to the heart of the matter, there was no need to think at all. This was beyond all thought, beyond all reason. She cared for him and she wanted him. She wanted to know the feel of his naked body pressed close to hers. She wanted to know the smell of him, the weight of him, the way he moved against her. She wanted to hear his cries of desire. She wanted to feel him inside of her. She wanted. And she was going to do this.

Darien turned off the light and walked out of the peach-colored room. She closed the door firmly behind her.

Chance was hard at work reviewing the results of laboratory tests on some of the charred remains from the fire. He did not look up as he heard her coming down the stairs.

"Thought you were going to turn in early," he said into the stack of papers on the table. "We have a long day tomorrow, what with the meeting with Edward and Jim, and the party at Sally's place."

It took several seconds before he realized that she hadn't responded, and he glanced up in her direction. She watched as his expression turned from deep concentration to surprise and then, finally, to awareness. Without taking his eyes off of her, he put down the pen.

Darien stood absolutely still at the foot of the staircase. She watched as his eyes wandered unhurriedly over the soft curves of her body, which the supple, clinging fabric of the negligee did little to conceal. His gaze was so intense that it was as if something tangible, something physical were passing between them. Where his eyes lingered, she felt his touch.

"Where is this going?" he asked finally, looking up at her.

She had an answer to that question. But it was an answer he would not want to hear, an answer he would not understand. That answer was better left unspoken.

"I don't want to sleep alone tonight," she said.

He considered that response. "It's not enough to know what you don't want, Darien. You need to be clear on what you do want. Look at me and tell me what you want."

She hesitated, but only briefly. "I want to sleep with you tonight, Chance," she said. "I want to sleep in your arms, in your bed. I want to make love to you."

He got up from the table and crossed to the foot of the stairs where he stood very close to her, looking down at her with eyes grown bright with passion, but not touching her. She did not flinch from his gaze, but held his eyes as the seconds passed.

Without looking away, he raised his hands to her breasts and caressed her through the slippery fabric, first stroking the gentle swell beneath the lacey trim of the negligee, and then tracing the curve of her breasts with practiced fingers until he reached the aching nipples that were straining toward his touch.

Darien closed her eyes against the shock of pleasure unleashed by his touch, and gave herself up to the fierce sensations evoked by the movement of his hands on her body through the silky fabric. She drew her breath in sharply as she felt his hands slide slowly down over her hips, over her stomach. And then she felt his caress between her legs, first feathery and delicate, then hard and demanding. Her body exploded with white-hot sensations. She put her arms around his neck and clung to him as he carried her up the staircase, turned down the narrow hallway, and into the blue bedroom at the end of the hall. Still holding her tightly in his arms, he placed a kiss, tender and lingering, on her scarred shoulder. Then he lowered her onto his bed.

The moon shone through the window and bathed Chance in a silvery light as he started to remove his clothes. She watched as he pulled his sweater over his head, revealing the now familiar broad shoulders and well-muscled chest, bronzed by the sun that had shown so warmly that afternoon on Mohegan Bluffs. He stepped out of his docksiders and kicked them aside. Her eyes followed his hands as they moved toward his belt, loosened it, and pulled it from the loops in his jeans with one smooth gesture. She watched again as he unsnapped his jeans and pulled down the zipper.

What would he be saying now? What words would he speak if he cared, if this meant something to him? He would say that during their time together on the Island, he had told her how he felt, both with his words and his actions. He would say that now he was going to tell her with his body, so that there could be no mistaking what was happening between them. That was what he would say.

He tugged at his jeans and they fell to the floor. Darien let her eyes follow them down the length of Chance's body. The hard, flat stomach. The narrow waist and hips. The long, powerful legs. And etched darkly against the moonlight, she saw the evidence of his arousal, grown hard and inflamed with desire.

He lay down next to her on the bed and pulled her to him. He smelled of the ocean, she thought as she brushed her lips across his chest. He smelled like the spray at the crest of a wave, like the heat of the sand, like the scent of the wind in the beach grass.

His lips found hers in a bruising, frenzied kiss that left her gasping for breath and longing helplessly for more. He pulled back for a moment, but she placed her hand on the back of his head and guided his lips to hers once again, hungry for the taste of his mouth, for the feel of his tongue.

Unashamed, she moved sensuously under his touch, giving free rein to the fierce desires that were surging through her, and learning now in Chance's bed all that had been implied but never fully realized in the urgent, oddly disturbing jazz rhythms of her music.

She heard his voice through a haze of passion. "Let's take off that nightgown, honey. You don't need it now," he said in a husky voice.

He sat up, put one arm around her, and lifted her effortlessly from the bed. With the other, he worked the shimmering yellow fabric loose and pulled it slowly over her head. She felt her long, silky curls brushing the bare skin of her back and arms, and the play of the cool night over her body.

Now he would have told her that it would always be like this between them, that their lovemaking would always be as wild and as tender as this first time, because their love was strong and would remain true. Yes, he would have said it just like that.

She opened her eyes and looked at him. "You are so beautiful, Darien," he said. "So very, very beautiful."

She smiled a smile that was only a small bit wistful.

Chance shifted, and she felt the weight of his body resting on her, the pressure of his hardness pressing against her, and then inside her. Each deep thrust triggered a fresh storm of sensation and pushed her closer to the edge of what could be endured. And each time he moved inside her, he would have whispered 'I love you. I love you. I love you.' She felt his powerful release deep within her, and then her body erupted in a wild, shattering, incandescent torrent of pleasure. She cried out in ecstasy, clinging to Chance, locked tightly in his arms if not in his heart.

They lay there together on his moonlit bed, dazed by the unbridled passion of their lovemaking and sated, for the moment, by the intensity of their release. In time, their breathing slowed and grew more regular. Chance turned to her and kissed her gently on her eyes, her nose, and then her lips. "Good night, my sweet Darien," he said tenderly. He brushed her hair from her face, and his hand lingered on her cheek.

He would have said, 'I will love you forever. Your heart is safe with me.'

"Goodnight, Chance," she said softly. She curled up against him, brushed her lips to his chest, and drifted across the boundary to sleep.

CHAPTER THIRTEEN

If she ignored it, surely it would go away, Darien thought. She kept her eyes tightly closed and didn't move a muscle. The knocking did not stop.

Sighing, she opened her eyes. The sun was streaming through the window. Why had her alarm not gone off? She turned her eyes in the direction of her clock and tried to focus her vision and her thoughts. Nothing looked familiar.

She heard the heavy door swing open and voices calling from downstairs. "Chance? Darien?"

Chance. Instantly, she recalled where she was. And who was there with her. And with horror, she realized who was calling their names. She turned to Chance and shook him vigorously.

"Chance, wake up," she urged. "Maggie and Ed are downstairs. Chance, come on, wake up!"

He opened his eyes slowly, smiled that lopsided smile, and reached for her as he had so many times last night. Small wonder neither of them were awake.

She dodged his embrace and pushed his hand away. "This isn't funny," she hissed. "Do something!"

"What would you propose that I do?" he asked.

"Go down there and keep them busy while I get into the shower," she said. "Hurry."

Chance got to his feet and slipped into the jeans he had discarded the night before. She shot him an appraising look. As was his way, he looked none the worse for wear. For once, she approved.

She waited until he had headed off down the stairs and she heard him greeting Edward and Maggie. She hoped he had the good sense to steer them away from the staircase.

Darien crept down the hall to her room and breathed a deep sigh of relief as she shut the door behind her. She would shower as quickly as possible, and then she would do what she could do to redeem the day. This was not a promising start.

Fifteen minutes later, Darien came down the stairs looking, she hoped, like the picture of the composed, confident professional she knew Edward expected her to be. She greeted the three people seated at the table, taking care to look each directly in the eye.

"Good morning Maggie, Edward, Chance," she said calmly. "Sorry to have overslept. Must be all this fresh ocean air."

"Must be," Chance said, with only the smallest hint of a smile.

She shot him a gracious smile that, she hoped, would mask from everyone but Chance the threat that lurked just beneath the surface of the smile.

Edward, oblivious to the charged atmosphere, gestured to an empty chair. "Maggie has kindly prepared us some breakfast," he said. "Sit down and join us, and when we've finished, we can talk while Maggie gets us settled."

Maggie was looking at her with frankly appraising eyes. Darien had an irresistible urge to squirm, which she squelched. Maggie glanced at Chance, who was busy spooning salsa liberally over his eggs, and then looked back at Darien. A deep furrow of concern appeared between her eyes.

"Hi, Darien. It's good to see you again," Maggie said. She stood up and came around the table to give Darien a quick hug. "I've missed seeing you at the law firm's events, but I understand that Edward's been keeping you busy."

Darien smiled. Despite the awkwardness of the moment, she was grateful as always for the warmth and kindness that Maggie showed her. The older woman was dressed in white trousers and an elegant green linen shirt. Her pale blond hair was twisted in a knot at the nape of her neck. Behind stylish glasses, her dark brown eyes sparkled with intelligence and sincerity.

Darien took a seat at the table. "Where's Jim Plattman?" she asked as she reached for a muffin. "I thought that he was coming out with you. He's been so anxious for information. He's insisted on being kept in the loop with every development."

"I know," Edward said, "and I appreciate the good work that you and Chance have done in providing him with updates. He called early this morning and said that he'd been unavoidably detained and wouldn't be able to make it to the Island until tomorrow."

"Will he be staying here with us?" Darien asked, spreading jam on the muffin and reaching for some orange juice.

"We'd be short a room," Maggie said, looking quizzically at Darien. "There are only three bedrooms in this house — yours, Chance's, and the master suite."

Darien could feel herself blush. She made the mistake of meeting Chance's eyes, and her blush deepened.

"We've put him up at the Inn," Edward said. "They had a cancellation for two nights and I think he'll be more comfortable there, anyway." He took a sip of his coffee and wiped his mouth carefully.

'I regret that he's delayed," Edward continued, "but it will give us some time to review the findings and to sharpen our presentation. We'll meet with him tomorrow morning. Then, time and weather permitting, I thought that we could entertain him with a dinner party."

"Sounds good," Chance said. "Why don't I catch a shower, and then I can take you out to the site, Edward."

"Excellent," he said. "And Darien, you plan to come with us, as well."

"Why don't we leave Darien here to keep company with Maggie," Chance said. "Her work isn't really relevant to the site, and you don't need both of us out there."

Edward hesitated. "All right," he said as Chance headed toward the stairs. He waited until Chance was out of earshot, and then turned to Darien.

"What's your impression of Chance?" he asked.

'He's capable, knowledgeable and thorough," she replied.

"That's been my impression. He has quite a good reputation."

"I'm not surprised," Darien said. "He's been most impressive. Since we've been on Block Island, he's lived up to his reputation in all respects."

"So it would appear," Maggie said. She stared deliberately at Darien, who just as deliberately studied her breakfast.

After they had left, the two women sat quietly at the table.

"It's a beautiful day," Maggie said. "Why don't we take our coffee out on the porch."

Darien nodded and followed her outdoors. She seated herself on a comfortable chair, took a sip of her coffee, and gazed out over the still, deep green water of the ocean. "You have a beautiful home," she said.

"I love it here," Maggie answered. "Over the years this house has come to be more of a home to me than our place in College Hill. It has more character, more personality. And I enjoy all of the seasons out here. Perhaps someday Edward and I will retire here."

They lapsed into silence.

"Darien," Maggie began. "I could preface my remarks by saying that you should let me know if I'm out of line, and I'll back off. But that would be dishonest, because I already know I'm out of line and I have absolutely no intention of backing off." She took a sip of her coffee and stared out at the ocean, composing her thoughts.

"I don't think of you as just another one of Edward's associates. I respect you and I like you, and over the years, I believe we've formed a friendship of sorts. And it's out of that friendship and a strong dose of concern that I'm speaking up now."

Darien shifted uneasily in her chair and twisted the emerald ring nervously around her finger.

"There's not a fuse made that wouldn't blow from the electricity passing between you and Chance this morning," Maggie said. "If you're worried that Edward noticed, you can relax. I don't think he suspected anything. But I noticed, and I'm concerned. I love that boy like a son, but I also know him like a son. Don't let yourself care for him, Darien. Not that way. It would be a mistake. He may be yours while you're together on the Island, but there'll be no holding him when this case is over. He's not that kind of man. He belongs to the one he's with at the moment, and he belongs for that moment only. And then he moves on. Chance has never learned the meaning of the word 'forever'."

Darien stood and walked over to the porch railing. Although it was early, the sun was rising higher in the sky and drenching the ocean in a soft golden glow. The sharp cries of the seagulls mingled with the sounds of the waves on the incoming tide.

It wasn't that she didn't believe Maggie's words. The woman was telling her what she already knew to be true. It was just that it was irrelevant. It was like trying to tell that sun not to come up this morning. It was like trying to tell that tide not to come in this morning. And it was like trying to tell those gulls to stay at home this morning. It was too late. Far, far too late.

Darien turned and walked over to Maggie.

"I appreciate your concern. I really do," she said. "But there's nothing to worry about. I understand how it is between Chance and me. I know what he's willing to give and I know for how long he's willing to give it. I don't expect anything more. I'll be fine."

"I wish I could believe that," Maggie replied.

"Believe it," Darien said with far more conviction than she felt. "What will not be fine, however, is showing up at Sally and George's party without a dish. Chance was supposed to be in charge of the cooking department, but since he and Edward have conveniently disappeared in the direction of the hotel, I think the job has passed to us.

"Change the subject if you wish," Maggie said. "But that won't change the reality of this situation and it won't change my opinion, either. It's not that Chance is cruel or even unkind. He's just heedless. Careless. He's busy enjoying today with no thought of tomorrow, and he's sure everyone else is doing the same. He hasn't the first notion of commitment. He won't take this seriously. But you will. Someone will get hurt here, and it won't be Chance. Please give some thought to what I've said."

"All right," Darien said, anxious to end the conversation. "I will. I promise. But right now I'm going to make a quick list of ingredients for my curried deviled eggs, and I'll head off to the grocer's to pick them up. I won't be long."

"I'll stay here," Maggie said. "I've brought up a new comforter for the bed in the blue room. It's in shades of deep blue and emerald green that should mix well with the color-scheme, but I want to see how it actually looks in the room."

The two women picked up the empty coffee cups and headed back into the house. Maggie walked over to a shelf and lifted down a bulky package. She reached inside and carefully removed the contents.

"This is the comforter," she said, unfolding a soft, down-filled quilt patterned in the blues and greens of the sea on a clear, sunny day.

"It's beautiful," Darien said. "It will go perfectly in the blue room."

Maggie put the blanket down and gave Darien a pointed look. "I thought that Chance was staying in the blue room."

Darien looked away. "He is," she agreed. Then she met the older woman's eyes. "Look, Maggie, I know what I'm doing and I'm more than old enough to do it. I'm sure you mean well, but this doesn't need to be your concern. The choice is mine, I've made it, and I'm prepared to accept the consequences. Please let it go."

"Point taken," Maggie said. "You know where to find me if you want to talk."

Darien nodded, and watched as Maggie walked slowly up the stairs to the blue room. The words she had spoken to Maggie had been decisive and strong. And when the time on Block Island was at an end, when it was time to walk away from him, she would have to be just that decisive and just that strong. He would leave easily, perhaps a bit sad on the surface to have their affair end, but untouched in any way that really mattered. For her, she suspected, it would not be so easy.

Darien turned resolutely toward the kitchen, tore the grocery list from the pad and then added the ingredients she would need for her dish. No need to follow Maggie up the stairs. In time, when she and Chance were alone again, she knew that she would learn for herself how the new comforter looked in Chance's blue room. She would learn that, and a great deal more, in that blue room to the left of the stairs.

A few hours later, putting the finishing touches on the eggs, she heard Chance and Edward pull in the driveway and come in the front door. She caught snatches of the conversation as she hurried to finish her work.

"Looks like you've been busy," Chance commented as they walked into the kitchen. "Edward and I want to spend a few hours with you before the party. He'd like to hear more details about your work and your conclusions. And we need to prepare for the meeting with Jim tomorrow."

He reached for an egg, but she shooed him away.

"This is for the party, not for you," she said firmly. "You'll have to wait along with everyone else."

"Chance slowly pulled his hand away. "I guess I can live with that. I've learned that some things are well worth waiting for."

She turned toward him. The warmth of his smile caught her by surprise.

Amazing, the power of that brief, silent smile. All of Maggie's words of caution, wise and well-intentioned as they might be, dimmed and faded.

"Just let me get my notes," she said. "I'm ready." And she was.

CHAPTER FOURTEEN

She would not have believed that anyone could have so many friends, not even Sally, with her warm and welcoming ways. There were people everywhere — grandparents, mothers and fathers, young singles, teenagers, toddlers — a tumble of people all engaged in animated discussion and laughter.

After so many years on the Island, Edward and Maggie appeared to know everyone and were greeted enthusiastically by their friends and neighbors. Darien and Chance left them behind and moved through the throng, trying to work their way to the table that held the food. The large platter of deviled eggs was clumsy to carry, and Darien was looking forward to setting it down.

"Let me take that," Chance offered, lifting the platter from her.

"That's not necessary," she protested. "I'm just fine."

"Is it against the rules for a man to help a woman with a big platter?" he teased, moving ahead of her and clearing a path through the crowd. "Wouldn't want to run afoul of any of your famous rules, Darien. Not right here. Not in front of all of these good people. I have my reputation to think of."

Darien studied the figure in front of her. He was dressed in a snug black tee shirt and soft, faded jeans. While she watched, the hard muscles of his back rippled as he shifted the platter to avoid a knot of heedless children. He looked incredibly handsome and unbearably desirable.

She laughed. "I have a feeling your reputation takes care of itself. And thanks, Chance. I do appreciate your thoughtfulness," she added.

"Much better," he said. "I'm happy to help. And," he added, "I'm looking forward to getting a taste of those closely-guarded eggs. Between you and Maggie, I couldn't even get a nibble. I need to know. Can the lady cook?"

"Let me give you advance notice," she declared with mock solemnity, "that I cooked for years for my grandparents. I like to cook. You just haven't given me an opportunity to get into the kitchen yet. Give me my chance and I'll show you what I can do."

"That sounds like a challenge," Chance said as he worked his way over to the table. "If it is, I accept. Take your best shot, woman."

The huge tables were loaded with food of every description. The appetizers were grouped in one area, side courses and casseroles in another, and the desserts were prominently displayed at the end of it all. Nearby, through the crowd, Darien glimpsed George and his buddies roasting a huge pig on a spit. The smell was absolutely delicious.

Chance deposited the eggs and then turned to Darien. "Are you hungry, or do you want to mingle with the crowd? We might be able to pick up some information on the fire. Or, if it suits you, we could go for a walk on the beach." A group of teenage boys came between them, laughing and gesturing as they moved along the food table.

After the boys had passed, Chance put his arm around her waist and pulled her closer. "Seems like time alone together is going to be a pretty scarce commodity for a few days," he said softly into her ear. "I really regret that. I'd like for us to have some time to talk."

That was not at all what she had expected to hear. She was not surprised to learn that he was looking for some time alone with her, but talking — where was that coming from? When it came to men and women, when it came to sex, Chance did not strike her as the talking type. He was definitely a doer. What did he think he wanted to say?

"Hello, Chance. It is Chance, isn't it?"

They both turned in the direction of the sultry voice that had interrupted their conversation. Darien found herself staring at a stunning young woman with long, glossy black hair worn loose and hanging down to her waist. The woman was dressed in a clinging scarlet silk shirt and elegant black trousers. Icy blue eyes stared briefly into hers and then swept slowly over her, taking in the casual white jeans and pale-yellow sweater. She raised those calculating eyes again to Darien's, and then with a toss of her hair dismissed her inconvenient but obviously inconsequential presence.

"Hi, Marnie," he said quietly.

"Hi, yourself," she replied, moving closer to Chance. "This party is definitely looking up. Where'd you disappear to the other night? One minute you were very, very much there, and the next minute, you were gone. And it was such a promising beginning. I can assure you that the end would have been even better." She smiled suggestively.

Darien felt her cheeks flame. That trip into town. That night he had come home late. Well, she had no claim on the man, and what he chose to do and whom he chose to do it with was none of her concern. That was how it was between them, and she understood the rules. She would stay out of it. She would maintain a demure silence. She would behave.

Marnie put a possessive hand on Chance's arm and smiled up into his eyes.

"He disappeared home, that's where he disappeared to," Darien said. So much for a demure silence.

"I believe I was speaking to Chance," Marnie said, never taking those hungry eyes from Chance's impassive face.

"You may have been speaking to Chance," Darien said coldly. "But you just got your answer from me."

Marnie moved in even closer to Chance. "Could you excuse us for a minute?" she asked in Darien's general direction. "I believe Chance and I have some unfinished business."

"No, I don't believe I could," Darien replied. "And I think your business here is very much finished."

"I went home, Marnie," Chance said, disentangling himself from her grasp. "The night was over. That was all there was going to be."

"What a shame," Marnie said, reaching into her purse and removing a business card. "For both of us. I hope all your nights won't have to end so abruptly. Some woman might be able to make it worth your while to stay up late."

She tried to hand him her business card, and when he didn't take it, she put it in his shirt pocket. Then she reached up and traced the curve of his cheek with a long, scarlet fingernail. "Call me," she whispered, touching the fingernail to his lips. "You won't regret it."

Darien could not believe the moxie of this woman. She felt Chance's arm tighten around her waist, and wasn't sure whether it was a gesture of restraint or reassurance.

"That's not going to happen, Marnie," he said.

"I wouldn't be so sure," Marnie said, casting an appraising glance at Darien and tossing her long, silky hair. "The first time a man leaves home is rarely the last. Do us both a favor, Chance. Don't lose that card." She turned and walked off in the direction of the bar.

Neither of them spoke for a few moments.

"I'm really sorry about that, Darien," Chance said. "Let's get away from this crowd. I want to explain."

"Nothing to be sorry about," she said with dignity, stepping away from him. "And you don't owe me an explanation. You don't owe me anything at all. I was out of line to get involved." She looked up at him and was surprised by the hurt she saw in his eyes.

"I don't recall saying anything about owing," he said. "This isn't about balancing the ledger or about a duty. It's about wanting things to be right between us. It's about wanting you to understand. It's about caring how you feel."

This really wasn't fair. She was trying her best to keep everything casual and on the surface. Whatever the price she might have to pay later, she had agreed for the present to play by his rules. Yet here he was, talking about her feelings. Talking about caring. He couldn't have it both ways. Absently, she twisted the old emerald ring.

"I told you, Darien, that nothing happened that night. And I told you why nothing happened. Do you remember?"

"There you two are! We've been looking for you!" Sally's warm greeting was barely audible over Bobby's excited shouts.

'Hey, big fella," Chance said as he lifted Bobby onto his shoulders. Then he turned to Darien.

"This discussion isn't over," he said. "Not by a long shot."

"Chance, come see the new trick I taught Flash!" Bobby shouted over the crowd. "C'mon, Chance."

Chance looked questioningly at Darien.

"I'll help Sally for a bit," she offered. "You go with Bobby."

"You could meet up back here in half an hour or so," Sally said. "They're taking the pig off the spit, so lunch should be served soon. And I could use some help, thanks," she added.

"All right then," Chance said to Bobby. "Let's go put Flash through his paces."

Darien watched as they threaded their way through the crowd.

"Didn't mean to interrupt anything heavy," Sally said. "What was that about, anyway?"

Darien shook her head in bewilderment. "That man makes up the rules as he goes along. Just when I think it's clear to both of us that I'm playing Old Maid and he's playing Solitaire, he shuffles the cards and we've started a new game."

"Not that it's any of my business, but maybe it's time you both stop playing and put your cards on the table," Sally suggested.

"Yeah, right," Darien said. "And what about all those aces Mr. Deckert keeps up his sleeves?"

"Trust isn't your strong suit, eh?" Sally asked with a grin. "Afraid to take a gamble?"

"Enough with the cards, already," Darien protested. First Maggie and now Sally. Why did everyone seem to feel that she needed advice? She was a bright woman with no shortage of common sense. Bright enough to know that she and Chance had put their cards on the table that first night in her office. She was simply playing out her hand the best way she knew how. And she didn't believe for a moment that there was any other way to play it.

The sun was low and preparing to set in a sky that was shot through with deep reds and golds. She had eaten far more than she should have, and had reached her limit on beer a good two hours ago. They were seated comfortably on the beach on a faded old blanket with two other couples. At times, they all spoke easily and quietly among themselves. Then, they would sit together in companionable silence, watching the ships barely visible on the horizon. Darien could not recall a time when she had felt more relaxed, more at peace with herself.

She reached over and traced a pattern with her finger in the sand. The air was growing cool, and the sand, which had retained the heat of the sun, felt pleasantly warm to her touch. She signed contentedly.

"Want to go for a walk?" Chance asked.

She shivered involuntarily. There was much in that invitation that was unspoken.

"Yes," she said simply. Yes to the walk. Yes to the man. Yes.

Chance stood and helped her to her feet.

"I enjoyed talking with you," she said to the other couples. "I hope our paths will cross again before Chance and I leave the Island."

"We'll make sure of it," said one of the men. "In fact, I have a book I intended to drop by for you. It's a historical book about Block Island. Has some pictures of the old hotel that you might find interesting. Not sure if they'll be helpful with the investigation, but you never know."

"That would be great, thanks," Chance replied. "I'd love to take a look at it. Mike Williams, right? Here's my business card. It has my cell number."

"I'll be in touch, then."

The couples turned back to their conversation, and Chance and Darien moved off in the direction of the sunset.

As they walked slowly along the shore, the party and the noisy crowd receded into the distance. The sun, acknowledging the inevitable, slid lower in the sky until it hung suspended just above the horizon, ablaze in color even as it gave way to the encroaching darkness of the night. Its reflection turned the water luminescent with hues ranging from deepest purple to soft rose. In the deepening twilight, the silence was broken only by the hushed whisper of the waves washing up on shore.

When they reached a secluded cove, he stopped, turned to her, and studied her face in the faint glow that was all that remained of the bright light of day.

"We didn't finish our conversation about Marnie," he said softly.

The mention of the other woman sounded a dissonant note. She didn't want to think about that.

"I told you," she said, "that you don't owe me an explanation."

"And I told you this wasn't about 'owing,'" he answered patiently.

"Don't do this, Chance," she said. "It's not necessary, and it's not fair."

"Not fair?" he asked.

"I've agreed to play by your rules. Don't confuse matters…"

"My rules?" he interrupted. He studied her face as if he might find the answer to a knotty puzzle in the slant of her brows or in the straight, tight line of her lips.

"My rules?" he repeated.

She stared back at him in silence.

"I don't know how 'rules' got into this. I didn't think we were playing. And I can assure you that if anyone is confusing matters, it most definitely is not me. I just want you to understand about that night with Marnie."

"I understand," she said.

"I don't think you do, Darien. We've been through this before. Your fiercely held convictions to the contrary, you cannot read my mind. Would it be possible just this once for you to hear me out without second guessing my motives or my explanation?"

His hazel eyes flashed with frustration and annoyance, but Darien did not think she could bear to hear what he had to say.

"You've already told me that nothing happened," she said finally.

"And I told you why nothing happened. Do you remember that part, Darien?"

'Yes," she said impatiently. "Yes, I remember. You said that you realized that everything you wanted was at home." As if she had a clue what that meant to him.

"Then what's with this 'rules' business?"

She looked at him. Why did he insist on going over this ground again? If he still didn't understand, explanations were futile.

"Look," he said finally, "can you suppose for the sake of argument that we aren't playing by my rules. What would be different? Tell me what would be different between us here and now." He reached out and followed the contour of her cheek with his fingertips.

His touch brought her up short, and she felt the unease and concern start to evaporate like the early morning fog on the Island.

What would be different? There would be tomorrow, she thought as she turned her face into the warmth of his hand and kissed the rough skin of his palm. There would be next month and next year. There would be the future.

He pulled her toward him and held her tightly against him, letting her feel his desire.

"Nothing would be different, not here and now," she said quietly.

"Then let's be in this moment," he whispered into her hair. "Let's let this moment happen."

Darien pulled away from him and took a deep breath. Without taking her eyes from his, she reached up and unbuttoned the pale-yellow sweater. Then, she slid it off her shoulders and let it drop to the sand. With her eyes still locked on his, she fumbled with the button that secured her jeans, pulled down the zipper, and slipped the white fabric down over her hips. She stepped out of the trousers and looked up at the man for whom she cared so deeply, the man whom she had trusted first with her secret and then with her body. The man that she was still afraid to trust with her heart.

She could feel his eyes on her, taking in the shimmer of the delicate ivory lingerie that glowed softly in dusky light of early evening. She drew closer to him, so close that she could see the pulse throbbing in his throat, so close that she could imagine she heard the slow, steady beat of his heart.

Unhurriedly, his hands moved down the straps of the satin bra and over the swell of her breast. She gasped at the now familiar rush of pleasure that coursed through her at his touch, and arched toward him as his hands continued their leisurely exploration down over the ivory trim of the panties, and came to rest between her legs. When he stroked her there, she reached up and pulled his lips to hers, kissing him deeply. They sank together to their knees, and then he lowered her down onto the soft folds of his jacket.

He lay down next to her and she felt his lips brush the ragged edges of the telltale scar. "I want you to feel pleasure where you've felt so much pain," he whispered through the kisses on the disfigured shoulder. "No more pain, Darien. Only kisses. Only this." His lips continued their feather-light caresses as his hands removed the ivory satin garments. And then he was moving onto her, and she felt the heat of his flesh against hers.

She was in free-fall, falling silently, falling swiftly through space. Yet in defiance of the rules that governed the universe, she was falling up. She was falling up to his lips that were seeking hers with such hunger. Falling up to his hands, that were caressing her with such urgency. Falling up to his body, hard and demanding. Falling, falling, and then, finally, shuddering with pleasure at her release.

They lay spent, tangled in each other's arms, listening to the muted music of the beach at dusk. The ocean breeze cooled her over-heated body, while the slow, steady rhythm of the waves formed a counter-point to the turbulent beating of her heart. He was heavy on her, still deep inside her. She turned her head and brushed her lips across his cheek.

Chance pulled himself up on one elbow and smiled that lopsided smile.

She wanted to ask him how he could do it. How he could bear to touch that scar, to kiss it. She could not even look at it. She undressed in the dark, and in the light of day, contrived never to see what was so very hard to avoid. It filled her with horror and repugnance. And yet, he could put his lips to that badge of shame. He could try to kiss away the grief and pain that remained undiminished by the passage of time. He could make love to her and make her feel, for those brief moments in his arms, as if she belonged in the world of the living. Did he have any idea what that meant to her?

Darien smiled back at him. She wondered if the answer to that question would be found in his mind or in his heart. Then he reached for her again, and that question, too, remained unanswered.

Maggie was in the kitchen when they returned, rinsing off the last of the dishes they'd used in preparing the deviled eggs, and stacking them in the dishwasher. Darien, aware of her rumpled, sandy clothes and tangled hair, and aware too of all that they suggested, nonetheless chose to meet Maggie's serious gaze directly.

"No need to do that now," she said. "We can take care of it first thing tomorrow morning, before Jim arrives."

Maggie continued rinsing dishes.

"I'm almost done here," she said. "I'll just be a few more minutes. Chance, why don't you stay and keep me company."

Darien looked from Maggie's closed face to Chance. She knew what was coming, and she was not going to leave him to face this alone. She paused, and Chance gave her a reassuring nod, looking pointedly toward the stairs.

"I think I'll stay and help," she said firmly.

"I appreciate the offer," Maggie said. "But Chance and I have a lot of catching up to do. Why don't you head up to bed and get some rest."

"Good night, Darien," Chance said. "Please."

"All right, then, I'll head up," Darien said uneasily. "See you both in the morning."

They listened to her footsteps receding on the stairway, and then heard the door to the little peach-colored room close softly. The silence stretched out between them.

"So, what's happening, Aunt Maggie?" Chance said.

"I was about to ask you the same question," Maggie said coldly.

Chance raised his eyebrows, clearly taken aback by her tone.

"I expect you already know the answer to that question," he said. "You don't miss much, and I gather we haven't been very discreet."

Maggie put down the dishtowel and faced him squarely.

"She deserves better than this. And despite all the evidence to the contrary, I continue to believe that you're capable of better, too. Your Mom and I have been shaking our heads for years at your reckless ways. I don't know how it ended all those other times, and frankly, I don't much care. But I do know how this will end, Chance, and I care. I care very much.

"With all respect, Aunt Maggie, this is none of your business. This is between Darien and me, and she's not complaining."

"What is the matter with you, Chance!" Maggie snapped in disgust. "Where did you get the idea that just because you can, you should?"

"I suppose I deserve that," Chance said. "But you really should have more respect for Darien. She doesn't need you looking out for her. Darien can take care of herself."

"I know what you're seeing, Chance, and you're right as far as it goes. Darien is a capable, tough, professional woman. She can take care of herself in a courtroom. And she can take care of herself in a boardroom. But she cannot take care of herself in a bedroom, Chance. Not in your bedroom. There's a lot you don't know about that young woman. She is very much alone. She has no family, no support system, no real friends. She will have no one to turn to and no way to deal with this. When you walk away, and you will walk away, Chance, it will go very hard with her. Think about it, and think whether these few nights of pleasure are worth all the pain you're going to cause."

Chance wheeled on his heels in exasperation and headed for the stairs.

"Don't you walk away from me, Chance Deckert!" Maggie said angrily. "And don't make the mistake of ignoring what I have to say!"

Chance's shoulders sagged as he turned back toward Maggie. He had never heard that hard edge to her voice. His confident smile faded under her unrelenting gaze, and he rubbed the back of his neck.

"I really care for her, Aunt Maggie," he said. "I care in a way I never have before. And it scares the hell out of me."

Then he turned and walked up the stairs to his room.

Maggie stood in stunned disbelief, watching Chance until he had left her line of vision. Then she picked up her dishcloth and turned back to the sink. She smiled to herself as she finished her work. That was the very last thing she had expected to hear from the young man she had known so well for so many years. The unimaginable had happened. Chance Deckert had met his match in more ways than one. And he was as wobbly and off-balance as one of those new calves on that ranch of his. Oh, Darien, Maggie thought. This should be very, very interesting. And she smiled again.

CHAPTER FIFTEEN

Jim Plattman unwrapped another toffee without looking up from the report he was studying, and carelessly stuffed the silver foil wrapper into his pocket. He chewed as he read.

"That's just a preliminary report, Jim," Chance cautioned. "It contains the facts we've gathered to date, as well as a good bit of educated speculation. But I think it will give you an idea of where we're going with the investigation."

"I've spoken at length with Chance and Darien and looked over their material, and I know you'll agree that they've come a very long way in a short time," Edward said. He looked at Jim over the books and papers stacked neatly on the dining room table.

Darien poured herself another glass of iced tea and studied Jim's absorbed expression, trying to gauge his reaction to their report. It had cost her a great deal of time and effort, not to mention all the emotional currency she'd spent, and it was important that he be pleased with the result. Both she and the firm had a lot riding on this work.

Jim closed the volume, stroked his ginger beard abstractedly, and then looked up at Edward. "This is good work," he said.

Darien realized that she had been holding her breath, and let it out slowly.

"Let's spend some time talking it through and see what we have." Jim pulled out his notebook and opened it to a fresh page. "First, do we know how the arsonist entered the hotel?"

"We've wondered about that too," Chance said. The firemen report that the door was locked when they arrived and they had to force it open. Windows were broken from the inside, so that wasn't the entry point. The head of the cleaning crew had a key, as did the foreman of the group working on renovations. We are trying to track down everyone else who might have had a copy of the key."

"Understood," Plattman said.

Chance consulted his notes. "There's no doubt that we're dealing with a fire that was set intentionally," he began. "For starters, someone blocked the fire truck from reaching the scene, so that the fire could take hold. No one can remember much about the truck that got in the way, other than that it was white and had blue lettering. We're having trouble tracking it down, but we'll keep on it. And the hotel's computer system was removed and downgraded just before the fire, so that the valuable equipment wouldn't be lost. That's classic." He took a sip of his iced tea.

"As we told you in earlier conversations, the smoke detectors were properly installed, but appear to have failed. We're still trying to figure out why. Fire damage may have prevented an audible signal, but that seems unlikely. The class teacher who called 911 reported seeing smoke, but did not hear an alarm. And unfortunately, the alarm was no longer connected to any service that might have been notified if were triggered."

"I don't see any sense to an alarm in a remote location that is not connected to a service," Plattman said.

"Agreed," Chance said. "And the sprinkler didn't work because the water for the fire suppression system had been turned off. We thought the workers might have done that, but they all report that they never touched the water valves. They would have had no reason to turn it off and every reason to leave it on."

"How about the wiring or the heater?" Plattman asked. "The tentative conclusion of the fire department had been that it was an electrical fire."

"They didn't really have much time to investigate, and I'm confident they would have reached a different conclusion if they'd had the resources. We checked it out, and the electrical system was old but functional. The wiring leading to the portable heater was fine. But although the heater was damaged in the fire, the lab was able to confirm that the safety devices had been tampered with. Likely, the heater and the nearby rags were pushed up close to an overstuffed chair to create a blaze and provide an obvious explanation for the fire."

"Also, we've confirmed that the heater and the rags nearby had been doused with an accelerant. The fire was set with a mixture of fuel oil and gasoline. All descriptions agree that it gave off the characteristic large quantities of black smoke, and burned a deep, cherry red. Also, I found rainbowing on the wood, which strongly suggests fuel oil. There's no explanation for the presence of that fuel oil, because the hotel's heating system uses propane."

"But did it ever have a heating system that used fuel oil, or any other system that might have accounted for what you found?" Jim asked.

"No. And I never did find a trigger, but I found a thin piece of wire near the source of one of the fires. I think it may have been started with a flare, the kind used when your car breaks down. Those things burn and don't leave a trace, except a wire that looks a lot like the one I found. I've sent it to one of my investigators to track down, but don't have the results back yet."

"And the other signs of arson?" Jim asked.

"As I said earlier, someone broke a window at the end of the building near where the main body of the fire burned, and another window at the other end of the hotel, where there is minimal fire damage. I think they wanted oxygen to feed the fire, and that would've worked, except that they got the fuel mixture wrong, and the oxygen couldn't really do its job. Also, there's no soot staining the glass, so it must have been knocked out from inside the hotel before the fire started, rather than blown out by the fire. Darien learned that a class of kids showed up on the beach on a field trip. I'm guessing that the arsonists were caught off guard and had to speed up their work, which made them careless. I'd have to say," he concluded, "that whoever set this fire was either under serious pressure to move quickly and so made some rookie mistakes, or was none too smart."

"That may well be," Jim said, reaching for another toffee. "But they were smart enough to cost Monitor a bundle of money if we can't prove that this is arson."

"Point taken," Chance said. "But that isn't going to happen. I've talked this through with Darien, and you'll hear from her that she's confident of our proof and sure she can make the case stick. All we need to do is find our guy, and we're getting close."

Jim looked up and peered intently at Darien. "So it would appear from the report," he said. "We'll get back to that later. For now, do you have any other schematics of the hotel, Chance? I'd like to look before we head out there."

"You've seen all my drawings there on the table," Chance responded. "But this morning Mike Williams, a local book collector who lives on the Island, dropped off an old book with illustrations of the hotel. I haven't had a chance to look through it yet, but you'd be welcome to see it."

"Bring it over, Chance," Edward said. "We'll all take a look at it."

They gathered around Jim as he turned the yellowed pages, and studied the photographs of the handsome old hotel and dignified patrons, while Chance pointed out the details relevant to the fire.

"Just a minute," Darien said as he turned the page. All heads turned to her, drawn by the excitement in her voice.

"Go back to the last page. Yes, that's the one. Do you notice anything, Chance? Remember back at the hotel, when you said there was something not quite right about the lobby? But you couldn't figure out what was wrong, what was bothering you? Look closely at this picture of the lobby."

Chance studied the picture intently. "The chandelier!" he said. "That old crystal chandelier definitely wasn't in the lobby after the fire. I guess I must have seen it in one of the photos Jim sent when I was preparing for the investigation. Then, when I got to the site, I felt that something was missing, but I couldn't put my finger on it."

"Exactly," she said. "There was some small, modern fixture there instead. I remember thinking that it just didn't look right in the lobby, but then I didn't think more of it."

She stopped short. They both knew the reason for her lapse, and the reason Chance had been distracted from following up on his impression. Mentally, Darien gave herself a shake. The memory of that day at the hotel was not something she could afford to dwell on. Not now.

"I'm sure that's what Sally had intended to tell us the first time we met," she said. "Remember, Chance, Sally had been about to tell us something when she was distracted by Bobby. Later, when we asked, she couldn't recall what it was. I'll follow up on it and see if she had the chandelier in mind."

Darien paused, considering. "This could be really important," she continued. "That chandelier is massive and bulky. It's unlikely, although not impossible, that they could have gotten it off the Island in this short period of time. I'd bet good money that the chandelier and the computer system are stashed somewhere right here on Block Island."

"Could be," Jim said thoughtfully, closing the book. "Any thoughts on where to start looking?"

"Not offhand," Darien said. "Edward, maybe you and Maggie could give some thought to that question. You know the Island better than any of us."

Edward nodded.

"All right, then," Jim said. "That's all very helpful. But let's move on." He turned and faced Darien.

"Now Darien, from the report, I gather that you've made some progress on tying the fires together."

"Actually, I've pieced together some additional information since we completed that report," she said.

"Okay, let's hear it," he replied.

"Without going into detail, unless, of course, you want me to, let me summarize what I've found. You've had fires at three sites. I won't review the similarities in the factual situations or in the details of the fires themselves. But I am confident that we will be able to prove that all three properties were owned and controlled by the same individual or individuals."

"That would go a long way toward building our case," Jim said, looking at her intently. "You hinted at the possibility in your report, but I didn't have the impression that you had any firm proof."

"Look at this," she said, pulling out a sheaf of documents. She passed them over to Jim.

"What are these?" he asked, putting on his glasses.

"These are the mortgages to the three properties. Look at them carefully. Do you notice anything unusual?"

Jim studied the papers carefully. After some time, he looked up and took off his glasses.

"Can't say that I do," he said.

"Neither did I, at first," she said. "But look at the notary line."

Edward and Chance got to their feet and stood behind Jim so that they could see, as well.

"They're all notarized by the same person. Those three properties are in three different parts of the state, and were purchased by three different partnerships in three different years. The mortgages were all issued on different dates. And yet, they are all notarized by the same person."

The group was silent as they absorbed this piece of information.

"That's not all," she said. I looked into the identity of the brokers who had arranged for the insurance with Monitor. The insurance for all three properties was brokered by the same agency. It's a group out of Philadelphia."

"Excellent, Darien," Edward said. "You're clearly on the right track."

"One more thing," she said, as Edward and Chance moved back to their seats. "I spent some time researching the records of the Secretary of State. I've been looking into the identities of the owners of the properties. Each is set up as a limited liability partnership. Although they appear to be three separate partnerships, I wanted to determine whether they have any partners in common."

"That's a good idea," Jim said. "Do you have any information on that yet?"

"I do," she said. I came across something that appears to be significant. One person's name appears as a partner in all three of the partnerships."

"Have you had the opportunity yet to track down any information about that individual?" Jim asked.

"No," she said, "but I'm doing what I can on the internet, and I have a legal assistant and an investigator looking into it."

Jim nodded, made a notation in his little notebook, and then turned to the group assembled around the table.

"That's a lot of good work accomplished in a short period of time," he said, looking first at Darien and then at Chance. "Most impressive. I feel encouraged by what you've reported, and I'll report back to my management that the case is shaping up nicely."

"I concur," Edward said. "Chance is getting the arson nailed down, and Darien is closing in on the identity of the owners. Given another week or two, I'm confident that they'll be able to name names, and you'll have a strong arson case to present to the court."

"Darien," he said, turning in her direction. "Finish up the investigation here, that's your first priority. But start thinking about who you want on your team when you're ready to begin preparing the legal case. The firm will make sure you have all the resources you need."

Edward turned to Jim. "Any thoughts, here, Jim? Anything else you'd like Chance and Darien to follow-up on?"

Jim leaned back in his chair and stretched.

"On some of your phone calls, Chance, you've talked about a kid. Bobby, I think his name was. You thought he knew something important about the fire. How's that part of your investigation going? Think he can be of any help to us?"

"Not much to tell," Chance said, "although Darien and I think he's the key to solving the puzzle. He clearly knows something, but he's terrified by whatever he saw or heard, and he's not talking. There's no doubt it has to do with the fire. He was in the vicinity of the fire with his class earlier on the day the fire was set, and hasn't been the same since. I'm hoping we'll be able to break through whatever's scaring him and get the story."

"With apologies for the interruption, I just want to let you know that I will fix lunch and serve it when you reach a good point for a break," Maggie said as she entered the room. She had been working in the garden all morning and was still in her muddy gardening clothes. "Just let me know. I'll take a quick shower and clean up, and then if you're ready, we could eat out on the deck. It's a beautiful day."

"Sounds good to me," Jim said.

"Excellent idea," Edward said. "We're almost done here. We just need a few minutes to plan our next steps." He favored Darien with an approving smile, and then turned his attention back to the task at hand.

From Edward, who was known for his reserve and formality, that smile was high praise.

She looked over at Chance and smiled with pleasure. The slow, lazy smile he gave her in return was ripe with promise. She shivered, and then made a great show of sorting through her papers. She was still smiling when she headed toward the kitchen to wait for Maggie and see if she needed any help.

Darien ate the hearty spread with pleasure, buoyed by the praise for their work, and conscious always of Chance's presence. This was, of course, simply one more in an endless line of business lunches with a business purpose, and she knew what was expected of her. And yet, she thought, glancing furtively at Chance, he transformed this occasion as he did all others, effortlessly but undeniably, and infused it with the elemental force that was the essence of the man. Everything, right down to the weathered wooden boards that created the frame of this patio, tilted inevitably in his direction. And she, Darien knew, was no exception. She was listing like a ship caught in a fierce nor'easter, and she had lost all will to send out an SOS.

"Wouldn't you agree, Darien?"

At the sound of her name, Darien's wandering attention returned abruptly to the conversation.

"Sorry," she said to Edward. "Could you repeat that?"

She looked hopefully around the table, trying to catch the gist of the conversation from their expressions. Edward was frowning, which made sense given her inattention, but Maggie was smiling knowingly at her and looked for all the world like she was about to chuckle. What was that about?

"I was saying to Jim that I thought we'd had a productive morning."

"Oh, yes," Darien said with great conviction. "Very productive."

"And I was saying that I expect he'll want to head out to the site of the fire this afternoon," Edward continued. He'll have a better feeling for Chance's work once he's actually seen the old hotel."

Although the gentle breeze carried with it only the sweet smell of the sun-warmed earth and early spring flowers, unaccountably, the acrid smell of smoke wafted about her and then, slowly, drifted off toward the sea. Darien shifted uneasily in her chair.

"Absolutely," Jim said. "I want to see firsthand what the burn pattern looks like. I also want to take a look at a few other things you've pointed out. I trust, Chance, that you've taken samples and preserved the chain of custody."

"You presume right," Chance said, "and Edward and I can run you out to the site right now, if you'd like."

Jim pushed his plate forward and gazed out over the glittering surface of the ocean. "That was quite a lunch, Maggie. I do appreciate all the trouble you've gone to. And the setting could not be more perfect.

But duty calls, so if you don't mind, I'm going to take your husband, Chance and Darien away from all this and put them back to work."

"It was no trouble at all, Jim. I hope you'll plan to join us for dinner this evening, as well. We're having some neighbors over for a cook-out, and I think you would find it enjoyable."

Jim smiled broadly. "You've got it. You know what they say about all work and no play. And I love good barbeque."

The cheerful banter around her was lost on Darien, as was the sound of the knock on the door. She was not going back to that hotel. Not under any circumstances. She was not going to smell the stench of smoke. She was not going to see the carnage left by the fire. And she most certainly was not going to see that staircase. She felt the familiar nausea rising in her throat and caught herself nervously twisting the emerald ring. Darien arranged her hands carefully in her lap and took a deep breath.

"Maggie?" Sally called from inside the house.

"We're out here," Maggie replied. "Come on out and join us."

Bobby and Flash burst through the door and headed straight for Chance. Sally followed, smiling apologetically and carrying a sleeping Lily in her arms.

"Sorry, didn't know you had company. I just stopped by to drop off some of the leftovers from the party. No way we could even make a dent, so I thought I'd share the bounty. I put them in your fridge. We'll be on our way now."

"No need to hurry away," Maggie said. "Sally, I'd like you to meet Jim Plattman, Edward's client from the Monitor Insurance Company. Jim, this is Sally, Bobby and Lily Olsen, and, of course, Flash."

Jim nodded politely to Sally.

Maggie turned back to her friend. "The crew is about to leave for the old hotel, and I'll be on my own here. Why don't you and Bobby stay and keep me company for a while?"

"Perhaps it would be best if I stayed here with Maggie," Darien said. She could hear the tremor in her voice.

Jim looked at her. "I really want all the team with me out at the site today," he said. "I'm sure you understand, Darien."

"I'm sure she does," Edward said. "Darien, you've put a lot of time into this investigation, and it will be helpful to have your observations and expertise at the site."

"Jim," Chance said quietly, "this is Bobby, the little boy we had mentioned earlier. I don't think Darien should miss the opportunity to visit with him a little. I can show you around the site."

"There'll be time for that another day," Jim said. "Right now, I want us all out at the hotel. And that includes you, too, Darien."

"And that's where we'll be," Edward said in a tone of voice that did not allow for the possibility of debate. "All of us. Let's go," he said again.

"I don't think that's a good idea," Darien said as firmly as she could. She could not meet Edward's eyes. "I think I should stay here with Bobby. It's very important that we talk. It would serve no purpose to have me out at the site. I'm of more use here. Trust me on this, Jim."

Edward's face was rigid with barely suppressed anger. He opened his mouth to speak, but Chance cut off his response. "I think she's right about this one, Jim," he said. "Her suggestion makes good sense."

"Darien," Edward said, pointedly ignoring Chance's remark. "I'd like to speak with you for a moment. Please excuse us," he said to Jim, as he pushed aside the glass door and walked off of the porch. Silently, Darien followed, and watched as Edward slid the door closed behind them.

"What the hell do you think you're doing?" he asked, his voice as harsh as his expression.

In all the years that Darien had known him, she had rarely seen Edward lose his temper. She had never heard him swear. She felt a trickle of perspiration run down her temple.

"Plattman is the client. He wants you out there. He doesn't care if you think that that's a good idea. He wants his team at the site and that's where we will be. All of us."

"I should stay here," she said quietly. "With Bobby. He clearly knows something about the fire and this may be a good opportunity to get him to talk." Let him agree. God in heaven, let him decide that it made more sense this way.

"I don't believe I heard you right," Edward said.

Darien saw the two crimson spots of color that stained his cheeks, and the way the vein at his temple was pulsing. She took a slow, deep breath to steady herself, and considered again the possibility of accompanying the men to the site of the fire. Cautiously, she let herself picture the charred remains of the hotel and the menacing staircase curving up into the darkness. In response, the earth wobbled under her feet.

"I said I'm not going," she repeated. Her voice was barely above a whisper.

"I don't understand this at all, Darien. Why would you defy a good client? You are representing the firm here, and if you value your place at the firm, I strongly suggest that you reconsider your position," he said.

She bit her lip so hard that it hurt. Edward's threat could not be clearer. He was drawing a line in the sand, and everything that she had worked for, everything that gave structure and meaning to her carefully ordered life, was hanging in the balance.

Darien walked over to the railing, playing for time. She watched as a wave formed not far from shore, swelling slowly at first, then soaring high above the surface, and inevitably, crashing back into the depths of the ocean.

Desperately, she ran through her options. She grasped each in turn, considered it, weighed it, and found it wanting. None of them worked. Not one. There was no way on this earth to satisfy Edward while keeping herself safe from the threats that lurked in the fire-ravaged hotel. There were no words that she could say. There were no moves that she could make. There was — nothing.

With that realization, her racing thoughts jolted to a stop. She stood dazed for a moment, and then turned bleakly toward Edward.

"Very well," he said. He turned, and she followed him onto the porch.

Jim, Chance, Maggie and Sally stood in an awkward cluster. Darien averted her eyes from Maggie's searching gaze.

"Darien will stay here for the moment, Jim," Edward said calmly. "She has a plan, and I think it's a good one. We'll catch up with her this afternoon."

Jim's brows furrowed, and he crumpled the toffee wrapper he was holding into a small, glittering ball. "That just doesn't make sense to me," he said, clearly puzzled. "But I'm paying you to make the calls, so I'm gonna go along with you on this one." And he followed Edward and Chance out the door.

"You're white as a ghost, honey," Sally said.

Darien took a deep breath. "All your fault," she said, reaching for a light, teasing tone that fooled no one. "Too much party at your house last night." She turned away from the questioning faces and wiped the perspiration from her forehead.

"Come on, Bobby," she said too brightly. "Let's you, me and Flash take a walk on the beach."

She heard the sound of Jim's rental car starting up in the driveway, and then listened as the roar of the engine faded into the distance. The roaring sound of the blood pounding in her temples, however, did not fade so easily. It lingered long after she, Bobby and Flash had run far down the beach. And it lingered while Maggie and Sally, who had followed at a more leisurely pace, joined them as they walked back toward the house. It lingered long after their guests had left and Maggie had returned to her garden. It wasn't until her second glass of wine, swallowed hastily and without enjoyment on the deserted porch, that her pulse seemed to return to normal and the roaring eased. She looked at her hands. Rock steady. But just to be sure, Darien poured herself a third glass.

CHAPTER SIXTEEN

"Did you have any luck?" he asked.

Darien squinted at Chance across the table. She was facing into the sunset. Between the diamond sharp glint of light off the ocean and the last horizontal rays of the sun that were glaring directly into her eyes, she was nearly blinded. Chance appeared gunmetal gray and indistinct, all shape and no detail. She shielded her eyes with one hand, but it did little good.

"Not really," she said, dropping her hand. "I feel like I get just so far with Bobby and then he pulls back. His guard is rarely down. I feel so sorry for the little fellow, and worried for him, too." She drained the nearly full glass of wine in one quick gulp, and looked up into Chance's startled eyes.

"With good cause, I think," Chance agreed, looking from the empty glass to her flushed face. "That's a pretty big burden for such a little kid." He rolled his glass between his hands, and she watched the swirling currents he was creating in the amber liquid.

"I did get him to talk some about the day of the school trip. He'd wandered off by himself searching for shells. That's when he came across the shell that you found hidden behind his curtain. From the description that he gave before he caught himself and stopped cold, I think he was very near the hotel. Probably somewhere to the east of the hotel as you're facing it. Not sure what's over that way, but it may be worth taking a closer look tomorrow."

"Is that before or after you speak with the police about the gas episode and the truck that was blocking your path?" he asked.

"Really, Chance," she said. "You're making a big deal out of nothing. You obviously didn't think it was important enough to tell Maggie and Edward. Why are you pestering me about going to the police?"

"You're wrong about that, Darien. Maggie found the broken glass from your door out in the shed and I told her what had happened. She and Edward are both concerned, and were only appeased when I assured them that you would talk with the police first thing tomorrow."

Edward. She did not want to think about his disappointment and his anger. She reached with shaky hands for the nearly empty bottle of wine. Before she could pour it into her glass, Chance caught her wrist and held it firmly in his hand.

"Don't you think you've had about enough of that wine, Darien?" he asked. "Unless I miss my guess, you passed 'a few' some time back, and now you're on the wrong side of 'a few too many'. Time for you to slow down."

She shook her hand free, poured the dregs of the wine into her glass, and took a long sip of the mind-numbing liquid. Then she looked up at him.

"Slow down?" she repeated. "Isn't that my line, Chance? You're supposed to talk about throwing caution to the wind, remember?"

She raised the glass again, but he wrenched it from her hand and tossed the remaining wine over the railing.

"This isn't the way to deal with it, Darien," he said.

"Deal with what?" Edward asked. He and Plattman came out onto the porch. "Can I offer you a drink before the guests arrive, Jim?" he said, turning to the client.

"Darien was just filling me in on her time with Bobby this afternoon," Chance said, replacing the empty wine glass out of Darien's reach.

"How'd you make out?" Plattman asked. "And yes, I'd love a drink. Preferably a good Scotch."

"Darien, anything for you?" Edward asked.

The cool demeanor went well beyond his usual formality. She would need to step lightly around him for now.

"Make mine — make mine whatever Chance is drinking."

"Bourbon on the rocks, straight up?"

"Sure. Bourbon." This drinking thing was new to her. Other than a discreet glass of wine at a business dinner, she couldn't remember that last time she had consumed alcohol. It had, she thought as she gulped down the burning amber liquid, much to recommend it.

"And I did make some progress with Bobby. He definitely was in the area where he would have seen what was happening at the hotel, and I'm more convinced than ever that he saw something important. We just need to find a way to make him feel safe enough to share what he saw. But we can talk more about that tomorrow. For now, I'm going to help Maggie prepare the food." She tossed back the remainder of the bourbon, put the glass on the table, and headed back into the house.

She could feel Chance's disapproving stare boring into her back. What was his problem? She was fine. She was just fine.

"From what I hear, you did some excellent work on this arson case, Darien." Maggie handed her a pile of napkins that were the green of fresh beach grass. "You should feel good about what you've accomplished here."

Darien placed the napkins carefully on the table. "Thanks," she said. "I do."

"Really," Maggie said skeptically "Could have fooled me. You look edgy. You have all afternoon. Anything I can do to help?"

Darien turned to Maggie with an unconvincing smile. "I'm fine," she said. "But thanks for asking." She started to arrange the flatware.

They worked together for several minutes.

"Who's coming to dinner?" Darien asked, trying to fill the awkward silence.

"A couple who are clients of Edward's. They're lovely people. They live in Boston, but come out to the Island during the summer. They may bring their daughter who works in Manhattan. She's, shall we say, colorful. And another local couple, both of whom are artists. I think you'll enjoy their company."

Darien nodded. "I'm sure I will," she said politely. She dropped a fork, and apologized as she fumbled to pick it up.

Maggie's brows drew together in concern, but she continued her preparations. "Edward is heading back to the office early tomorrow," she said. "I think I'll stay out here until late afternoon to finish up a few projects, if I won't be in your way. Then I'll go back, as well. I can use the old car we keep in the garage."

"That's fine."

"Why don't you clean up and change," Maggie suggested. "Not much else to do here. The menu is simple. I don't like to fuss when I'm on the Island. I can finish up here myself, and I'm already dressed."

Darien felt Maggie's questioning, worried eyes on her as she climbed the stairs. She would have to do better than this. Perhaps another glass of the bourbon would help?

She entered the small peach room unsteadily. She glanced hastily at the contents of her closet and selected a black jersey and matching black linen trousers. She pulled out her good black sandals and added simple gold jewelry to the pile on her bed. That would do it.

A cold shower first. Then to dinner. And then, to bed. If nothing went wrong, she could get through tonight. She would not think about how she would get through the rest of her time on the Island. She would not think about Edward's anger. She would not think about the fire. She would be in this moment and in this place, but not of it, until she was safely back in Providence.

Darien had barely made it back down the stairs before she realized that something had gone very wrong indeed. She recognized the voice before the saw the arrogant, fine-boned face and the ice blue eyes. The colorful daughter had arrived, and she was none other than Marnie. Colorful, Darien thought, was a charitable way to put it. She herself could think of several more suitable descriptions. Piranha came to mind. Scorpion would do nicely, too. Darien did her best to put on a polite smile and walked into the room.

"Darien," Edward said politely, rising to greet her. His gaze held hers for a moment, and then he looked away. "These are some neighbors on the Island, Ruth and Jeff Fortas. And these are our friends Dorothy and Dan Auburn, and their daughter, Marnie. This is Darien Dalton, a senior associate at my firm."

Darien murmured polite greetings. Then she turned to Marnie. The shiny black hair was caught back at the nape of her neck with a clip, and hung down her back in a sleek cascade. She was wearing scarlet again, but this time she had a strapless camisole that left very little to the imagination, and a short, tight, silky skirt. Her legs were bare, and the toenails that were visible in the high-heeled sandals were blood red, as were her manicured nails. Darien could not recognize the name of the scent she wore, but she sure recognized the smell. It smelled like desire, plain and simple.

"I believe we've met," Marnie said. She smiled smugly at Darien. Then she seated herself on the couch very close to Chance. Darien watched as Marnie leaned over to retrieve her drink. The little bit that had been left to the imagination before this maneuver was now displayed for Chance's benefit. Darien could have kicked her. Smiling grimly, Darien seated herself on the remaining chair, which was across the room.

"Edward speaks very highly of you," Dan said. "Tell me about your practice."

Stifling a sigh, Darien obliged with a description of her work. Then Dan reciprocated with a description of his. From time to time, she glanced over at Chance and Marnie. The woman was all over him. Darien drained her wineglass and readily accepted Dan's offer of a refill.

Dinner passed in a merciful haze. Conversation ebbed and flowed around her, and she chatted politely with the two artists, who had been seated across from her. Next to her, Chance shifted uncomfortably in his seat. She'd bet her last dollar that that woman had her hand on his thigh. And over brandy on the patio, while she discussed Boston's sports teams with Jim, she could hear Marnie explaining to Chance that she was free the next several weekends, and really had no fixed plans for the summer. The provocative expression in her eyes must have been visible clear to the other end of Block Island.

When the company rose to leave, Darien's relief was nearly palpable. She smiled, shook hands and made polite comments. At long, long last, this day would be done. Her near-brush with the fire-scarred hotel, and the lingering feelings of dread unleashed by that threat, had drained her to the point of exhaustion. Edward's barely contained anger had only exacerbated the situation. The alcohol had helped, in its way, but now she needed to be alone.

"Let's go for a walk on the beach." Chance's words were more of a command than an invitation.

She did not know how she was going to walk up the stairs, let alone down the beach. "I'm tired, Chance," she said. "Let me help Maggie clean up, and then I'm headed for bed."

"That's not necessary," Maggie said. "Edward and I can clean up. You two go ahead and let us take care of things here." She gave Darien an encouraging smile.

Without waiting for a response, Chance took her arm and propelled her down the narrow stairway to the beach below. She did not have the strength to resist.

She walked mutely along the moon-drenched beach, unmindful of the restive breeze that was churning the ocean into foamy whitecaps and rustling the sea grass. After a time, he stopped, sat down in the sand, and pulled her down beside him.

"I hardly got to talk with you tonight," he began, putting his arm around her and drawing her close. "Marnie is one persistent lady. She doesn't take 'no' for an answer."

Darien closed her eyes and curled into him. She was so very, very tired. And during the short walk on the beach, the dull throb in her head had kicked up a level.

"Sounds like she has big plans for you this summer, Chance. Are you planning to stick around?"

"With Marnie?" he asked. "Are you joking?"

She didn't think she knew how to joke about something like that. Marnie was gorgeous. She was willing. And she was without baggage, without rules, without a history that diminished the present.

"Look, Darien. With all these people around, it's been hard to be alone together. We need that time," he said. He stroked her wind-tangled hair and held her close.

"I want you to stay here on the Island with me after the investigation is over." He was silent for a few minutes, giving her time to absorb the proposal.

"I'm planning to spend some time at one of the old Inns on the ocean. They're still pretty quiet during the week at this time of year. I know Edward wants you back in the office preparing the case, but he owes you a few days before you get started. He owes you at least that much. Stay with me."

It made no sense. He still wanted to be with her. Darien considered, trying to think through the pain in her temples. Why did he want to complicate his life, to take on all her memories, all her ghosts, when there was such an easy solution so close at hand? He was no fool, and should not be making foolish choices.

But there it was, however unlikely — the invitation. An invitation to what?

That wasn't a difficult question to answer. An invitation to spend a few more days in the life she'd been living since she'd come to the Island. An invitation to continue, for a brief time, the life she'd led since she'd relinquished the safety and security of her office, her apartment, her solitude, her rules. The life she'd led since she'd left behind the old life, the life that was so tidy, so carefully circumscribed and predictable, the old life that held no surprises.

That had not been such a bad life. She'd been successful at her work, she was respected and admired at the firm. She had her music. It was true that the nightmares haunted her, but she'd managed to bind those specters to the darkest hours of the night and keep them there. She had been doing fine.

It had been a mistake to leave that life and come to the Island. She knew that now, and had suspected it from the first. Here, she'd put her job on the line. Here, she'd found love that existed largely in her mind and her imagination, and only marginally in his heart. And here, her ghosts had shattered the fragile constraints that confined them to the night and had burst forth into her days, spreading their poison at will and leaving her trembling in their fearsome wake. The terror. The nausea. The wild pounding of her heart and the dizzying tilt of her world. She felt bruised and rubbed raw, lacerated by it all. It was quite literally unbearable. Was there anything or anyone on this earth that could induce her to accept such an invitation?

Darien pulled back from Chance and studied the face that she had come to know so well. She thought of his tenderness and his humor. She remembered the hope that she had felt in his arms, and the passion that she had known in his bed. And she knew that not even that, not even the gift of a few days of bliss with this man for whom she cared so deeply, was enough to hold her in this world. She could not do it. It was as simple as that.

In the pale light of the moon, Chance watched the expressions that passed over her face. "You're running away again," he said.

"I'm right here," she said. "I haven't moved."

"You don't need to," he replied. "You run first with your mind. Your body only follows."

She traced a pattern in the shifting sand. She did not need to hear a lecture. She was quite certain that he couldn't tell her anything that she didn't already know.

"Don't run, Darien. You owe it to yourself, if not to me, to stop running and to get some help."

"Some help?" she echoed.

"Come on. You're an educated, intelligent woman. You must know that anyone living through the horror of that fire would run into some serious problems down the line. And I have to believe that you know, too, that there's help for those kinds of problems. There are doctors who specialize in treating traumatic stress disorders. You live in a city with excellent medical centers. I'm sure you could get all the help you need in Providence. And yet…"

"Just what kind of help would that be, Chance?" she interrupted, speaking through the throbbing pain in her temples. "What kind of help do you think there is for me? The kind of help that would bring Abby back? The kind of help that would bring my mother and father back? The kind of help that would erase that day for all time, the 'no fire' kind of help, the 'no death' kind of help? Where do you suggest I find that kind of help, Chance?"

He could see her closing off before his eyes, drawing back into herself as the fragile bonds of intimacy and trust between them froze solid and started to shatter.

"Not that kind of help, Darien," he said. "That kind of help doesn't exist this side of sanity. But the kind of help that would let you become…"

"Become what!" she cried. "What do you think is left for me to become?"

"Become you," he said. "The kind of help that would let you become yourself, become the person I've seen when you forget that muted, careful little person you've created out of whole cloth. Become the person you were intended to be, the person you'd be if you could leave behind all the useless rules and limitations and boundaries you're so busy protecting."

"Protecting!" She could barely choke out the words. "I haven't 'protected' a damn thing, Chance. 'Protecting' is not in my repertory. I would think that you could have figured that out by now." She looked up at him, and the anguish in those amber eyes jolted him like a stray bolt of lightning.

"This is who I am Chance, and it's who I'm going to be for the rest of my life. What you see is all there is. You see a person who let her family die. All of them. That's the guilt I have to carry for the rest of my days, and I do it in the best way I know how."

"You let them die?" he repeated. "Is that what this is all about? You let them die? My god, Darien, you were only six years old. From what you've told me about that fire, there was nothing an adult could have done, let alone a six-year-old child. Think of Bobby. Picture him in your place, in that fire. What could he have done to save anyone? You're alive only because that fireman grabbed you from the stairs. You didn't save yourself, and you couldn't have saved them, either."

"I was there. I'm alive, and they're not. That's really all that matters, isn't it?" she said wearily.

"And what about me, Darien?" he asked. "Do I matter?"

"What do you mean?" she asked. "What does that have to do with this discussion?"

He moved toward her and wound his hand in her hair, forcing her to look up at him.

"It has everything to do with this discussion," he said. "Seems to me you have some choices to make, Darien. You've taken a rough blow, and nothing can change that for you. But you can change your future. You can choose to spend the rest of your life hiding behind your books at work, pouring all your feelings into your music and spending your nights grappling with ghosts, or you can face your misbegotten guilt and move on with your life. If you choose life…"

Darien struggled to turn her face away from his.

"If you choose life," he repeated, tightening his grip in her hair and moving his face closer to hers, "I'll be there with you. You can count on that. If you choose your guilt and your ghosts — well, I reckon that's about all the company you'll need."

He released her, got to his feet, and walked away.

CHAPTER SEVENTEEN

He was wrong, of course. Darien closed her eyes against the early morning light that was shining weakly through her window. She knew that, knew it in a way he never could know, never could understand.

Choices. She rolled over in bed, turning her back to the irritating light. Did he truly believe his own words? Could he possibly be that naïve? She grabbed the covers and pulled them over her head in a futile attempt to block out the sun.

She had no choices. A choice assumed options, and she had ceased to have real options long ago. If ever she had doubted that proposition, her time on Block Island had provided solid and searing proof.

Struggling out from the tangle of the covers, Darien got to her feet, rubbed her tired eyes, and made her way to the shower. She turned the faucets with a swift, jerky motion, and stepped into the cold, sharp needles of water with grim determination. She was going to solve this damn case, and then she was going to get off this island as quickly as possible and never look back. She would return to her job, assuming she still had a job when this was over. She would return to her old life. And she would never, never again invite this kind of fear and confusion into that life. Never.

She emerged from the shower, dressed, and pulled her brush through her tangled, damp hair. She worked quickly, methodically, oblivious now to the beauty of the peach-colored room and to the scent of the ocean breeze drifting through the curtains. Then, without so much as a glance in the mirror, she strode out of her room, down the narrow hall, and walked briskly down the stairs.

Edward typically was the first to arrive at the office, and she had counted on his following this same pattern on the Island. She needed some time alone with him before Maggie, Chance, and most of all, Jim Plattman, could intrude on the conversation. She needed to try to set things right.

Edward was seated on the porch, watching the ocean and sipping a steaming cup of coffee. She poured herself a cup, and then joined him. They sat for a few minutes in uncomfortable silence.

"I owe you an explanation," she said.

"I don't think there could be any explanation for your behavior yesterday, Darien. You rebuffed a reasonable request from a client. You undermined my credibility. And you did some serious damage to my good opinion of your work. Quite a day's work."

Darien did not flinch. She faced him squarely.

"I know, and I'm truly sorry for all of that. I don't have an excuse, Edward. There is an explanation, but…"

Edward took a deep sip of his coffee and then shifted in his chair. "I'm not interested in excuses or explanations at this point," he said.

"That's just as well," she said, "because I'm not giving any. You've known me a long time, Edward. You know who I am and you know what I'm about. And now, I need you to know me well enough to understand that if there were any way I could go out to that hotel, any way at all, I would. It's not that I won't go. I can't."

"That makes no sense," he said.

"And I don't expect it to. But it's the truth. I've never given you reason to doubt me in the past. You have trusted me, you have depended on me, and I've come through for you every time. I'm asking you to give me the benefit of the doubt. I think I've earned that much from you."

Edward put down his coffee and got to his feet. He turned and looked down at her.

"Perhaps," he said, and then he went back into the house.

She sat there for a moment, staring out at the shifting currents that rippled across the gray-green expanse of the ocean. Then she stood, squared her shoulders, and walked back into the house.

Darien leaned over the kitchen table to scrawl a hasty note for Chance and Edward. She was heading over to the Olsen's house. There was no doubt in her mind that Bobby held the key to this mystery. He knew something and she was going to find out what he knew. Today.

"Where are you off to?" She felt his hand on her shoulder and steeled herself against the warmth and comfort of his touch.

"I'm going to see Bobby," she said, her back still to him. "I think we need to push harder to find out what he knows. It's not helping him to back off from that question, and it's not helping us, either." She thought her tone sounded impersonal, business-like. Good.

He dropped his hand. "I see," he said. His tone mirrored hers. "I'll come along."

"That's not necessary," she said.

"Oh, but it is," he countered. "We're here to do a job. Bobby trusts me, and this'll go better if I'm there."

Much as she wanted to, she couldn't deny the truth of what he said.

"You have a plan?" he asked.

"Let's talk in the car," she answered. "I don't want to waste any time."

She tensed, waiting for the predictable rejoinder. Maybe some snide remark about wasted opportunities. Or some dig about rules.

"Sure," he said.

Momentarily disconcerted by his unexpected response, she hesitated. Then she grabbed her jacket and headed out into the early morning mist.

"I'll drive," she said decisively. So much, it seemed, was beyond her control here. She would assume whatever control she could. She started up Edward's old car, backed quickly out of the driveway and headed off in the direction of the Olsen's.

Busy with her explanation, she nearly missed the house and swerved sharply into the driveway. The car stopped abruptly and the screeching breaks announced their arrival.

Sally opened the door and Flash dashed out, barking loudly.

"Nice entrance," Sally yelled over the din. "What do you do for an encore?"

"Sorry," Darien replied as she opened the car door and stepped out into the cool morning mist. "I wasn't paying attention. Got any coffee on?"

"Sure, come in," Sally said.

Darien and Chance followed her into the house. "Bobby, guess who's here?" Sally shouted, trying to make herself heard over Flash's enthusiastic barking.

They went into the family room to Bobby, who was curled up in a chair in front of the television. Darien gave him a warm hug.

"Hey sport," Chance said, ruffling Bobby's soft hair. "We'll catch up in a minute. Darien and I are gonna talk with your mom first."

Bobby nodded, turning back to his cartoons.

Darien followed Sally and Chance back to the kitchen. She selected a chair at the opposite end of the table from Chance and then sat at the edge of her seat, her back ramrod straight and her hands folded carefully on her lap.

Reaching for the coffee pot, Sally poured three large mugs and set them on the table with some muffins. Darien ignored the questioning look from her friend. Yes, the temperature between Chance and her had dropped several degrees. And no, Darien was not going to explain. She was not even going to acknowledge it.

Sally looked from Darien to Chance, and then back again to Darien. She put a tentative smile on her face. "George said he's meeting with your team this afternoon to go over some aspects of the fire," she said finally. "Thought you'd be with Edward, preparing for the meeting."

"We'll be back in plenty of time," Darien responded. "But this morning, we were hoping to spend some time with Bobby. Is he still home from school?"

Sally's smile faded. "Yes. His teacher is sending lessons home for the time being. We were planning to do some school work today, but I thought I'd give him a break and let him watch cartoons for a while. George and I are planning to wait a bit and see if he'll feel comfortable going back. If not, we'll have to turn to Plan B. Trouble is, nothing has changed, and there is no Plan B."

Darien nodded sympathetically and lowered her voice. "Chance and I have been giving this some thought. We agreed that we might make some progress if he'd take a ride with us down to the beach near the hotel. The proximity to the place where it all happened might get him talking."

"We'll watch him carefully, and if he gets too frightened, you know we'll turn right around and bring him home," Chance said. "But we thought that maybe he'd feel comfortable enough with us there to open up some and tell us what he saw."

Sally hesitated, chewing on her lower lip and twisting a stray curl around her finger.

"You said yourself that things aren't improving," Chance reminded her. "At least it's worth a try. Nothing else has worked. We won't push it. If he's too upset, we'll leave. You have my word on that."

"All right," she said reluctantly. "I guess it's okay. I'd come with you myself, but Lily's down for a nap and there's no one who can watch her this morning. But please be careful. I'm not sure that this is a such a good idea."

"We will be," he said reassuringly.

"Hey, big fella," Chance said as Bobby walked hesitantly into the room. "What say you, me and Darien have an adventure today?" Chance asked.

"Can I, Mom?" Bobby asked.

"Okay, but be sure you get these grown-ups home by lunch time. We don't want to make them miss work, do we?"

Bobby nodded in agreement. "I'll make sure they get home on time."

"Let's go then," Chance said. He helped Bobby into his coat, and then lifted the child on his broad shoulders. "Low ceiling!" Chance yelled as they both ducked to clear the door.

In spite of her misgivings, Sally gave a small smile of amusement. Then her expression turned serious. "You watch out for him, okay?" she said to Darien.

"Absolutely," she replied. "He's safe with me."

"I know," Sally said. "Just an excess of caution, I guess. Bobby just seems so shaky lately. If you need to reach me, my cell will be on all day."

Darien headed out to the car, where Chance was already behind the wheel. Today. She would get the information she was waiting for from the office back in Providence, she would find out what Bobby knew, and she would tie up the loose ends. Soon, this would all be a bad memory. A bad mistake. She would go home.

She wouldn't need to look in the direction of the hotel, she told herself. She would concentrate on Bobby. No need to concern herself with anything else. She wiped her damp palms on her jeans.

"So, Bobby," Chance began in an off-hand tone of voice. "I've been thinking about that shell you showed me. The one that was behind the curtain in your room. Do you remember the one I mean?"

No response came from the little boy in the back seat.

"Thing is," Chance continued, "I have a hankering for a shell just like that. I'd like to take it far away back home to Montana, and show all my family what pretty shells they have on Block Island."

Bobby remained silent.

"What do you say, son?" Chance asked. "Will you help me out and show me where you got it?"

"I don't want to go back there," Bobby said in a small, quavering voice.

Chance and Darien exchanged glances.

"Just for a few minutes?" Chance asked. "Wouldn't you go back just for a few minutes to show me where to look? It sure would mean a lot to me."

Bobby shifted nervously. "No, please, not there." He hesitated for a moment, and then he brightened. "Let's go to the sailboat, Chance. Let's have a sail. I can help!"

"I'm kinda disappointed," Chance said. "I sure was counting on getting one of those shells to take home."

Bobby wavered. He pressed his fists into little balls, and his mouth formed a thin, tight line. "All right. I guess so," he said uncertainly. "Just for a real quick minute, though. I'll just show you real fast."

Darien's heart ached for the child. She reminded herself that this was the right thing to do, even though it would be hard on him. Right for him to get this burden off his thin shoulders. And right for her to get this case behind her.

"That's great, thanks!" Chance said. "It's near the hotel, isn't it?"

"Yeah," Bobby said, slouching further into his seat.

"I'll park out that way, and then you can direct me. We'll be real quick."

They rode on in silence. As they rounded a curve, Darien saw the charred outline of the hotel in the distance and quickly averted her eyes. The flash of vertigo that followed left her breathless and dizzy. She breathed deeply and tried in vain to steady herself.

"We're here," Chance said, as he guided the car into the hotel parking lot.

Darien stepped out of the car and directed her attention to Bobby. He was pale, and his tiny hand grasped hers.

"Over this way," he whispered, pulling Darien onto the beach near the hotel. "I found it right over there."

Chance followed them to a little inlet very near the hotel. He looked around to get his bearings. Darien looked at Bobby. Bobby looked at the ground.

"Can we go now, please?" Bobby asked in a barely audible whisper. "You know where now. You can come back tomorrow."

"Why are you in such a hurry to leave, Bobby?" Chance asked gently. "Is there something that you're afraid of?"

Bobby dragged his sneaker through the sand.

"Darien and I know that something is wrong. Your Mom and Dad know, too."

At the mention of his parents, Bobby's head jerked up and a look of alarm contorted his face. Darien put a cautionary hand on Chance's arm.

"Whatever you're afraid of, it's too much for a young man like you to handle on your own," Chance said. "You need to trust the grown-ups. We can help you and keep you safe. Please tell me what happened here."

Bobby was silent.

Chance knelt down until he was Bobby's height and was face to face with the little boy.

"Do you trust me, Bobby?" he asked.

Bobby nodded solemnly.

"And do you know that I'm your friend?"

Bobby nodded again.

"Good," Chance said. "Then let me help. That's what friends do for each other."

Bobby started to cry. Chance put a reassuring hand on his shoulder.

"I'm scared," he blurted out.

"You don't need to be scared anymore," Chance said gently. "But I can't help until you tell me what happened."

"I saw two men," he sobbed.

"That's the way," Chance said. "That's a good start, Bobby. Now, did you know those men? Had you seen them before?"

"I don't think so," Bobby said.

"Okay. And what were those men doing?"

"They were carrying a bunch of stuff. Cans of something that smelled funny. Some rags. And some more things that I can't remember."

"Smelled funny like what, Bobby? Like when you go to the gas station with your dad? Funny like that?"

"Maybe," Bobby said.

"Okay," Chance said after a pause. "And what did they do?"

Bobby's eyes widened with fear. "They saw me and they came over. They were very mad at me. They told me that I better forget I ever saw them there. They said I better never tell anyone I saw them there. Ever! They said they knew my Mommy and my Daddy, and if I told, something terrible would happen to them. Something really, really terrible!"

He was sobbing too hard to talk now. Chance held the little boy in his arms. "It's okay, Bobby," he said. "It's okay. Your Mom and Dad will be safe. No one is going to hurt them. I promise you that."

Chance looked over at Darien. "I bet if we were to get a description of those two men, they would look a lot like the two men who blocked my way on the road," she said.

"Probably the same ones that fooled with the gas in Maggie's house, too," Chance said.

They waited until Bobby's sobs had quieted.

"Bobby, can you tell me where they came from?" Chance asked.

"They came up from the ground," Bobby said. "Like the ghosts on the cartoon shows. They just came right up."

"Are you sure about that, son?" Chance asked. "People don't just come up from the ground."

"Yes, they did too. I saw it," Bobby insisted.

Chance and Darien exchanged puzzled glances.

"Where, honey?" Darien asked. "Where did they come up?"

"Over there." Bobby pointed to a secluded spot in the cove set far back against the cliff and near the hotel. An outcropping of rocks spilled across the area.

"Let's take a look," she suggested. They all walked in the direction of the rocks.

Chance surveyed the area and walked over to a large pile of randomly stacked rocks. A smooth, faded expanse of wood was barely visible next to the rock pile.

"Look at this," he said.

"Looks like a hatch of some sort," Darien replied. "It probably leads to the basement of the hotel. I bet it was used for deliveries years ago."

"I studied the blueprints of the hotel and I've been over every inch of it. There is no storage room down there connected to this hatch."

Darien considered this piece of information. "In the twenties," she said, "during prohibition, there were a lot of rum runners around here. Vast fortunes were made. As I recall, that's about the time this hotel was constructed. I wouldn't be surprised if they built a room with access to the shore to facilitate a little trade on the side. They wouldn't be likely to put that room on the blueprint."

Chance looked dubious. "One way to find out," he said. "Let's open it up and see where it goes."

Now it was Darien's turn to look doubtful. "I'm not sure that's a good idea, especially with Bobby here. It may not be safe."

"If those two men came out of here, it was safe enough," Chance noted. "And I thought that you were the one who was in a hurry to tie down the facts, Darien. Finish it up and make a clean getaway. No time to waste. Isn't that true?"

She was stung by his words, and stung, too, by the frosty tone in which they were spoken. She had no ready retort. He was right. She had made her choice, and although she had not put it into words, he had heard it, loud and clear.

"Maybe best if I go alone and you and Bobby wait up here for me," Chance said.

"No," Bobby said, grabbing Chance's hand. "I want to be with you."

Chance looked at Darien, who gave a reluctant nod.

"I'll go first," he continued. "If at any time it looks unsafe, we'll turn back. Okay with you, partner?" he asked Bobby.

"I guess so," Bobby said.

"I'll just go back to the car for a flashlight. It'll be dark in there."

He was back before common sense could prevail and she could marshal her arguments against the wisdom of this move. Chance tugged on the handle of the heavy metal hatch, and with a loud creak, it gave way, revealing a short flight of rickety wooden steps that descended steeply into the darkness. He started down the stairs, and Darien and Bobby, clinging tightly to each other, followed closely.

In the dim light cast by the flashlight, Darien worked her way down the crumbling stairs. "Look at the cobwebs, Chance," she said into the gloom. "They're hanging in tatters. Someone has used these stairs recently. And judging by the damage, I'd say it was more than one person."

"Yeah, I agree," Chance said. "And the dust on the stairs is disturbed. Wherever we're going, it's a good bet that someone else has gone there in the last few days."

They continued carefully down the stairs. "Look here," Chance said, directing the flashlight to a spot on the stairs. Darien saw an oily looking substance shining dully on the step. Chance reached into his pocket and tossed her his Swiss army knife. "Take a sample of that and put it in one of the evidence bags in my jacket pocket," he said.

He held the light steady while she worked. Bobby hovered anxiously at her side, his features drawn into a worried frown. She worked as quickly as she could, and when she'd completed the task to Chance's satisfaction, she stuffed the items quickly into her pocket and reached once again for Bobby's hand.

"It's okay," she said as they started back down the stairs. "We're almost done here. We'll be heading home before you know it. Maybe we can take that sail then."

Abruptly, Chance stopped. Darien, with Bobby close behind, took the last step down and found herself in a damp, musty-smelling room that, save for the small circle of illumination that shone from the flashlight, was black as the ocean on a moonless night. They stepped through a puddle of water, formed as the rain seeped in through the hatch and trickled down the stairs, and moved deeper into the room. The eerie silence was broken only by the sound of their breathing.

Chance shone the beam of the flashlight around the room. The wavering circle of light cast sinister shadows. Bobby moved closer to Chance.

"From the direction that we traveled, we are definitely under the hotel. Can you hold this while I get a match?" Chance asked. A dingy lantern stood in the pallid yellow glow of the flashlight.

Darien held the light steady. She heard him strike the match and closed her eyes against the flare of fire. When she opened them, the room was bathed in a weak and flickering light, although the recesses remained shadowed.

Chance whistled. "What have we here?"

A jumble of modern computer equipment was carelessly scattered on the floor, as was an obviously antique, elegant crystal chandelier. And resting nearby they saw a pile of cans that smelled strongly of gasoline.

"Well, that's one mystery solved," Chance said. "They never did get this stuff off the Island. They stashed it here. Someone must be planning to come back and get it out when they judge it's safe."

"Look over there, Darien," Bobby whispered, pointing toward the far end of the illumination. "What's that?"

Darien's eyes traveled in the direction that Bobby had pointed. "I'm not sure," she answered. "Let's go take a look."

Together, they walked in the direction of the computer equipment, and Darien stooped to pick up the shiny object that had caught Bobby's eye. She carried it over closer to the lantern, in order to observe it more carefully. It was a paper wrapper of some sort, silvery and shiny, and from all appearances, had not been there long. She turned it over and studied it.

Chance heard her gasp.

"What is it, Darien?"

He was unprepared for the shock and cold terror in her eyes when she looked up.

"We have to get out of here, Chance," she cried urgently. "Now!"

He was next to her in a heartbeat and took the glittering object from her trembling hand. He didn't need to study it. It was instantly familiar. He was looking at a candy wrapper. A toffee wrapper, to be exact. A very special silver wrapper, used on fine toffees. He had seen a lot of those toffees recently.

"Damn it, Darien," he said through clenched teeth. "How could I be so stupid? He knows everything. What we've found. What we're thinking. How close we are."

A figure stepped silently out of the shadow at the far edge of the bleak, dank room. It was a stout figure, a figure with a full ginger beard and a head of curly ginger hair. The dim light of the lantern glinted off of the steely black revolver that the figure held pointed very precisely in their direction. Darien pushed Bobby behind her and moved closer to Chance, and together, they confronted Jim Plattman.

CHAPTER EIGHTEEN

"Chance, Darien, Bobby," he said. "The 'A' team, present and accounted for. Excellent work. Sadly, a bit too excellent for your own good."

No one spoke. Darien could sense Chance taking the measure of the situation, weighing their options, looking for their best move.

"Ah, Darien," Plattman continued. "I had such a good deal going. Not for me the indignity of retiring on the paltry pension that Monitor bestows on its employees. No, no. I have money put aside, money to spare, money to burn, you might say." His laugh, raw and humorless, echoed ominously in the underground room. "Sorry for the little joke," he said. "I couldn't resist."

Plattman took a few steps in their direction.

"It was such a sweet little deal," he continued in a conversational tone of voice. "Easy, too. I find the undervalued properties. I create the partnerships to purchase those properties. We use Monitor as the insurer, and Monitor's friendly underwriter who specializes in valuing hotels is delighted to take a pay-off to boost the valuation so that I can get excess insurance. And then I arrange to have the property torched. Result — a tidy little profit. No hassle. No risk."

"Why don't you put that gun down, Jim," Chance said. "No one needs to get hurt here."

"I'm going to have to disagree with you there," Plattman said. "You really didn't have enough to connect me to this operation, but you were getting uncomfortably close. All that I needed was enough time to tie up a few loose ends before I could join my money far from the reach of US law. I'd be free and clear. But now…"

"So that's what the gas and the truck were about," Chance interrupted, holding Jim's eye and edging a bit closer. "Delay. You called in the gas leak, right? You didn't intend for anyone to die then, and no one needs to die now."

"I was playing for time," Jim said. "But then this happened. So my job is to 'un-happen' it, in a manner of speaking. Speaking more directly, you have made yourselves inconvenient, and you will have to disappear."

"You don't want to do this," Chance said. "You haven't hurt anyone yet."

"I don't see that I have much choice now," Plattman said mildly. He sounded for all the world as if they were having a nice chat over tea, rather than talking about murder. "It's gone too far now. You know too much."

Darien could sense Chance tensing beside her, coiling like a viper ready to strike. She waited, hardly daring to breath, trying to think what she could do to defuse the situation.

"It was a clever little side-business you had going there," Chance said, taking another step toward Jim. "But you pushed it one fire too far."

"Maybe so," Jim said. "When the company got wise to the pattern of fires, they directed me to hire a team to work the case. They insisted on you, Darien. That worried me, because I knew how good you are. I'd seen the results you produced when you were on my side, and I didn't relish the thought of having you working against me. And then, Edward added Chance here to the mix. I did some research on him, and concluded that he was trouble. But there was nothing I could do at that point. I couldn't argue without calling suspicion to myself. So,

I decided to play the game and manage the situation until I had the insurance payouts."

"And you might have pulled it off if you hadn't come down here for one last look," Chance said, taking another step forward.

"That's quite enough, Chance," Plattman said, waving the gun menacingly in Chance's direction. "Stop talking, and speaking of stopping, one more step and I'll blow your head off where you stand. You can count on that."

Chance hesitated. He was almost next to Plattman now. He put the lantern down on a rickety table.

"And was taking the computer system and the chandelier part of your plan, too, or did your henchmen get a little greedy on you?" he asked.

Chance was going to do something. She could sense it. And with that gun pointed right at him, he was not going to live to tell the story.

Carefully, she dropped Bobby's hand and reached into her pocket. Staring straight ahead and trying not to move a muscle, she groped in her pocket until she felt the cool metal against her hand. Chance's knife.

She looked up at Plattman. All of his attention was focused directly on Chance, as was the gun. There would not be a better time. As stealthily as possible, she tossed the knife across the room. It landed with a dull thud.

Plattman whirled in the direction of the noise, and Chance was on him in an instant. They fell to the ground in a tangle of bodies, struggling fiercely, each trying to control the gun.

Darien shoved Bobby behind several cartons at the far end of the room. "Stay here," she cried. "Don't move, Bobby."

Something heavy. She needed something heavy that she could lift. Frantically, Darien moved her hands over the shadowed shelves at the far end of the room. She touched something — hard metal, cold and solid — and grasped it in her trembling hands.

The deafening explosion of a gunshot reverberated in the underground chamber. Darien spun around toward the men. In the tangle of arms and legs, she could not tell what was happening. Then, to her horror, she saw Plattman struggle to his knees, and start to rise unsteadily to his feet.

With a shrill cry, she threw herself in his direction, swinging the metal bar. The sickening thud of metal connecting with his skull told her that she had hit her mark, even before she heard Plattman's scream of pain and fury.

The force of the blow threw Plattman sideways. As he fell, he threw his hands up in a futile attempt to gain some purchase and stay on his feet. His flailing hand struck the lantern, which toppled off the table and landed on some rags that had been carelessly piled against the wall. In the time it took for Plattman's inert body to hit the floor, the rags burst into flame. The sickening stench of gasoline quickly permeated the small underground room.

Darien took several steps back. Her mouth opened in a silent scream of horror that echoed loudly again and again in her mind. She gazed in a deepening stupor at the fire snaking its way across the piles of papers stacked neatly on the floor. She stared, mesmerized, as the flames twisted, writhed, first reaching out and then curling back upon themselves. The room, no longer dim, glowed with a sinister, incandescent, white-hot light, tinged with shades of red and yellow. Black smoke obscured the ceiling. She tried to understand what was happening, but reason and rational thought hovered just beyond her reach.

The dream. She looked around the room, dazed. This must be the dream. Different, somehow, but the dream nonetheless.

She took a few more tentative steps away from the fire and then stopped, confused. Where was the staircase? There was supposed to be a staircase.

"Darien!" The stricken voice played at the edges of dream. "Darien!" She felt something tugging at her hand, shaking her. The heat was intensifying. Where was that staircase?

"Darien, Chance got hurt. You have to help Chance."

Chance? Darien looked down in the direction of the insistent tugging. She saw Bobby, his eyes wide with terror, his sooty cheeks smudged with tears.

"He's going to be in the fire!" Bobby sobbed.

Darien's bewildered gaze swept the room slowly and came to rest on Chance, perilously close to the blazing fire. He was trying in vain to sit up. As she watched, he fell back weakly with a soft moan that was barely audible over the roar of the fire. The front of his shirt was soaked in blood.

Slowly, the present separated from the past and moved to the foreground, grew more substantial and vivid. Not the dream? She shook her head, unsure what was real and what was memory, but increasingly aware that lives may depend on her ability to distinguish between the two.

Still struggling with a lingering sense of disorientation, Darien turned to Bobby. He was fiercely determined. He kept tugging at her sleeve and pushing her toward the fire.

"Please, Darien, Chance got hurt! Help Chance!"

Hesitating, Darien reached out and touched Bobby. He was solid, substantial. She touched his cheeks and felt the moisture from his tears. The dream receded further into the background and then vanished. He was real and so was the fire. And if that were true, they were all in deadly trouble.

Darien turned, fully alert now, and took in the scene. The fire was spreading rapidly. She needed a plan. She would only have one opportunity to get it right.

"I want you to go to the staircase, Bobby," she said urgently. "Then walk up those stairs quickly and don't stop until you get to the beach. Okay?"

Bobby hesitated, clinging to her hand.

"I need you to help me now," she said firmly. "I know you want Chance to be safe, and so do I. I'm going to get him out of here, Bobby, but before I can do that, I need to know you're safe. Please do as I say. Now. And when you get up there, use this cellphone and call 911. Tell them it's an emergency. Tell them there's a fire and tell them where we are. Can you do that for me?" She handed him her cellphone.

Bobby nodded uncertainly. She watched as he walked haltingly to the staircase, and then heard him running up the stairs toward safety.

Darien turned her attention to Chance. He was lying on the ground, very still, on the other side of a restless curtain of fire that shifted unpredictably. It was impossible to guess which way the flames would veer next. She would have to go through those flames to get to him, and then pass back through them to get to the stairs. There was no other way.

Darien scanned the room, searching for something she could use. She spotted an old, faded blanket that had been tossed over a tall pile of boxes. She stood on her toes and stretched to grasp it. Reaching high above her head, she was able to snag a ragged corner and pulled it down, together with a pile of boxes that tumbled onto her.

Kicking and pushing the boxes aside, she ran to the bottom of the staircase and immersed the blanket in the pool of water. When it was fully saturated, Darien lifted the dripping blanket over her head and wrapped it firmly around herself. And then, she turned to face the fire.

The wave of panic broke over her with a fierce power that had remained undiminished by the passage of time. Darien shuddered. Her heart beat wildly and erratically, and she found it hard to breathe. She was sick with nausea, weak with fear. Color bled from the world and left it strangely gray and lifeless.

She took a step forward. Then she took another. As she walked into the waking nightmare of the fire, she reached through the stunted woman, and then past her through the fire-scarred child, to find strength and courage. And she kept walking. She felt the flames licking at the blanket, smelled the acrid stench of burning fabric and heard the fire-wind around her. The heat was intense. And then, she felt her foot brush something. She peered out of the blanket and looked down at Chance.

Darien fell to her knees beside him. She put her hand to his throat and felt a strong, steady pulse. But the wound continued bleed. He had lost so much blood already. She had no time to lose.

With a quick, decisive motion, she pulled off her jacket and her shirt. She folded the shirt and pressed it to his wound. Then, she placed the jacket over it, and secured it by tying the sleeves tightly around him.

Reluctantly, she turned her attention toward Jim. She rolled him to the wall, as far as possible from the fire. There was nothing more that she could do for him. She ran back to Chance.

"Chance," she called as she touched his face. "Wake up. We have to get out of here." She searched his face for any glimmer of a response. There was none. "Chance!" she repeated. "Chance!" She choked on the smoke. It was getting difficult to breathe.

She looked up anxiously. The fire was spreading. Then she turned back to Chance. He was so very pale, so still. She would have to drag him out back through the fire. There was no other way.

Darien spread the damp blanket on the floor, and half pushed, half rolled Chance onto it. She wrapped it securely around him, and then turned once again to face the fire. She tugged hard on the blanket, and to her relief, it slid along the floor. Struggling for breath, she pulled harder, easing him toward the searing flames. The heat was growing unbearable.

"Get down." She could barely hear the voice over the noise of the raging fire. "Down. Hit the floor!" the disembodied voice ordered.

She peered through the fire and the smoke. Hazy figures appeared to shimmer in the heat of the fire. They motioned for her to get down.

"Darien, get down on the floor." The voice sounded familiar. It was… George.

The fireman motioned again for her to get down. Silently, she thanked Bobby and whoever it was who had invented the cellphone. Then she slid to the ground beside Chance. The scorching heat dissipated instantly in the hard rush of water that spewed from the firehouse. Her hand groped for Chance and found him. And then, she joined him in darkness and oblivion.

CHAPTER NINETEEN

They say that he who hesitates is lost. She was betting everything that old adage was untrue. Surely, life was not so unforgiving. Surely, there were second chances.

Darien took a sip of her tea and then wrapped both of her hands around the heat of the mug. The slanted rays of the early-morning sun did little to warm the breeze blowing off the ocean, and it was still cool on Maggie's patio. Absently, she replaced the tea on the small table at her side and rubbed her temples.

Despite all the visitors, she had had the time and solitude to do a lot of thinking in those long days since the fire. For so many years she had run from her thoughts, living on the surface of her life and not daring to consider too closely what lurked beneath. And now, since the fire, it seemed she could not stop thinking. Her thoughts tumbled wildly about while she tried to order them, make sense out of them. She had a lot of catching up to do.

She had thought a lot about the child who'd lived through the fire all those years ago, and had emerged deeply scarred in both body and mind. She'd thought about the woman that child had become and the choices she had made. And most of all, she had thought about Chance.

This much, she knew with certainty. She wanted to stay on the Island with him. She wanted to accept his offer and share those few days with him at the Inn. She wanted to talk with him, to hike the soaring cliffs with him. She wanted to spend time in his company, laugh with him, play with him, share her thoughts and her dreams with him. And she wanted to spend the quiet, moon-drenched nights in his bed. She wanted to feel again the passion and the tenderness that she had known in his arms, the weight of his body on hers, the feel of him deep inside of her. The wanting had grown more insistent and urgent as the days since the fire had passed. She wanted it that badly.

Darien stood and walked restlessly across the porch to lean on the railing. There were no clouds to mar the azure blue of the sky. The sun glistened off the gentle swells of the ocean, and the breeze that ruffled her unread papers carried with it the scent of the ocean. She closed her eyes and breathed deeply. Then she ran her hands nervously through the wind-blown tangle of her hair.

She had been such a fool. Such a coward, really. Too afraid to face her fears and move beyond them. Too foolish to know this was someone she could trust. She stared moodily out to sea.

It was probably too late. She had blocked him at every step with her countless rules, and had driven him away by second guessing everything he had tried to say. He had given her a choice that night on the beach, the last night they had been alone together. She had chosen safety. Now she might have to live with that choice.

Still… So much had happened since that night. So many changes. Maybe there was a chance. Maybe.

"Can I freshen your tea?"

Darien turned from the ocean and from her musings, and smiled at Maggie.

"You're spoiling me, Maggie," she protested, and it was true. Since the day of the fire, Maggie had hovered anxiously over her, worrying over her like a mother. Even after Edward had been obliged to return to Providence, Maggie had remained on the Island with Darien. They had spent their evenings talking long into the silent, pre-dawn hours.

Now she placed her hand on Darien's shoulder and gave her an affectionate squeeze. "I doubt that," Maggie said. "And even if I am, it will be short-lived. I just got a call from the hospital and they're releasing Chance back to the Island today. I expect we'll both be busy spoiling him for a while."

Darien didn't think for a minute that the casual look she pasted so firmly on her face was fooling Maggie. So, he was coming home. The time for thinking was drawing to an end. She was going to have to take charge of her destiny now and act on all that she had learned.

But there was one other thing she knew, and she found comfort and strength in that knowledge. She would be alright. Whatever the outcome, whatever happened now between her and Chance, she knew that in time she was going to be alright. In the days since the fire, she'd struggled to face the guilt that stood between her and the help she needed, and that was a good start. In time, she was going to be able to get that help and use it to heal herself, however slowly and haltingly. She had taken the first difficult steps down the path. If necessary, she could finish the journey alone. But please, please, let it be with him.

"Edward called earlier," Maggie said. "He wanted you to know that Plattman has been released from the hospital and was taken into custody. He wants to talk with you and Chance when we get Chance home. And Sally and Bobby want to visit, as well. Apparently, Bobby has a gift for each of you, and you know Sally — she's been baking up a storm for Chance's homecoming."

"Yes, we'll call Edward, of course," Darien said.

"I'm worried that it's going to be a long day for Chance, and we want to be careful not to tire him. He's been through so much," Maggie continued.

"Of course," Darien said. "We'll see that he's not disturbed and that he gets plenty of rest." Even to her own ears, her voice sounded distracted and distant.

Maggie studied her closely. "I'm leaving to pick up Chance and bring him back to the Island. Just wanted to make sure that you were okay before I left."

"No problem," Darien said. "I'll see you then."

Maggie had been gone for a few hours when Darien heard a car pull into the driveway. The doorbell rang and Sally, Bobby and Lily walked in. The quiet house erupted in noise and activity. Flash, freed from the confines of the family car, dashed ecstatically from Bobby to Darien and then back again, punctuating his activity with loud, excited barking. Lily, prompted perhaps by the barking, began to crow with pleasure. Bobby and Sally rushed to her side and hugged her, and both began talking at once. Darien smiled and hugged them all back.

"Where's Chance?" Bobby asked eagerly, looking around.

"He'll be here shortly," Darien said. "Maggie just went to get him at the hospital."

Bobby grinned. "That's great! Mom, do I have to wait until Chance gets here before I give Darien her present? Is it okay now?"

Sally was headed in the direction of the car to unpack the cake she'd made for the homecoming. "That's fine, honey," she called back over her shoulder. "Every day when we'd get ready to visit you, Bobby and I would talk over whether to bring the gift that day or to wait until Chance got home so that he could give you the gifts together," she explained to Darien. "I guess he's about waited-out."

Bobby carefully unzipped his little backpack and pulled out an object swathed in bubble wrap. Solemnly, he walked over to Darien and gave her the parcel. "This is for you, and I hope you feel better soon," he said, looking at the bandages covering the burns on her arms.

"Thank you, Bobby," she said. She unwrapped the gift and then she held up the beautiful shell so that she could inspect it in the light. "It's just perfect," she said, hugging him. "I'll treasure it, and it will always remind me of my friends here on Block Island."

"I hope you'll do more than remember us," Sally said as she carried the cake to the table. "You know you have a standing invitation to visit. There's always room for one more in our house. Or two, for that matter," she said, giving Darien a pointed look. "Two is good."

The women heard the car in the driveway at the same time.

"Speaking of number two…" Sally started, but stopped when she saw the flush that spread across Darien's face. She gave Darien an encouraging smile.

Darien paused, squared her shoulders, and then walked toward the front door.

He did not look like a man who had spent four days in the hospital. He was a little pale under his tan, but if not for the arm that was tucked securely in a sling, he could have been returning from an adventurous sail.

Bobby and Flash both ran to him, and he scooped Bobby up with his good arm and hugged him tightly. "Hey, sport," he said, putting him down. "Good to see you."

"Chance, I have a something for you!" Bobby exclaimed. He ran off to get the present.

"Hey, Sally," Chance said. "Good to see you. Is that your handiwork?" he asked, nodding happily in the direction of the cake. He ruffled Lily's hair gently.

"You say your hello's and then you head right up to bed and get some rest," Maggie ordered. "There'll be the devil to pay if your mother finds out we let you…"

"Now Aunt Maggie," Chance interrupted, "the first thing I'm going to do is sit out on the porch and get some fresh air. I'm not used to being cooped up indoors. And the next thing I'm going to do is drink a long, cold beer. And then, I'm going to drink another. I don't ever want to see another container of milk with a straw sticking out of it. And then…" He cast a meaningful glance in the direction of the cake.

He stopped when he saw Darien. She watched as his eyes moved over her, and felt them linger on the white gauze bandages wrapped around her forearms. "Hello," he said. She could not read anything in his voice.

"Hello yourself," she said, walking over to him and hugging him carefully. "Very convincing," she said, nodding in the direction of his sling. "Some people will do anything to get a little sympathy."

"Not to mention a little beer," he said with a grin. "You're looking pretty pitiful yourself," he added, nodding in the direction of her arms.

"That's nothing," she said quickly. "I'm really..."

"Fine," he said. "I know, you're really fine. You're always fine."

She stopped for a minute, hurt by his words.

"I really am fine," she said firmly. "They're barely burned. More like a sunburn than anything. The doctor wrapped them as a precaution."

"Chance," Maggie interrupted. "If you're not going to go to bed, please settle yourself somewhere. Sally and I will serve the cake, and against my better judgment, I'll get you that beer." She headed off in the direction of the kitchen.

Chance headed out to the porch, and the entourage followed.

"Look what I got you, Chance," Bobby said, handing him a package.

Chance unwrapped his shell and examined it carefully. "This is really perfect!" he exclaimed. "It will look so good in my room in Montana. I'm going to put it on my desk, right next to my computer, so that I can see it whenever I'm working. It'll remind me of Block Island, and of a certain young man who is a very fine sailor."

"Maybe I could come and see it sometime," Bobby said shyly.

"Sure. I have a nephew just about your age, and I think you guys would get along great together. And I believe we have a pony that would be just your size," Chance said.

Bobby's eyes glowed with pleasure.

Maggie returned with the beer and cake, and all three women watched with amusement as he all but inhaled the cake and sucked down the beer.

"Can't imagine how a person could get better on the food they feed you in the hospital," he said. "What a sorry excuse for a meal that is. I've been thinking about that beer for the past four days. And it's every bit as good as I thought it would be."

Sally stood up and gathered the children and dog. "Don't want to tire you out, Chance. I just wanted to drop off the cake and welcome you home. It's good to see you looking so well."

Sally paused a moment, and her expression grew serious. "I don't know how to thank you both for what you did for Bobby."

"No thanks necessary," Chance said. "Darien and I owe our lives to your family, to Bobby's 911 call, and to George and the other firemen. We're the ones who're grateful."

"Enough of this love fest," Maggie said in a tone that brooked no argument. "You need to rest, Chance. Now."

Darien walked Sally to the door. "One piece of advice, for what it's worth," Sally whispered. "If you want him, get in there and fight for him, girl. Subtlety is lost on that man. You've said it yourself. But he's a man worth fighting for."

"I'm not sure I know how to fight like that," she said.

"Of course you do. It's genetic," Sally said with a smile. She gave Darien a big hug, and then was out the door.

When Darien returned to the porch, she found Chance and Maggie in the living room, clustered around the speaker phone that Edward had installed for conducting business out on the Island. Chance was calling Edward, while Maggie glared her disapproval.

"I told him this could wait," she complained to Darien. "He is just impossible."

"Well, Edward," Chance was saying. "I'm weak from lack of decent food and suffering the ill effects of being poked and prodded at all hours of the night and day, but other than that, I'm good to go."

"I'm pleased to hear that," Edward said. "And are you there, Darien? Are you feeling well?"

"Yes, thanks," she said. She stifled the temptation to tell him that she'd feel a whole lot better if she knew that his good opinion of her, and her place at the firm, were secure. She'd spoken with him daily since the fire and he'd been conscientious about providing her with updates as he and his colleagues completed the investigation, but once he'd established that her injuries were minor, it had all been about the case.

"First, let me start by saying that I commend the excellent work that you both did on this case. Chance, there will be a bonus for you in your paycheck. And Darien, the partners have taken note of your fine work and want me to pass along to you our pleasure at your outstanding performance, and our intention to reward that performance at the right moment. We'll discuss that further when you return."

"Thank you, Edward," she said. She felt the tension in her shoulders relax. That probably was as close as he'd come to telling her that all was forgiven and that she was welcome back. And that was good enough for her.

"I also want to let you both know how shocked I was…" His voice wavered. He composed himself, and started again. "How shocked I was to learn that our client was the arsonist, and how much I regret that your lives were put in peril by this investigation."

"No one could have known," Chance said. "He was an insider, so he was a pro at setting up the con and covering his tracks."

Maggie touched Chance's shoulder lightly.

'Edward, I think it's time for Chance to get some rest," she said.

"All right," Edward agreed. "I'll call tomorrow. I'm planning to come back out to the Island tomorrow evening, in any event, and we can tie up loose ends then. And Maggie, I'll call you back later." He cut off the connection.

Moving deftly out of the path of Maggie, who was about to put an arm firmly around him and escort him up the stairs to rest, Chance turned to Darien.

"Now the other thing I've been thinking about in the hospital," he said, "is Mohegan Bluffs. The longer I was in the hospital, the more I wanted to get back there. It's far and away my favorite place on the Island and, I'm sure, a place that's guaranteed to help a wounded man heal quickly. It's that fresh sea air and all." He winked at Maggie, who was frowning fiercely in his direction. "And I want to go now, while it's still sunny and I still have the memory of that beer to carry with me. Are you up for it, Darien?"

"Absolutely not," Maggie protested. "Under no circumstances. You just got out of the hospital, young man. You are in no condition to go wandering around Block Island. And with that arm, it's not safe for you to drive."

"Now you know," he said patiently but firmly, "that it was not much more than a flesh wound. If I'd been from any place but Block Island, they would have kept me in the hospital for a day at most. In New York or LA, they would have patched me up and sent me home. The only reason I was in that hospital for four days was because the doctors here do not see gunshot wounds. This was undoubtedly the most exciting thing that's happened to them in a very long time. And," he added, "I have a chauffeur. Right?" he asked, turning to Darien.

As if she could deny him anything now. "If Chance feels up to it, I guess it's okay," she said to Maggie. "I'll drive, and we won't stay long."

Maggie looked from Chance to Darien, and then back again. She sighed in exasperation. "There's no hope for it when the two of you gang up on me," she said. "All right then, but don't let him tire himself out, Darien. And you be careful driving with those bandages. You don't have an ounce of sense between the two of you."

The drive to the Bluffs seemed to take forever. The silence between them grated on her nerves, which were none too steady to start with.

"Mind if I play some music?" she asked. Without waiting for a response, she reached for her phone and selected a play list. Sarah Vaughn started to sing "What a Difference a Day Makes."

Chance smiled. "This is right back where we started," he said.

"I guess that's true," she answered. "It's the same song we played on the trip down to Point Judith."

But she had come so very far from where they'd started. Then, the music had been a means to an end, a way to lose herself and avoid any thought of the fire scene she would have to face and the memories she would have to confront. Now, the hopeful mood of the melody struck a responsive chord. Now, the words were imbued with a special meaning. And Chance — what did the song mean to him? She glanced his way, but his eyes were closed and his expression was inscrutable.

She drove on to the parking lot, and mindful of her promise to Maggie, parked as close to the stairs as she could get. Chance stepped out of the car and looked around appreciatively. Then he grabbed a blanket from the trunk, smiled that crooked smile that she remembered so well, and headed for the stairs. Darien followed close behind. She could not take her eyes from him, from the way the sunlight glinted off his hair, from the easy grace of his stride. She would etch this into her memory, and if this were to be their last time together, she would have this moment to carry with her always.

They reached the bottom of the staircase, and Chance walked down the beach a distance before spreading the blanket on the sun-warmed sand, close to the shelter of the cliffs. He settled himself comfortably on the blanket. Without a word, she sat next to him. When he reached out for her and put his good arm around her, she curled into him and rested her face against his chest. Please, she thought to herself. Please.

"I've thought about this place so often since we were here," he said at last. "There's so much I'll never forget."

She did not look up, did not move a muscle. She wanted to stay this way, this close to him, for as long as possible. This was hers to savor.

"I'll never forget the joy on your face when brought me here to the Bluffs," he continued. "I'll never forget how excited you were to share it with me. I loved that you loved it, that you could find so much pleasure here."

He paused for a few minutes, looking out to sea. "There's so much more I'll never forget, Darien," he said softly. "I'll never forget holding you that night when we danced. I'll never forget nearly losing you to the gas. I'll never forget making love that first time. And I'll never forget your courage at the hotel, the way you saved both Bobby and me from the fire. Knowing all that fire meant to you, knowing what you must have been feeling — I'll never forget any of that." His arm tightened around her.

She could not remain silent any longer. She could not bear the uncertainty. She had to do something.

Darien lifted her head and looked into his eyes. "Are you still planning to stay at the Inn for a few days?" she asked.

"No," he said. "No, I'm not. I'll stick around for a day or two. There are people I want to see before I leave. And there's a little boy that's been promised a sail. But after that, I'm heading back to Montana."

She flinched as if she had been hit. It was over. She had her answer, and she could not blame him. She had given him so little reason to stay with her, and so many reasons to leave. She looked away, blinking back the hot tears that stung her eyes.

He pulled his arm away, and she felt him digging around in back pocket of his jeans. Then he pressed something into her hand. He closed her hand carefully around it, and sat back, waiting.

She arranged her face into a bland expression and turned to look at the unexpected gift.

"What is it?" she asked, peering at the piece of paper in her hand. She read it to herself. 'Electronic Ticket,' it said. She picked out the word Montana. And then she saw her own name.

"It's a plane ticket to Montana," Chance said. "It's yours, if you'll take it. There are some people there that I want you to meet, and they all sure want to meet you. I hope you'll spend a few days with us and get to know us."

She stared dumbly at the ticket.

"I don't make a practice of bringing women home, Darien," he said. "This is different. You're different. Tell me you'll come."

She still could not speak over the lump in her throat.

"What are you thinking? Are you worried about the time off from work? After all that's happened, I know Edward won't object. Are you nervous about meeting my people? My family's easy to love, and I know they'll love you. Or — is it us, Darien? Is that why you're hesitating? Are you still unsure about us? Unsure about me? Because if that's what you're thinking…"

She smiled then, and raised her eyes to his. "You're so busy trying to second guess my thoughts," she said. "You think you know what's on my mind, but your strong convictions to the contrary, you're mistaken. And even if you could read my mind, you wouldn't learn anything worth knowing there. Read my heart, Chance. You'll find your answer there."

He laughed out loud. "Using my own words against me, counselor? Guilty as charged." Then his expression turned serious. "What's in your heart, Darien? What will I find there?"

Without waiting for her answer, he pulled her to him and kissed her deeply. The kiss was searching, hungry. Darien kissed him back with a passion that mirrored his own.

She said, "You'd find someone who cares deeply about you. You'd find someone who wants to give those feelings a chance to grow. You'd find someone who believes there could be a tomorrow for us."

She had said it all as clearly as she could. If he cared, if he loved her, now he would say…

"I love you, Darien," Chance whispered.

And he would say…

"You can trust me," he said softly in her ear.

And then he would say…

"Your heart is safe with me," he told her.

And she knew it would be true.

Acknowledgements

A big thank-you to Sonali Shaw for designing the perfect cover for this book. I still smile every time I look at it.

Special thanks to Adam Shaw for his skillful, caring and patient work turning my manuscript into a paperback book. I would not have known where to begin.

A warm thank-you to my neighbor and friend, Marilyn Fenichel, for her helpful suggestions and close reading of my manuscript. Our two-person writers' group is enjoyable and productive in equal measure.

And finally, many thanks to Lorraine and Howard Veisz for their encouragement and exceptional fact-checking skills. They kept me honest. All remaining errors are mine alone.

About the Author

Ricci Cummings was born in Niagara Falls, New York, and resides with her husband, Glen, in Connecticut. She is a former clinical social worker and a retired corporate litigation attorney who serves on the boards of local not-for-profits that focus on the well-being of our children, families and communities. Ricci is an amateur birder who is co-editor of *Chickadee Tales*, a compendium of essays about the New Haven Bird Club and birding. She relishes the serenity she finds in nature when walking, canoeing and sailing. She loves to read and write, and admits to being an inveterate daydreamer. Ricci also is a proud mother, mother-in-law, and grandmother of Martin, Ayla, Sydney, Jacob and Stella.